DECEPTIVE JUSTICE

DECEPTIVE JUSTICE

A VICTORIA JUSTICE MYSTERY

ANDREA J. JOHNSON

First published by Level Best Books 2025

This novel is entirely a work of fiction. The names, characters and incidents portrayed in it are the work of the author's imagination. Any resemblance to actual persons, living or dead, events or localities is entirely coincidental.

Andrea J. Johnson asserts the moral right to be identified as the author of this work.

Author Photo Credit: Brad Buckman

First edition

ISBN: 978-1-68512-989-7

Cover art by Level Best Designs

This book was professionally typeset on Reedsy.
Find out more at reedsy.com

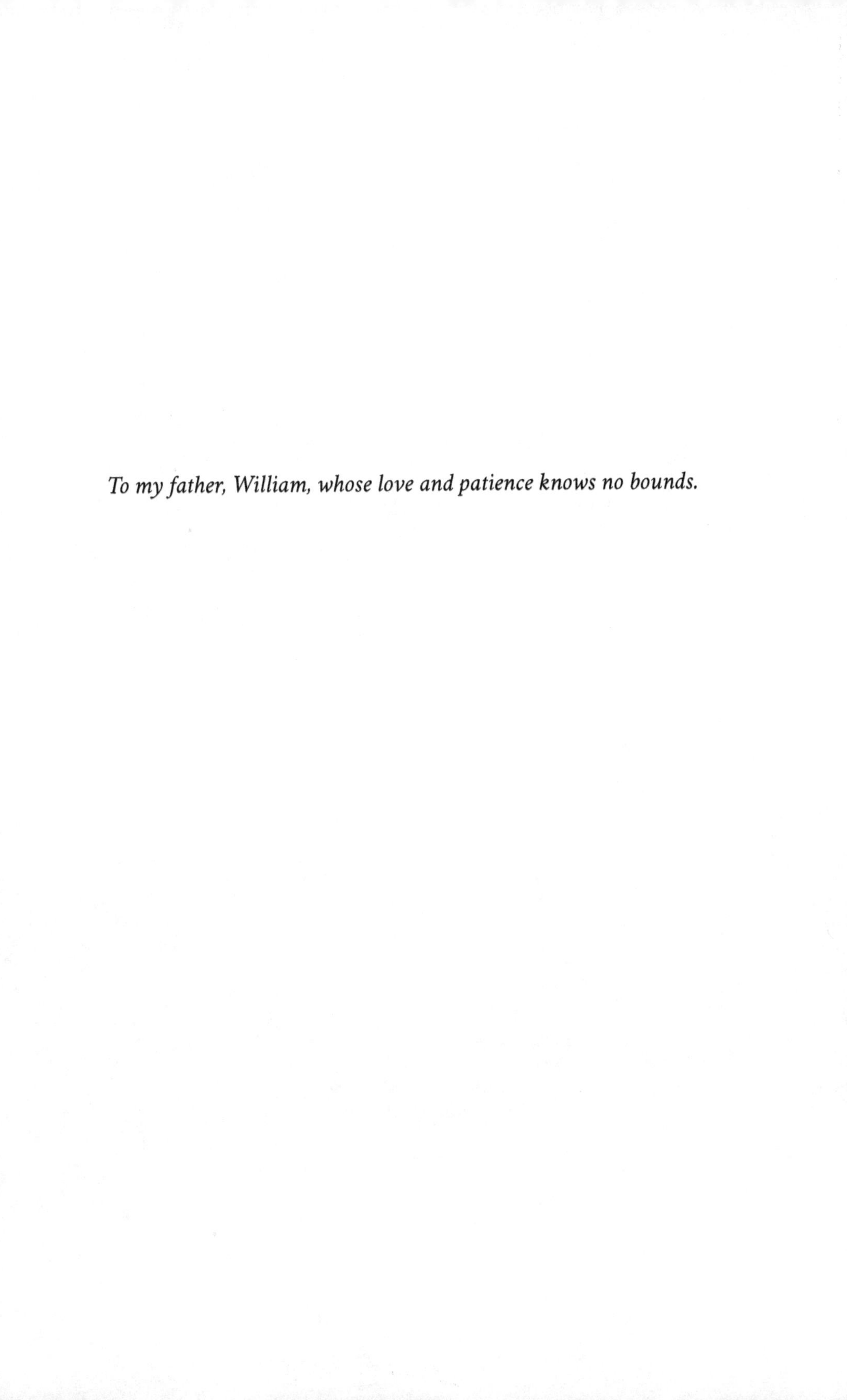

To my father, William, whose love and patience knows no bounds.

Praise for Deceptive Justice

"Victoria Justice is a smart, savvy court reporter who finds herself on the trail of a killer. When danger touches those closest to her, Victoria kicks into high gear in a dogged search for answers. A fun, read with twists and turns you never see coming!" —-Pamela Samuels Young, award-winning author of *The Law of Karma* and *Failure to Protect*

"Deceptive Justice is a rousing romp of clues and quips even before the crime occurs. Becurled, spunky, and short in stature, Victoria Justice is also courageous and crafty. Readers will find themselves laughing out loud as Victoria bogarts her way into a case the police think is cut and dried and marvel at the way she goes into action when her friends and family are in peril.

"With an insider's knowledge of trial proceedings, Andrea J. Johnson plunks the reader into the authentic dynamics of courthouse culture you won't see while serving on jury duty. Set firmly in the structure of a cozy mystery, the characters and strong writing will keep you engaged and entertained."—Cheryl A. Head, author of the Charlie Mack Motown Mystery series

Chapter One

We'd gathered at the site of a potential massacre.

I swallowed back the knot of sickness that churned in my stomach. Eight months earlier, feet from where I stood, a hotel had gone up in flames on Bickerton, Delaware's world-famous boardwalk during the height of tourist season. Thirteen people had been severely injured and the building destroyed.

The prosecution claimed the defendant, Ignacio Cardoza, was a disgruntled employee who'd set the building ablaze after a contentious dismissal. Fortunately, the charred wreckage had long since been cleared away, and a new rustic framework rose in its place. Yet, the mood of mayhem still hung in the air and contorted the remaining storefronts into salacious reminders of the carnage. Now, the jury had come to view the crime scene, hoping to forever exorcise the demons by bringing justice to light.

"This is a bum move, Wells," Public Defender Jonathan Erving whispered to the prosecutor. The two suits walked shoulder to shoulder toward the gazebo where I stood on the step, desperate to find an inconspicuous place to set up my steno machine.

Johnny gripped his colleague's shoulder once they stopped in front of me. "The only thing this trip is going to prove is that anyone could have started that fire and that it is impossible for my client to have done squat without being caught on camera."

"Don't be too sure, Erving," countered Deputy Attorney General Grant Wells as he slapped Johnny's chest with the back of his hand. "How does that saying go? A picture is worth a thousand words, but an emotional appeal is worth a thousand more."

Out of all the county's state-appointed attorneys, Erving and Wells were my favorites because of their youth, professionalism, and passion. Both men were cocky but honest and refrained from the cutthroat trial tactics that led to rant-filled sidebars. Even still, I had to side with DAG Wells on this one—no amount of paint, plaster, or landscaping would erase the knowledge of what happened.

"Hey, Victoria," called PD Johnny Erving. "Where should we stand?"

As much as I disagreed with the public defender's view of the case, Johnny definitely had the edge over his competition when it came to personality and aesthetics. His perpetual five o'clock clock shadow, dimpled chin, and curly superhero hair left the female jurors swooning while his athletic persona kept the men respectful.

"You guys can stand anywhere within arm's distance." I pointed to a spot on the gazebo's platform a few feet behind me.

"Arm's distance? Yours?" Johnny held up his beefy arm and flexed. His suit did nothing but wrinkle in response. "Or mine?"

This brought a deep belly laugh from DAG Wells, who thrust his crotch toward the center of the gazebo. "How about mine?" He snickered to his colleague.

Gross. Did I say professionalism earlier? Scratch that.

I rolled my eyes skyward and pretended not to notice. They couldn't have thought I'd find that funny? Maybe they figured there wasn't much I could do about the matter. Even though we were on official court business, we were nowhere near the Superior Courthouse. No matter. Let the two of them have their little boys' club. If lurid humor and making fun of my diminutive stature took some tension out of the solemnity of our endeavor, so be it.

Standing at five foot nothing, I tended to blend into a crowd, which was a blessing and a curse as a court stenographer. The irony of taking the verbatim record meant I had to capture the proceedings while remaining neutral. To do my job well, I had to go unnoticed. However, that very need and ability to disappear meant no one took me or my job seriously.

Teachers teach. Writers write. Plumbers…plumb. Those jobs have quantifiable descriptions. Since civilians can't decipher my shorthand abbreviations or comprehend how a machine the size of a breadbox helps me write at speeds of 240 words per minute, I become the target of jokes—or worse, seen as a relic soon to be replaced by voice recognition technology.

"You boys ready to put this pony on the track?" Judge Henry Dean Maddox sauntered over, and the attorneys snapped to attention.

A mix of Ichabod Crane and Shaggy from *Scooby Doo*, Judge Maddox had a reputation as a maverick. This is not to say he took proceedings lightly or that he didn't know the law. On the contrary, he was the head judge for our courthouse, the longest-seated judge in the state, and he knew the importance of a clean record—should appeal issues haunt him later. Rather, his wild reputation came from the judge's tendency to buck formality. He'd often stumble onto the bench in running shoes and wrinkled robes with a mug of coffee in hand, then spend half of his remarks misquoting old movies. Today wasn't much different, except he'd ditched the robe for a black Adidas tracksuit since criminal law prevented him from conducting matters during the jury's view of the crime scene.

"Yes, Your Honor. We're ready." DAG Wells ran a hand through his mop of blond hair and offered up a three-fingered Boy Scout salute. "And thank you for this opportunity, sir."

"No problem, Wells. I'll ask the bailiff to drag out the jurors and give them their instructions. We need to get started before any looky-loos or press start working the perimeter."

Ugh. I'd forgotten about the possibility of busybody reporters. Only an idiot would attempt to conduct a criminal trial on the beach—not that Judge Maddox was an idiot or that we were directly on the beach. We'd gathered under the massive wooden gazebo that marked the center of Bickerton's historic boardwalk. The whitewashed structure, usually reserved for concerts and speeches, towered at the end of a cul-de-sac that abutted the popular landmark. Perfect wooden planks stretched a half mile in each direction along the coastline—a sight soon blocked by the curious faces of twelve jurors and four alternates eagerly awaiting instructions.

Since the first twelve days of our trial had suffered the monotony of a courtroom, most jurors had wide eyes and upturned lips that signaled excitement for the early morning field trip. But a few, like me, yawned and eyed the perpetually cloudy April sky for the threat of rain. A briny breeze heavy with moisture whipped through our group, so I hunched my back and slipped behind the spindly figure of Judge Maddox and the two stocky attorneys.

Even though the gazebo's pitched octagonal roof protected us from the worst elements, I cringed at the idea of getting wet simply because DAG Wells had some cockamamie notion that a jury visit to the crime scene meant a sure-fire win for his case. Truth be told, jury visits were a rarity in the legal world—after all, it's the prosecutor's job to visit the scene and determine the evidence, not the jurors. And for that reason alone, most judges would have shut down such nonsense; but, being our resident rogue, Maddox granted the attorney his unorthodox wish even though diagrams surely would have sufficed.

With that seed of dissatisfaction taking root in my brain, I flopped onto the steps of the gazebo—thankful I'd worn a pantsuit—turned my back to the horizon, unfolded the tripod of my steno machine, and resisted the urge to groan as I waited for the bailiff's pseudo call to court.

"Ladies and gentlemen, this view should be regarded as a part of the trial," said the bailiff, Arnold Knight. "Even though we are not in the courthouse, think of today's events as taking place in a courtroom without walls. Look around, make a mental note of the scene. See how this lines up with the testimony. But, to ensure everyone views this evidence with the same eye, please do not attempt any reenactments. No pictures, no measurements."

He paused to square his shoulders and hike his gun belt over the peak of his belly. The motion was clearly meant to convey the seriousness of the day's endeavor, and Arnold's intimidating height helped drive that point home. However, his rosy skin, pudgy cheeks, and salt-and-pepper beard undermined the whole thing, leaving the impression that Saint Nick had stopped by for a lecture.

"Do not communicate with each other about any subject connected to the trial." Arnold wagged a finger at the jury. "Simply observe. File away any observations made and use them during this afternoon's deliberations. Remember, you can't ask questions of the judge or the attorneys." He jabbed a thumb at our quartet. "They are only here to make sure this tour succeeds without bias to either side, and I am in charge today to protect you from their influence. You have sixty minutes to conduct your inspection of the former hotel's perimeter, its proximity to the various boardwalk surveillance measures, and the delivery alcove along the side alley of the facility where the fire is estimated to have been set." He tilted his head toward the wood and steel structure sprouting from the hotel's old lot about fifty yards down the boardwalk. "Your boundaries have been marked. Follow the troopers, and head out."

As the crowd dispersed, I flicked off my steno writer. My duties as the court stenographer meant I had to be on hand in case the attorneys wanted to make a motion about any improprieties, but what was I supposed to do for the next hour? The defendant had been given the option to stay behind at the courthouse. I wished I'd been given the same courtesy.

But as much as I wanted to attribute the day's inconvenience to other people, the root of my bad mood was our proximity to the water. Most folks would have enjoyed the rising sun reflecting across the surface of the ocean in a golden streak that looked like a yellow brick road to nowhere. Not me. Large bodies of water made me queasy and brought on panic attacks—only recently, after a brush with death, had I sought help with the phobia.

Even still, we hadn't found a wholesale cure, so I was hesitant to leave the safety of the gazebo, not daring to look at the wide swath of cool blue liquid that painted the coastline for miles in each direction. Part of me thought the trip would be a smart experiment, a risk calculated for maximum success since I'd have colleagues and work to shield me, but my mood soured and my skin prickled.

I'd chosen wrong.

I fidgeted on the steps and tried to keep my eyes focused on the shops that lined the main drag of Oceanside Drive. We'd arrived at the boardwalk a little before 8:30 a.m., and the court had gained the town's permission to seize sole jurisdiction of the area for about ninety more minutes.

I could hear a few of the vendors banging around behind the metal gates that covered their colorful storefronts. Others unloaded stacks of boxes from carts or set out placards outlining the day's specials. While the area was by no means busy like it would have been on a full-blown summer weekend, there were enough distractions for a Monday morning to keep me occupied.

So, I concentrated on a young male juror who'd straggled behind so that he could peek into Pepperton's Popcorn. The store's buttery sweet emissions of caramel corn danced along the sea breeze. The carefree gesture eased some of my gloom and prompted me to rise from the gazebo steps to further assess my surroundings.

Judge Maddox had disappeared, maybe he'd retired to one of the state-issued vans that had transported us over, or maybe he'd gone for a jog—one never quite knew with him. Arnold, the bailiff, mingled among the jurors spread out along the north side of the boardwalk. He stood guard while they examined the scene, which the State Police had sanctioned off with a series of metal barriers and large orange cones.

"Dude. C'mon. You can't be serious with that thing?" The high-pitched note of irritation in Johnny Erving's voice caught my attention. The defense attorney had his back to me, but the subject of his objection proved obvious—Grant Wells had lit up the longest, fattest, and smelliest cigar I'd ever seen.

"What?" DAG Wells replied through a thick, billowy cloud of putrid white smoke. He stood triumphantly in the center of the gazebo with his free hand casually stuffed in his pants' pocket. "We have a ton of time to kill, and I need to relax."

"Then go somewhere else." Johnny coughed. "You know I'm allergic to cigarette smoke."

"Good thing this isn't a cigarette. And what kind of person is allergic to smoke? Isn't that some kind of made-up thing like an aversion to aftershave or all those rock stars who claim they can only eat green M&Ms?"

"You're a piece of work, bro. You're totally doing this on purpose." Johnny backed away and covered his nose. "You had your fun. Now get lost."

"You know I can't leave the area." Wells plastered on the sly grin of a used car salesman. "I might accidentally mingle with the jury."

"What about Victoria?" Johnny stretched an arm toward me. "Would you dare ruin the lungs of this lovely—" But before he could finish the sentence, his body heaved and a pool of vomit erupted from his mouth. He hunched forward just in time to narrowly avoid getting the foul concoction on his suit.

"No way." Wells clutched his chest and started to laugh in loud honks. "I couldn't have planned that better if I tried."

Johnny clamped a hand over his mouth, his face bright red, and ran down the gazebo steps toward the public bathrooms on Oceanside Drive.

"Real classy, Wells." I hissed as loud as I could without drawing attention to us. "I don't know what's going on with you guys, but leave me out of it."

I spun on my heels, but the prosecutor caught my arm and held me in place.

"Hey, hey. Victoria, look." He dropped the cigar on the floorboards of the gazebo and stomped on it a few times. "I'm sorry. There's no ill intention here. I was just trying to blow off steam. This has been a long trial, and I figured the jokes would help with the friendly competition of it all. You can understand that, right?"

"Don't try to make yourself look good on my account." I snatched my arm from his grip. "You need to apologize to Johnny."

Wells narrowed his eyes, but he didn't say anything in response. Not that I would have heard him anyway because, in that moment, the manically catchy Candy Kitchen theme song blasted from the loudspeakers outside the shop's garish rainbow-inspired storefront. The jingle was a cross between the treacliest kids' song and the planet's cheeriest Christmas tune with a circus organ and a tuba as lead accompaniment. God bless them though. Whenever I heard the song, my desire for fudge spiked.

"You should probably tell them to turn off the music," I growled through clenched teeth, determined to remain civil despite my discomfort.

"Not a chance." Wells shook his head so that his floppy blond bangs framed his arrogant brow. "The conditions should be as authentic as possible. I want the jury to be reminded of all the women and children who were put in danger by the defendant's vicious acts."

"Unbelievable." I cocked my head to the side and rolled my eyes at him. He might have been doing what's in the best interest of our community, but, for once, I didn't have to listen to it. Without a word, I snatched up my steno machine by its tripod and walked west along Oceanside Drive, away from the gazebo, to do a little window-shopping at Candy Kitchen. Perhaps the sight of homemade fudge would vanquish my dark mood.

As I neared the storefront, my pulse quickened. Their metal gate sat slightly ajar, making it easier to see the different varieties of dark chocolate and gooey peanut butter goodness in their bright rainbow boxes. I rushed toward the glass to get a closer look and bumped into the bony frame of a willowy, freckled-faced woman traveling in the opposite direction. She wore a black shawl and sunglasses, but I recognized her immediately.

"Phyllis Dodd?" My jaw dropped.

She was the last person I expected to see. Once the head chemist and director of Bickerton's Controlled Substance Lab, she'd been sentenced to a year in prison and eighteen months of probation for allowing an unauthorized civilian to enter the facility and extract drug items for the purpose of sale. Between the shutdown of the lab for security modifications and the outsourced testing, Phyllis had cost the state millions of dollars. That alone should have landed her in jail for decades, but there she stood.

"Well," Phyllis let the word linger in the air, her voice arctic, "if it isn't our mayor's little miracle, Victoria Justice. Professional note taker." She gestured at the steno machine I held pressed to my chest.

Phyllis knew my mother, Corinne Justice, before she became mayor. They were sorority sisters until Phyllis's drinking problem put a rift in their relationship. Ma was reluctant to talk about it, especially after everything that happened at the lab in recent months. However, Phyllis once told me Ma had her kicked out of the sorority—a betrayal I'm sure the chemist hadn't forgiven.

"Lovely to see you too, Ms. Dodd." Sarcasm oozed from every syllable. "Shouldn't you be working on your tan in one of our state-sanctioned facilities?"

I could go toe to toe with the best of them.

"Hilarious." Her voice emerged devoid of amusement. "I earned an early release for good behavior due to overcrowding, not that it's any of your business. Now, if you'll excuse me, I'm late for work." She pushed past me and walked down the street toward Readalong Bookstore. As I watched her walk inside, I couldn't help but feel a little sorry for her. To go from respected scientist to retail salesperson must have been a tough transition...but it only goes to show what becomes of the choices we make.

I suddenly didn't feel in the mood to look at candy, and the idea of spending another thirty minutes walking around with my steno machine in tow seemed silly, so I wound my way back to the gazebo.

When I returned, DAG Wells had taken over my spot on the steps. He sat with his head down, elbows on his knees, legs wide, his narrow jaw slack like someone had stolen his puppy.

"Is Johnny doing okay?" he asked.

"I wouldn't know." I set my steno machine on the ground and took a seat beside him. "I meant what I said when I left. You guys need to remember what we're here to do."

"You're right," said a third voice.

We both looked up to find Johnny Erving with a gun in his hand.

My heart stopped.

Chapter Two

Wells, legs shaking, half rose from his seat. "Holy sh—"

"Shut up." Johnny thrust the weapon toward us, causing Wells to recoil and crouch beside me. "I'm the one holding the gun."

"Stay still," I whispered to Wells as we cowered together on the steps. A light trickle of nervous sweat beaded between my breasts. Ironically, this wasn't the first time I'd been held at gunpoint. Less than six months ago, a courthouse employee had tried to kill me as part of a cover-up for the murder of my mentor and a slew of others. Therefore, I quickly recognized the dumbfounded look of betrayal that washed across Wells's angular features.

"Please. I'm sorry. I can't—" Wells sputtered. His hands gripped my shoulders, and he positioned himself behind me as if to hide. "I'll give you anything you want."

"Gotcha." Johnny pumped a fist in the air and lowered the gun. "April Fools', sucka."

I stared at the barrel until it dropped out of sight, but I didn't dare breathe. A flock of seagulls mewed overhead, filling our silence. Wells flinched like he'd been hit.

"Chill. It's not loaded." Johnny flipped the underside of the gun toward us as proof. "No clip. The chamber is clear."

"Whoa." Wells chuckled nervously, his head protruding over my shoulder. "Nice comeback. You had me going for a second." He then pushed me aside and stood to pound a fist against his colleague's knuckles. "Where did you get the gun?"

"The bailiff is a fellow Lambda, he let me borrow it after I told him about our—"

"Are you two crazy?" My words came out as a squawk because my nerves were fried. If my steno machine hadn't cost several grand, I would have picked it up and bashed them both over the head with it. "What if the jury had been close enough to see that stunt? Judge Maddox is going to kill you."

"Relax." Johnny reached out to pat me on the head, but I slapped his hand away. "Maddox is walking around putting on a stern face for the jurors and won't find out unless somebody tells him. And you're not going to rat on me now, are you, Ms. Justice? This was payback for the cigar and the vomit. You get that, right?"

"Look, Johnny, this is not about me. We have civilians here." I waved a hand toward a couple of employees sweeping outside of Pepperton's storefront, which separated us from the jury's cordoned-off area. "Not to mention, the State Troopers who could have viewed the action as a threat."

But that wasn't the worst of it, a nanosecond after the words left my lips, I heard the sound of our doom.

Click!

The snap of a camera shutter echoed from behind, and we all turned to find a cellphone trained on Johnny Erving, who still held the gun by his side.

"What in the Sam Hill?" Johnny roared at the interloper as he hurried to stuff the firearm into the rear waistband of his trousers. "Back off. We're conducting official court business."

"Doesn't look that way to me," replied the intruder. "The photo practically captions itself: 'A Mockery of Justice: the PD's PDA for G-U-N-S.'"

Click! Click! Click!

"Enough." I stepped in front of the camera before our voices drew unwanted attention. Apparently, I was the only one who recognized the amateur photographer as Mike Slocum, the lead investigative reporter for *The Bickerton Bugle.* A few months back, he'd helped me untangle the clues behind the murder of our town's most prestigious judge, and I hoped that meant he'd be willing to take it easy on my coworkers for the sake of avoiding another courthouse scandal.

"Delete the pictures, Mike. This isn't the time or place, and you know it."

"No way." His mouth curled into a cartoonish smile. "The people have a right to know, especially given the magnitude of this trial and the adverse effects the defendant's actions have had on— "

"Gimme that." Johnny lunged at the smartphone, but the gangly young reporter danced to the side like a prize fighter, then bounced before us, wiggling the device, daring the attorney to test him again.

Grant Wells, who still stood near the gazebo steps because he'd hidden under his suit jacket at the sight of the camera, was stupid enough to take Mike's bait. Arms outstretched, like an infant chasing a toy, he dove low to tackle Mike.

Of course, he missed and landed squarely on his face, but the heavily telegraphed move acted as enough of a distraction that Johnny made a successful grab for the phone. Unfortunately, Mike's grip was firm, and he was strong despite being less muscular than his athletic opponent. As a result, an awkward tug of war ensued as the duo grappled over possession in a series of loud grunts and moans.

"That's enough. Knock it off." The clipped remarks were delivered in the unmistakably sarcastic southern cadence of Judge Henry Dean Maddox, who approached our motley crew from the sea side of the gazebo. "Doesn't this just make my day."

Mike and Johnny froze in place, but their hands remained deadlocked on the phone.

"Sir?" Wells responded from the ground. He'd recovered enough from his dive to be sitting upright, but he was still disheveled and a little disoriented based on the lines of bafflement across his brow.

"Pull yourself together. This isn't a frat house." Maddox snapped at the dazed prosecutor and motioned for him to stand. "I don't know what's going on, but all of you are about a millisecond away from flushing this entire case down the crapper." He stepped into the center of our gathering and put his hands on his hips. "Is this how you treat the sanctity of our judicial system when everyone here, from the troopers to the van drivers, has gone out of their way to give you an unprecedented opportunity to bring the jury face to face with the evidence? I should hold you both in contempt. If I had a nickel for every time an attorney around here screws—" The judge's scowl hardened as if noticing Mike for the first time. "And who the heck are you?"

"Judge, I can explain." My skin grew hot with embarrassment at the nasally sound of my voice. I didn't often speak during court proceedings since my job was simply to protect the accuracy of the record, and for that reason alone, I should have played dumb. But in an effort to mask Mike's identity as a member of the press and to salvage a case that might otherwise end in controversy, or worse, a mistrial, I joined the rest of the idiots in the day's misdeeds by lying to the judge.

"He works nearby. He's...my boyfriend."

"Boyfriend?" Mike dropped his guard and lost control of the phone to Johnny, who immediately tapped at the screen in pursuit of the incriminating pictures.

"Good grief, Victoria." Maddox threw up his arms with an exasperated sigh. "As if things aren't tenuous enough. You know what? I don't even want to hear why you thought this would be the perfect time for a love connection. Just get him out of here. I'll deal with you when we get back to the courthouse." He lifted his chin toward the attorneys. "Frick and Frack, come with me. I'm getting to the bottom of this. And for heaven's sake, put that thing away," he snatched the smartphone out of Johnny's hand and stuffed it into the pocket of his track jacket, "before one of the jurors sees it and starts whining about why they can't have theirs."

Mike opened his mouth to protest, but I grabbed him by the arm.

The judge and his charges stormed off toward the south side of the boardwalk, which extended the distance between them and the still occupied jurors. Grateful for the reprieve, I dragged Mike down Oceanside Drive away from the gazebo. We stopped in front of Candy Kitchen, where the shop's theme music would hopefully mask any chance of someone overhearing our conversation.

"What did you mean by *boyfriend*?" Mike's already dark features clouded over with an odd mix of confusion and concern that I didn't quite recognize.

"Get over yourself, Mike. That was just a ploy." I released his arm and punched him playfully in the chest so that he'd let the lie go. "What are you doing here?"

"What are you doing letting the judge confiscate my phone?"

"What else was I supposed to do?"

"Tell the truth." He shook his head and rested an arm on the bank of pay phones anchored to the wall outside the sweet shop. "You were threatened by a coworker…again."

My blood ran cold when I flashed back to the gun in Johnny Erving's hand. Mike was right in guessing that the experience had dredged up angst caused by the former coworker who nearly took my life, but was this scenario the same? And if not, should the whole trial be tanked over one man's poor judgment?

"The truth isn't always black and white." I gritted my teeth and joined Mike beside the pay phone pavilion. "There are shades of gray."

"Then you can't fault me for doing my job and reporting the facts." Mike bit his bottom lip like he was attempting to censor himself. "All I know is that the situation looked real—and even knowing that it wasn't, doesn't change the level of danger and stupidity taking place. Johnny Erving deserves to be fired or, at the very least, exposed as an imbecile and first-rate jerk." Mike turned to face me. "Explain what possible motive could justify such an act."

"No comment."

"You don't trust me?"

"No comment," I repeated with an edge to my voice. "You never answered my question. What are you doing here? Troopers were supposed to have secured the area."

"Looking for stories is what I do." He ran a hand across his closely cropped Afro. "Plus, I live a few blocks over on a houseboat docked at the inlet, so I was enjoying a peaceful stroll through my neighborhood when I saw what I thought was a robbery in progress. Sorry if showing concern for a friend's well-being is a capital crime." He spread his fingers in a sarcastic set of jazz hands. "The real question is, why would you cover for those guys. You think they'd do the same for you?"

He had a point. In the short time we'd been on the boardwalk, those guys had managed to patronize and insult me, but this wasn't about them or the gun. This was about protecting the record and making sure that the trial didn't get derailed.

"It was a prank. You heard Johnny say it." I folded my arms to signal the resoluteness of my stance. "Sure, as pranks go, it was highly irrational, totally ill-conceived, poorly timed, and morally bankrupt. But no one was hurt, and I'd hate for this town to lose its opportunity for a long-awaited verdict because of one idiotic decision."

"That's your interpretation." Mike swung around and lifted one of the pay phone's receivers from its cradle. "My interpretation is that truth prevails. Why has your moral compass changed? You've seen with your own eyes that Johnny Erving's judgment is as bad as his client's and that our state officials can't be trusted."

"I'm not saying Johnny shouldn't be punished. I'm saying the town shouldn't have to go down with him. Can't you just wait until after the verdict to report on this? All we have left are the jury instructions and closing statements. Deliberations should start sometime this afternoon."

Mike pinned me with a desperate stare. "There's no one I'd rather bend the rules for than you," he sighed and punched a phone number into the keypad, "but when I've come to you in the past few months for insight into other trial issues, you've boxed me out."

"You know I have to remain neutral. I can't just..."

I could hear the phone ringing as he lifted the receiver to his ear.

"Regardless," he rolled his eyes, "you've made a point of dodging me with no explanation whatsoever. But now, out of the blue, I'm supposed to compromise my work ethic? I don't think so."

"Mike, be reasonable—"

He held up a hand to silence me and spoke into the receiver. "Hello? Allen? Slocum here. I've got a story I need you to get up on the website, pronto. I was hoping we'd have photos, but maybe I can get backups from the Cloud by tomorrow's print deadline. In the meantime, this will have to do."

Before I recognized what was happening, Mike pulled a small, gray, rectangular-shaped object from the inside pocket of his windbreaker. He held it up to the receiver, and the object pinged. Then, clear as if the defense attorney were still standing in front of me, I heard Johnny Erving's voice say, "I'm the one holding the gun."

This can't be happening.

Mike had audio of the whole interaction and was going live with the story.

So much for friendship.

Chapter Three

"Yes, Your Honor." I gripped the padded leather armrest of the captain's chair that sat opposite Judge Maddox's desk. "Mike Slocum is a reporter for *The Bickerton Bugle*, but I had no idea he was going to be there, and I didn't invite him. I only said he was my boyfriend in hopes of getting him alone to talk him out of reporting what he saw." My nose twitched at the smell of my own fear. They weren't going to like what was coming next. "Unfortunately, I failed. He called his office and played a recording of the incident just before we came back here."

"But, sir, that's an easy fix. We can call *The Bugle*, right?" DAG Wells scooted to the edge of his seat and spoke to the judge as if the rest of us weren't there. "If we have control of the photos, we've neutralized it, right?"

"Yeah, like that matters." Johnny slouched in his chair and let out a loud snort. "Were you listening, or were you too busy calculating how to spin it?"

Wells whipped around to face the opposing attorney. "I'm trying to be proactive."

Judge Maddox held up a hand for quiet and paced the tiny space behind his desk. There were four of us in chambers with him—Johnny, Wells, me, and the trial's bailiff, Arnold Knight. The room grew warmer as the judge completed his first circuit.

"Sounds like it's only a matter of hours before things go public." Maddox closed his eyes and massaged his temples with both hands. "You people are lucky that we were able to pull the jury away before they caught wind of your foolishness. Otherwise, all of our butts would be hanging out to dry."

My stomach roiled at the thought. No doubt, a full confession of my conversation with Mike was what the moment required.

Arnold Knight, the bailiff who'd overseen our boardwalk visit, sat to my right and stared at the floor with his arms folded. He had been pulled away from his duties with the jurors to answer for his role in providing the gun. He hadn't said a word since we left the beach. I should have been furious about the role he played in this chain of events, but he seemed like the kind of guy easily duped by the flash and dash of a jerk—I mean, jock—like Johnny.

Wells, on the other hand, was a twitchy mess. He reeked of perspiration and seemed scattered amongst the impossible tasks of sucking up to the judge, doing his job as prosecutor, and smoothing things over with his friend.

Friendship, however, was the furthest thing from Johnny's mind if the whispered argument that took place during the heavily guarded van ride back to the courthouse was any indication. Johnny sat in the corner and stared daggers at Wells, who had apparently cracked during his seaside conversation with the judge and blabbed about the incriminating pictures on the confiscated phone, forcing Johnny to reveal the gun hidden in his pants.

Maddox was, of course, incensed because knowledge of our activities put him in the sticky situation of having to decide whether to report the whole incident now and saddle an already controversial case with rumors of a scandal, or take the path of a maverick and barrel ahead with the trial, reporting Johnny's misdeed once a verdict came in.

My nails dug deeper into the slick fabric of the armrests. I hated that my own stubbornness might obstruct the service of justice, so I steeled myself for the questions to come and accepted the fact that Mike was right. The truth always comes out in the end.

"How much audio does this reporter have?" asked Maddox.

"Not a lot, but enough to set the scene. The word 'gun' is used at least once. And of course, with the photos being on a smartphone, he'll probably be able to download them from some sky-high server even if they've been deleted." I swallowed. "Speaking of which, I'll need to get that phone back."

Everyone looked at me dumbfounded, but it was Arnold Knight who smartened up first. Gone was the jolly smirk and the rosy skin seen at trial.

His countenance had become a series of hard gray lines on pale skin.

"What can I say, Your Honor?" He'd dropped the presentational tone he'd used during the call of court and let his native New Jersey shine through. "I'm sorry. I wasn't thinking. Helping PD Erving with pranks is, like, second nature. I've been doing it for years, ever since we discovered we're both Lambdas." Arnold looked over at Johnny, who averted his gaze. "So, you know, when a brother says he needs help with a prank, you come through. I mean, if we'd been in the courthouse, the thought might not ever have crossed my mind, but being outside, I didn't consider—"

"Frankly, my dear Arnold, the water has already broken under that damn." Maddox stopped pacing and scratched at a scar that emerged from the cuff of his track jacket. "Let's not waste time with excuses. We're too close to the end to let this train run off the rails. Wells, are you going to push a motion for a mistrial? The gun got pulled on you, but this is also your prosecution. The only thing keeping us from seeing the trial to its conclusion are the jury charge and closing statements."

"No motion, Your Honor. Our case is air-tight. If you're willing to proceed, so am I." Wells reached over and held out a hand to the public defender, who made a show of ignoring it.

"Johnny, I'm going to make you an offer you can't refuse." Maddox knitted his brows together for a moment. "I'm sure it will bite me in the butt. Still, I think the ends justify the means. I'm going to let you give your closing statement. But after that, I don't want to see you in my courtroom ever again. If we get a verdict today, send someone else from the PD's office to stand with your client. I figure, even if the jury votes guilty on only half the counts, we'll have at least two months before the sentence hearing. That should give your people plenty of time to get a replacement up to speed. Work with Victoria to get the complete set of trial transcripts. I don't want any mistakes here."

"Thank you, Your Honor. I won't let you—"

"No goodnights yet, John-Boy. Don't you dare think we are going to let this situation slide. The Justice Department will be prompted to open a thorough investigation on your so-called prank, so I suggest you get out of here and start working on your close. It will probably be the last one you give for a long time."

The attorney growled and made a slow show of unfolding himself from his chair. He hip-checked the seated prosecutor's shoulder on the way out and slammed the door hard enough to rattle the series of diplomas and accolades Judge Maddox had lined along that wall.

"Which brings me to you, Arnold." Maddox placed his palms on the desktop and stood so that he leaned over the wooden structure to look down at the man. "Since your unit reports directly to mine, it pains me to inform you that you've been relieved of your duties, effective immediately. Another bailiff will be assigned to oversee the jury in your stead. You are on administrative leave until the allegations surrounding the unauthorized use of your firearm have been investigated. The service weapon in question has been confiscated, and you will be barred from the building until further notice."

"But wait, Your Honor." Arnold shot from his seat. "I told you I wasn't thinking straight."

"This is not a negotiation." Maddox shook his head and pressed a button on his desk phone. "Ethel, send them in."

The disembodied voice of the judge's secretary confirmed his request, and seconds later, two short but sturdy gentlemen from the Capitol Police stormed into the room and seized Arnold by his biceps.

"C'mon, guys." Arnold protested. "Not like this."

But, I guess there was no room for negotiation with them either because they hoisted him along by his armpits until he had the good sense to walk out the door on his own.

Chapter Four

When the prosecutor and I entered the courtroom, we were greeted by a tsunami of sound. Every pew in the gallery overflowed with people engaged in animated chatter. Their voices reverberated through the antebellum-style rafters and solid oak finishes. The noise, though jarring, was to be expected since the *State of Delaware v. Ignacio Cardoza* was our small town's version of *The Towering Inferno*. We'd already spent most of the three-week trial with a courtroom full of tenacious reporters, curious citizens, and outraged victims. But on this particular Monday afternoon, there was a bizarre buzz underlying the din—one that went beyond the nervous energy that comes with awaiting the call to court.

Had Mike's story hit the internet in the couple hours since we'd gotten back from the boardwalk and hashed things out in judge's chambers? And if so, what bearing would it have on the day's proceedings?

I hugged my stenotype and laptop tight to my chest to shield myself from the thought as I followed DAG Wells down the aisle. He held his head high, seemingly oblivious to the odd pulsation in the air. I followed suit and focused my sights straight ahead, where Johnny Erving was already at the defense counsel's table whispering to his client, Ignacio Cardoza.

The defendant was in his early thirties with sallow skin, a light beard, and a close-cropped haircut that faded away on the sides. He wore the cheap polo shirt and khakis public defenders obtained for clients still in custody and sat unchained, nodding calmly as his attorney spoke. He'd been through the judicial system before on similar arson charges, though those previous fires had been minor in comparison.

But that hadn't stopped DAG Wells, who'd filed a pretrial motion seeking to introduce parts of Ignacio's record as evidence. He'd hoped to prove the defendant's prior bad acts were a sign that Ignacio had the potential and the desire to escalate his already dangerous behavior. Judge Maddox, however, denied the motion in limine, and the jury was never made privy to the defendant's sordid history.

Once I pushed past the bar, I nodded at the trial clerk stationed below the judge's bench and headed across the well to my seat in front of the witness stand. I sat mere feet from the empty juror box. A hush fell over the room in that moment—perhaps folks sensed my arrival signaled the proceedings were about to start—except for one person who used that second to let out a low whistle. I set my steno machine on the floor and bent down to double-check that the tripod's legs were firmly extended in place. This turned my mane into a curtain of bushy curls from behind which I could covertly search for the source of the sound.

Mike Slocum.

I should have known.

He sat in the front pew behind defense counsel's table. He jotted something on his notepad, then looked straight in my direction as if he could see through my makeshift veil. The slight upturn of his full lips hinted at a coy smile that would have been sweet under any other circumstances, but I shuddered. Hopefully, he had no plans to disrupt the proceedings with some revelatory outburst.

"All rise."

A new bailiff—clean-shaven and reedy—called court to order. Whereupon, Judge Maddox climbed the elevated platform and took his seat on the bench while I opened a new file on my computer and marked the time, 1:13 p.m.

Focus up. Duty calls.

Maddox motioned to the young bailiff. "Let's bring in the jury."

Twelve jurors and four alternates filed out of a doorway on the side of the room farthest from the defendant. With them came the delightfully sweet aroma of coffee and donuts, but their expressions were anything but pleasant. Gone was the wonder seen earlier that day. Most kept their gazes downcast, presumably to avoid scrutiny from the packed gallery.

As a group, they skewed over thirty and dressed casually, though a few name brands suggested upper middle class living. The defense had done a good job at selecting a diverse jury, considering the dated beliefs about race that still pervaded our seaside hamlet. Of the four men and eight women who made up the jury proper, three Black and two Latinx faces turned toward the judge when he cleared his throat to address them.

"Good afternoon. Once again, has the jury been exposed to any media coverage in this case, such as radio, TV, newspaper, or the internet?" Maddox stared intently at the sixteen somber faces seated in the elevated box. When a collective, "No, Your Honor," rang out, I could have sworn I heard a slight sigh of relief from Maddox before he resumed. "Let the record reflect a negative response."

I did so by hitting SKWR*UR/SKWR*UR on my steno keyboard so that a short, preprogrammed parenthetical appeared in the text that was being captured and translated via Bluetooth to the computer-aided transcription program open on my laptop.

The judge then explained the purpose of the jury charge, i.e. the instructions of law, to the jurors and read through the lengthy text so the parameters for their deliberation were clear and on the record.

I'd been a court reporter for half a decade, so capturing a jury charge was second nature. Besides, every decent reporter had briefs, a/k/a abbreviations, or shortened word forms for all of the standard terminology like "presumption of innocence" PRUPBLG and "beyond a reasonable doubt" KWRORD. Most juror instructions were merely a compilation of those standard rules of law set forth in a manner to best address the defendant's indicted charges.

The folks in the gallery remained surprisingly quiet and their attention zeroed in on Maddox, but the restless energy from earlier still percolated beneath the calm. I glanced at the attorneys with the hope that the tensions from chambers weren't further feeding the atmosphere of unrest, but their discontent remained. Wells sat with his back as straight as a poker. An odd carnival barker grin presented a strange contrast to the furrow that marred his brow.

Johnny, on the other hand, made no effort to hide his discomfort. When the judge read through his client's counts of arson, criminal trespass, reckless burning, reckless endangering, and burglary, he clenched his jaw until his neck grew taut.

Ignacio was the only calm face among those seated center stage. He took notes as the judge concluded his instructions and provided a shy nod to those jurors who dared to meet his eye.

"Now we will hear closing arguments from counsel." Maddox motioned to the prosecutor.

DAG Grant Wells stood, buttoned his double-breasted suit around his trim frame, and took the podium that had been set out in the middle of the well so the attorneys could address the jury directly. He bid them a pleasant afternoon and thanked them for their service before diving into the heart of the matter.

"The State has shown that the defendant walked from downtown Bickerton to the boardwalk every day to start his 5:00 a.m. shift at the historic Rainbow Sands Hotel. We offered the testimony of several coworkers who confirmed the defendant often arrived to work drenched due to the four-mile trek and would therefore change into his uniform prior to the start of each shift. The wardrobe changes consistently caused him to arrive late to his post at the bellman's desk. This is the reason documented for his eventual dismissal, and the proposed impetus for his retaliation by fire."

Johnny Erving coughed loudly at the end of this last statement as if he wanted to call B.S. under his breath. But when the prosecutor stilled, no other sound came, so Wells brushed a strand of blond hair from his eye. The move was slow and deliberate, like he'd paused his speech for just that purpose.

"You heard from the State Fire Marshal's Office that the person who started this fire did so during the early morning hours and relied on common combustibles such as rags and loose paper to fuel his work." Wells held up the marked exhibit containing the written report. "You also learned that the fire was set without accelerants like turpentine or gasoline, and we'd submit that fodder over fuel fits the modus operandi of the defendant, whose lack of transportation wouldn't permit carrying items that could limit his mobility."

With those words, Wells made a big show of turning to look at defense counsel's table as if daring Johnny to offer another interruption, but the public defender and his client sat silent with blank stares. A few jurors snickered at the gamesmanship that had clearly entered the proceedings. This was the shady theatrics they understood from shows like *Judge Judy*. Never mind the fact that people like Judge Maddox, whose lips were pursed as if on the cusp of complaint, found both moves completely juvenile.

"Our experts," Wells continued when he caught the judge's evil eye, "then pinpointed the fire's origin to the alley side service entrance of the hotel used for loading and unloading. They determined the fire was set in the middle of a large stack of towels and paper supplies stored in the basement level of the building. This was an area where the defendant knew the fire suppression system was less sophisticated and could be turned off by hand onsite rather than electronically through the hotel's security office as per the residential levels of the facility."

He walked to the trial clerk's table, where the case's larger pieces of evidence lived, and held up two poster boards. One contained an enlarged file photo of the alleyway leading to the hotel's service entrance, and the other showcased its front-facing façade from the days when the building was the crown jewel of our beloved boardwalk.

"We have eyewitnesses who can put the defendant near the boardwalk at the time of the fire. Two empty matchbooks were found mere feet from the back alley service entrance of the hotel, and they carry the name of the bar that's across the street from the defendant's residence. We also have footprints leading to the area of the hotel where the fire was confirmed as set. Those prints match the tread of the shoes the defendant was commonly seen wearing. Shoes that had rundown heels and other telltale markings consistent with someone who'd worn that footwear to excess."

Wells set the photos beside the podium and continued to outline the damning evidence against the defendant. It wasn't long before he was talking so fast that capturing his words was like trying to juggle a trio of active chainsaws. My fingers flew across the steno keys as muscle memory took over. Words like TKREBG "direct evidence" and HRURPBLGS "ladies and gentlemen of the jury" popped onto the screen while my mind raced ahead to anticipate what the attorney might say next. Fortunately, machine shorthand wasn't like typing on a QWERTY-style laptop. My keys were placed in three tight uniform rows so that several of them could be pressed in unison to form a full word or phrase like chords on a tablet-sized pipe organ. This logistical edge ensured I stayed within seconds of the prosecutor's manic delivery without breaking a sweat.

At the end of Wells's speech, I held up a finger to stall PD Erving's approach to the podium. I needed to shake out my hands and check that my laptop was still translating the shorthand in real time. While I worked, Johnny seized the moment to do what I like to think of as his heroic quick change. It's a move he usually did in front of the jury when he introduced himself and his client for the last time.

Since public defenders are often considered villainous, Johnny made a point of throwing on a pair of thick rimmed glasses and slicking back his unruly chestnut curls to show he could be as straightlaced and aligned with justice as the prosecutor. The desired correlation, of course, being that his clients weren't criminals but rather innocent victims of circumstance. I once found this schtick amusing, but now I saw the vile deception inherent in the act.

When Johnny had run one last hand through his hair to complete the transformation, I gave him a nod, and he launched into his closing without preamble.

"We've heard three weeks' worth of testimony about the cause and origin of the fire, but we haven't heard anything other than theories when it comes to *who*. The state wants to paint you a pretty picture where all of the dots are connected, but there's no proof my client was in the hotel's loading area at the time of the fires or that he started them. It just does not exist—no photos, no video, no eyewitnesses to the event."

Johnny, ever the athlete, liked to move around the courtroom when he gave his summation, which made it difficult for me to capture the record once he walked away from the mic. So when he made a move to round the podium and approach the jury box, I gave him a one-word warning.

"Counselor." As always, I strove to preserve the record without becoming a part of it.

"Sure," Johnny directed the word to the jury and didn't acknowledge my presence, but he did lean an arm against the podium so that he remained in range of the mic, "the prosecution has lots of circumstantial evidence that helps shape the story they are trying to create—the footprints being the primary example. Yet, they gave no proof as to when those tracks were made. So, is it really that shocking that someone who once worked at the hotel would have left a footprint or two somewhere on the premises? Particularly when we consider that it was only a week between my client's dismissal and the destruction of the hotel."

Johnny took off his prop glasses and held the stem against his lips for an exaggerated moment as if to physically signal the jurors' need to ponder the question he proposed.

"And what about the matchbooks?" His voice swelled, and he threw his hands above his head with a flourish. "No fingerprints were found on them, and the bar in question is frequented by locals and tourists alike during the summer season." Returning the eyewear to the bridge of his nose, he raised an eyebrow. "I would submit the prosecution has failed to prove there is a direct connection between my client and the crime. I would also suggest that they're trying to use the false motive of revenge to convince you that their lack of evidence is justified. Reflect on the instructions the judge gave you. Motive alone is not sufficient evidence of a crime. You need proof. The fact that they cannot put my client inside the hotel at the time of the fire..."

Johnny slammed the side of his fist down onto the wooden surface of the podium.

"...*that* should be the key to your decision. Remember, every person charged with a crime is presumed innocent. That presumption requires a verdict of 'not guilty' unless you are firmly—not kind of, not sort of—but firmly convinced by the evidence that the state has proven their case beyond a reasonable doubt." He picked up the poster boards that the prosecutor had left on display by the podium. "Whoever destroyed the Rainbow Sands Hotel did so sometime around 3:30 a.m. during the height of the August tourist season when onsite surveillance, or at the very least someone's cellphone, would have surely captured the wrongdoing. Yet, no such evidence exists."

Cellphone footage. Isn't that ironic? The idea that the case could hinge on something like the lack of video made me tear my focus away from Johnny in search of Mike Slocum. He sat forward in his seat and scribbled furiously. His nostrils flared, and he turned to meet my questioning gaze as if he'd come to the same conclusion.

Despite our clash today, I considered Mike a friend—a confidant even—and I'd turned my back on him over some moral obligation that wasn't even my own. Was his intrusion a sign that we all needed to be more vigilant when it came to protecting each other and what we believed in? After all, if someone had been brave enough to stand up and speak out that fateful night, would we even need this trial?

This minuscule nugget of discontent burrowed into my consciousness as my hands worked feverishly to capture the rest of the public defender's closing and the final counterpoint by the prosecution. Things moved swiftly thereafter, with the judge instructing the jury on their deliberation procedures and the importance of a unanimous verdict. Maddox then excused the alternate jurors and asked the trial clerk to swear the bailiffs assigned to supervise the remaining twelve.

As we watched their somber faces recede into the darkened confines of the jury room, I was struck by the paradox embedded within the task we'd given them: The jury now wielded the immense and fearsome power to decide a man's fate, but could only do so based on snippets of the truth presented by equally flawed men.

I didn't envy those jurors for a moment.

With the jury gone and the courtroom cleared pending the verdict, the guards chained Ignacio's arms and legs together with an intricate array of jangly metal bracelets and hauled him to the small holding area located behind a heavy metal door just off the courtroom.

CHAPTER FOUR

Deliberations had officially begun.

* * *

Something was wrong.

We'd only been sitting in the courtroom for a couple of hours when the light above the jury room door lit up.

As I stared at the beacon, a lump formed in my throat. I had known this moment was coming, but I hadn't expected it so quickly. My experiences had proven that deliberations of this magnitude took a full day, if not three or four. Many jurors requested evidence, submitted questions of law to the judge, or asked for the court reporter to read back testimony. That's why I'd sat in the courtroom scoping my transcript—well, that, and the desire to avoid the prospect of running into the hordes of reporters roaming the courthouse lobby awaiting the jury's decision.

The courtroom—though only occupied by me and the attorneys at present—took on an eerie chill as the bailiff slipped inside the deliberation room to turn off the light. A minute later, he emerged with a tight-lipped expression that said nothing and everything all at once.

"Counselors," the young bailiff bellowed, "are you prepared for me to bring in the judge? The jury has reached a verdict."

Chapter Five

Judge Maddox settled onto the bench. His robes, though slightly rumpled per usual, billowed around him onto the dais and expanded his thin frame into an opposing figure seemingly floating above his audience.

"Foreperson," he nodded at the juror closest to the empty witness stand, "has the jury reached a unanimous verdict?"

"Yes." The foreperson, a mature woman of color in her late fifties with a husky voice and a square jaw, stood in response to the judge's call. She held a paper in her hand, which trembled slightly as she spoke.

"Very well. You may take the verdict, Madam Clerk."

Our trial clerk, a pale, wrinkly woman with crescent-shaped spectacles permanently stuck to her nose, stood and motioned the defendant to do the same. She then picked up a copy of the indictment and turned to face the foreperson.

"On the charge of criminal trespass in the first degree, does the jury find the defendant at the bar guilty as charged or not guilty?"

"Not guilty."

I looked at Ignacio Cardoza, who stood dutifully with his hands at his sides, but his eyes closed when the first answer sounded as if he'd fallen into a silent prayer of gratitude.

"As to the charge of reckless burning in the first degree, guilty as charged or not guilty?"

"Not guilty."

Ignacio bowed his head at those words. At the same time, a loud wail came from the back of the courtroom as the gallery of outraged victims and tenacious reporters began to voice their discontent. Judge Maddox banged his gavel twice to thwart the interruption, but the manic energy I'd intuited earlier seeped into the proceedings and glommed to the edges of the foreperson's responses.

"As to the charge of arson in the first degree, guilty as charged or not guilty?"

"Not guilty."

Ignacio looked up then, as that was the charge with the lengthiest minimum sentence. Tears streamed down his face, and he gripped his attorney's shoulder. The wail from the rear of the room once again pierced the air, louder and more feral. The attorney that had replaced the now banished Johnny Erving didn't even blink. His face was as still as stone. His eyes never wavered from the judge. DAG Grant Wells sat equally as impassive to the point where I didn't think the man had taken a breath.

As the clerk continued through the last three counts of the indictment, getting a "not guilty" response on each, I could hear muffled sobs in the jury box slightly behind me and to my left. Meanwhile, the voices in the gallery had grown from a single wail to a collective roar.

Upon completion of the verdict, DAG Wells sprang from his seat. "I demand the jury be polled."

The judge acknowledged the prosecutor's request and asked the clerk to question each juror individually.

"Madame Foreperson, is this your verdict?"

"Juror No. 2, is this your verdict?"

"Juror No. 3, is this your verdict?"

A chorus of "yes" resounded through the courtroom while the defendant covered his face with his hands, unable to dislodge the mask of elation that had formed there.

It was over…and the jury had let him go.

Chapter Six

"With the overwhelming amount of evidence presented at trial," Mike Slocum shouted over the din, "how could you possibly justify today's verdict?"

The jury's foreperson stood outside the courtroom, cornered by Mike and the cadre of cameras and television reporters who had formed a bottleneck around the double doors in the rear to catch the jurors as they exited. The dark woman narrowed her eyes and set her broad jaw so that her chin jutted forward with an air of defiance, but she eventually answered the question posed to her.

"A guilty verdict would have been a violation of our duty as jurors," her husky voice rang sharp, "which was to apply the law. We weren't asked if this guy had the means or the motive or the know-how; we were asked to convict if persuaded by the evidence beyond a reasonable doubt. And quite honestly, what does that even mean?" One of the cameramen flicked on a bright light in response to her question, and she held up an arm to shield her eyes. "We all had doubts and theories about who did it. But at the end of the day, we decided not to condemn one man just because we needed someone to blame."

I hung back, knowing the questions would only grow more probing. My hope was that the media vultures would get a couple of soundbites and buzz off. No chance of them getting anything from Judge Maddox, who had left the bench seconds after the verdict had been deemed unanimous. He'd done so through the special door at the head of the courtroom that led to his private chambers. The defendant had quickly taken his leave as well, escorted by three large guards through the metal security door so that he could be whisked back to Trident County Correctional Institution and processed out as a free man.

The lawyers, however, dawdled behind the bar, the wooden partition that separated the gallery from the well of the courtroom. They knew it was the one line the reporters couldn't cross. I would have done the same, but the hour was nearing 5:30, and I was eager to put the day behind me. So, I stood in the middle of the aisle with my laptop under one arm and my steno machine in hand as each juror passed through the gauntlet.

"Based on the outraged reactions of some of the victims here today, are you having regrets about the verdict?" asked a woman in a sharp red dress suit, who I recognized as Ana Ortega from the WSYS nightly newscast. She'd directed her question to a gruff-looking male juror who donned shiny black cowboy boots and a matching plaid shirt.

"What does it matter?" he answered. "In this country, not guilty doesn't mean innocent anyway. That man is marked for life regardless of what we say. The least we could do is spare him the jail time."

The more I watched, the more I recognized a commonality in the jurors' answers. They all seemed to have concluded the prosecution failed to meet its burden of proof—no one saw him do it, so who's to say he did?

As a plump, rosy-skinned woman in a cardigan walked out, a bearded reporter in a navy blue trench coat hurled a question in her direction. "But what about your duty to uphold the law? Can you honestly say justice prevailed here?"

"Yes, we were asked to uphold the law," her face reddened as cameras clicked and flashes descended on her, "but I don't understand your question about justice because the two aren't always the same. Justice would have been to vote guilty so the community got its closure. Adhering to the law meant allowing the defendant to go free because the evidence failed to prove the case. I'll admit it didn't feel right, so I prayed about it." She swallowed hard as if deciding whether to say more. "Justice belongs to God. Only He can decide our fate. Man is fallible and must therefore err on the side of caution. And that's when I knew, I couldn't pronounce that man guilty."

This seemed to cow the voraciousness of those who'd gathered to capitalize on the crime, and I used the juror's moment of religious superiority to slip into the crowd unnoticed. I'd almost gotten through the throng when a coarse hand gripped my elbow.

"You're not getting away that easy." I looked back to find Mike Slocum at my shoulder.

"You know I won't talk about the trial." I wriggled from his grasp. "If you want a copy of the transcript, call my office."

"Is this the ending you were hoping for?" he asked.

"Are we on the record?"

"Of course, not."

"Really?" I cocked my head to the side and balanced my equipment on my hip. "I feel like I have to check after this morning. Why didn't you tell me you had an audio recording of the prank?"

"You would have freaked out even more." He shrugged and let his posture slump. "I'm not a monster. This was simply about the truth. I mean, look what happened here when the full picture wasn't laid on the table."

His dark eyes, wide and pleading, met my own. I nodded and relaxed my stance. He had a point, and the irony that Ignacio walked free because no one provided the kind of visual or aural evidence Mike had provided for his web article wasn't lost on me.

"Fine. I get it. You were right. We can't save the truth for moments of convenience. I thought I was doing the right thing." I glanced back at DAG Wells, who looked like he was on the verge of losing his lunch. "Things managed to be screwed up anyway, and I just don't want to fight anymore. Okay?"

"Whatever. I just want my friend back. Is that too much to ask?"

"Of course, not. I'm sorry." I pulled out the cellphone confiscated by the judge and returned it to Mike.

"Me too."

A slight nudge from behind jostled Mike forward. As he recovered his balance, Ana Ortega weaved around him and lobbed a question in my direction.

"As someone who saw this trial played out behind the scenes, what did you make of the verdict?" She waved to her cameraman to join her.

"No comment." I turned to walk away.

Ana followed me down the courthouse hall. "Is there anything you can tell us about the defendant's demeanor when he left the courtroom?"

"No comment."

"What do you make of what the jurors have been saying?"

"No—"

"Back up, guys. Just backup." Mike stepped between me and the camera that Ana had beckoned into action. "You're swimming in dangerous territory. You know as well as I do her work as an officer of the court makes it unethical for her to discuss the case. She couldn't have been any clearer. She doesn't want to talk."

Mike used his forearm to hold the gathering crowd back so I could break from the fray and walk down the corridor toward my office.

Fed up by the presence of the press, I bit my lip to keep from cursing. I couldn't say what I wanted to say, which was that most people were selfish and idiotic. Place a dozen individuals together in tight quarters for long enough, and they'll find someone—or something—to hate. In this case, it seemed that *thing* was the law.

But the jurors were right, justice didn't happen in a vacuum. Lives were won and lost every day in the courtroom. Most people never thought about this because more often than not, justice was manufactured, the imperfect made perfect by the hubris of mankind.

Mike caught up with me just before I hit the double doors that led into the personnel area where the court reporters' office was located. "You okay?"

"Yeah, I just need to relax. Ideally, somewhere away from here."

"Would you like to join me for dinner?"

"Back off. Now's not the time." DAG Wells bellowed as he breezed by us with a troupe of reporters hot on his trail. He'd probably attempted to escape unnoticed while they feasted on me. Half a dozen reporters, including one with a cellphone on a selfie stick, followed him down the hall, firing off questions:

"The Bickerton Bugle's website says Public Defender Jonathan Erving was the perpetrator of an ill-conceived gun prank during trial proceedings. Is the judge aware of his actions?"

"Where did he get the weapon?"

"Do you plan to press charges and settle the score, so to speak, after today's unexpected loss?"

I glared at Mike. The firestorm had begun. Between the bad verdict and the pending scandal, the courthouse wouldn't be safe for anyone in the coming days.

"I'll have to pass. My mother needs…some help at her office." This was a lie. I had no intention of walking down to the Mayor's Office after a day like today, but I did have plans to meet a friend at my favorite café across the street. And with the mayhem Mike had caused in the last eight hours, I didn't need a squeaky third wheel ruining my fun.

"Fair enough." He backed away and offered a gentle wave. "I'll email you about the transcripts. In the meantime, don't be a stranger."

I gave a non-committal smile. Screw that. Truce or no truce. My momma didn't raise no fool. You were less likely to get burned if you simply stayed away from pot stirrers.

* * *

Cake & Kettle's gray and gold striped awning was a welcome sight as I stepped out of the courthouse into the crisp spring evening and scurried across the street before I could be spotted by the handful of reporters milling around. The café was known for its authentic British cuisine, but I loved the place for its imported teas and homemade confections. I opened the door to the familiar jingle-jangle of the welcome bell and inhaled the subtle aroma of cinnamon and cardamon.

Heavenly. All the joys of home with none of the dishes.

My good friend Jillian Galbraith, the brassy divorcee who owned the shop, carefully navigated her way through the maze of velveteen settees, decorative side tables, and ornate ottomans. She carried a metal tray, containing an elephant-shaped teapot and a mountain of English-style scones, over to a familiar face seated in one of the three wing-backed chairs near the rear.

Once Jillian had set the tray on a nearby coffee table, she waved me over. We'd initially met each other six years ago in the time before I became an official stenographer. Those were the days right after college when I'd spent a year interning for a dear family friend who happened to be a judge at the courthouse. Back then, Jillian was a nerdy-looking brunette married to a promiscuous guy named Shaun. These days, she was a well-exercised blonde with an edgy pixie cut and wild green contacts she claimed made her look younger than her thirty-three years.

"We were worried you'd be stuck at the courthouse. That wacko verdict is all over the internet." She wrapped her arms around me in a tight hug, then perched on the arm of the chair occupied by the person I had come to meet. "Ashton was just telling me he's never met Cardoza, but he had a brief look at the case in late August back when they thought the fire might be gang-related."

Ashton North stood upon mention of his name and leaned in to give me his own hug. This one picked me up off my feet because he was a massive six-foot-four to my petite five-foot frame. Although broad-shouldered and muscular, Ashton was as gentle as they came. We'd grown close after my brush with death at the hands of a rogue courthouse employee. And despite his dishonesty about the role he played in the event, he'd eventually helped capture the culprit even though he'd lost his job as a State Trooper in the process.

"Are you okay? You look exhausted." Ashton helped me remove my leather jacket and gestured to the seat across from him. "I took the liberty of ordering your favorites. Lemon-ginger tea plus scones with clotted cream, strawberry preserves, and lemon curd."

I reached for one of the golden domes without plate or preamble. "After a day like today, you guys don't know how much I need this."

Jillian hopped up from the arm of Ashton's chair and patted the sleeve of his pale blue Oxford. "I'll run and grab you some coffee. Would you care for a Chelsea bun?"

"Two, please."

"Sure thing, love." Jillian sashayed toward the pastry counter at the front of the café.

"Did the press give the DAG a hard time for failing to prosecute," Ashton picked at an invisible piece of lint on his jeans, "or did Johnny's gun prank cast doubt on the verdict?"

"Both issues exploded separately." I stopped mid-chew and met his gaze. I appreciated his efforts not to ask me about the trial directly. "Most of the questions went to the departing jurors, but…"

I split my half-eaten scone open and slathered it with lemon curd and clotted cream. After a gooey sweet bite, I finished my thought.

"…there's probably not much anybody could do about Johnny even if they managed to prove his behavior outside the courtroom could have mucked up the trial. The defendant isn't going to complain since he got the desired outcome, and the prosecution can't appeal the verdict based on the guarantees given to the accused under the Fifth Amendment."

"Interesting." Ashton ran a hand through the shag of his copper-colored crew cut. "I also thought I heard your voice on the recording they posted on *The Bickerton Bugle's* website. Were you there when the gun was pulled?"

Oh, boy. I should have known this was coming.

"Sorry, I can't tell you how fast these baked goods have sold out today." Jillian rounded Ashton's wing-backed chair with a huge ceramic mug—*thank goodness*—and a small plate filled with a spongy-looking dessert. "We're all out of Chelsea buns, but I nipped you some mascarpone-filled coffee and walnut cake from my personal supply. Taste it and see if you love it."

Jillian handed Ashton his order, and I used the distraction to calculate an appropriate answer because I knew he'd overreact and want to confront Johnny. In the months following the attack by my corrupt coworker, Ashton had proclaimed himself my protector and invited me to casual outings like this one to check on my mental health. He also worked with me on my aquaphobia during our Sunday morning outings to the various waterfront attractions our town boasted due to its proximity to the Atlantic Ocean and Delaware Bay.

I was fine with that on the surface because I'd never really had a friend growing up. I'd completely skipped middle school and was bullied for my size as a high schooler—nearly drowning in the process—which led to my overall distrust of people. But I'd grown up and become more than capable of deciding my own fate.

Of course, having another gun pulled on me thrust me right back into the fear mindset that had gripped me nearly six months ago, but I'd persevered under pressure today because I knew Ashton wouldn't always be there. So, uncomfortable or not, I had to continue to stand up for myself...even in moments like this.

"All met?" Jillian gave me a wink. She'd been privy to many a tense moment like this between me and Ashton. "I'll be behind the register if you need me."

When she'd gone, I reached for the elephant teapot—my favorite from her assorted collection—and spoke with finality as I poured my tea. "The gun wasn't loaded. I'm not pressing charges. Johnny's going to have enough trouble now that word has—"

"That's unacceptable—"

"Ashton, I've had enough for one day."

"I don't care." His nostrils flared.

"I just want to put this behind me."

"We will once I—"

"This wouldn't even have been an issue if it wasn't for Mike Slocum."

"He was there too?" Ashton slammed his mug on the table with a clatter.

"He made the recording and reported the incident."

Ashton groaned and crossed his arms so hard his biceps strained against his shirt. The two men barely knew each other, save for a few brief cross-interactions with me, but this revelation seemed to infuriate Ashton more than the news about the gun.

"Mike apologized. It's done." I blew lightly over my piping hot tea and racked my brain for a change of subject.

"He could have left you out of it."

"Perhaps, but he was trying to do the right thing and report the whole story."

"Sounds a bit self-serving on his part if you ask me."

"For the record, I hadn't." I sipped my tea and savored the peppery tang. "How's the job hunt going? You promised me good news."

"Del State called me for an interview." The lines of tension around Ashton's bright blue eyes softened, and his thin lips curved into a smile. "I shouldn't say too much. I don't want to jinx it, but they asked me to come in for an interview Friday morning. Are you willing to meet me afterward for lunch? I'll take you someplace fancy."

Before I could answer, the door chime rang. Since we were the only ones in the café, my attention wandered to the source of the sound.

"That's a scone?" said a brash male voice. "Aren't they supposed to be three-sided? Looks more like a biscuit to me."

I peered around Ashton's chair as best I could, and I spied a familiar figure—tall, dark, and lean.

Curses. Mike Slocum.

He stood by the squat set of bookshelves Jillian used to mark the eatery's order area. He had his back to me and seemed preoccupied with examining the desserts in the glass pastry display, but that gangly set of ebony limbs could only belong to one person.

Next to him, a curvy, sienna-skinned woman in her mid-sixties, wearing a fitted maroon pantsuit, drummed her acrylic nails on the counter. Her tawny pageboy swayed side to side as she shook her head at Mike's indecision.

As if things couldn't get any worse, my mother was with him.

With my moment of peace disrupted, I excused myself and walked over to them.

"Hey, Ma, since when do you hang out with the press?" I fired a sharp look at Mike, who was still in negotiations with Jillian about his order.

"Oh, stop being so dramatic. He's your friend." She smoothed the collar of my shirt and brushed a frizzy lock of hair from my cheek. "I saw him standing outside the courthouse on the way over here, and he asked me for my reaction to the—by the way, you need to start answering your phone. I shouldn't have to rely on Jillian to figure out where you are. I've been texting you nonstop about that gun incident. What was the public defender doing with a gun?"

"Ma," I held up both palms to stop her from spiraling into a full rant, "the whole thing was a prank outside the presence of the jury."

"That doesn't matter." She clutched my hands to her ample bosom. "You could have been hurt—and that trial was a sham by a sham artist. If the defense attorney can get away with waving a gun around in broad daylight, it only stands to reason his client could get away with burning down businesses in our historic district. The city council demands a copy of the trial transcript. Something must be done about Johnny Erving and that verdict."

"I take it this is off the record?" Mike chimed in with the cream of a half-eaten profiterole dribbling down his chin. "Kidding. Thanks for the coffee, Madame Mayor."

"Please, call me Corinne."

He grabbed a to-go cup off the counter and lifted it in a cheers gesture, but did so to someone over my shoulder rather than to Ma. When I turned in the direction of Mike's gaze, I noticed Ashton had risen from his seat and appeared as if he was ready to spit nails.

Busted.

"You're here with Ashton?" Ma gasped.

I edged her away from Mike for a more private conversation. "Yes, and I suggest you don't wait up."

I had no intention of staying out all night. I just wanted her to remember I was an adult with my own agenda. The only reason we even still lived together was that I was her only immediate family, and I worried about her being in her sixties and living on her own.

"Not a chance." Ma stood her ground. "I don't think it's wise for you to be seen in public with a disgraced trooper even if—"

"Mike, wait." I reached out to grab his arm, but he'd already made a beeline for Ashton while Ma continued to air old complaints. So, I abandoned her and dashed after the reporter, who stood little chance against the taller and broader former cop.

"Surprised to see you here, Corporal North—or should I say, Citizen North."

"Well, if it isn't little Jimmy Olsen come to save the day." Ashton's voice oozed with sarcasm, but he kept the volume casual, probably because we had an audience in Ma and Jillian, who both still stood by the counter. "I should warn you. There's no story here, so why don't you find someone else to record without their knowledge?"

"C'mon, guys. It's been a rough day for the whole town." I nodded toward the empty wing-backed chair at the other end of the coffee table. "Let's sit down and have a drink."

"Do you really want this guy around after he's connected you to another scandal?" Ashton clenched his jaw and remained standing.

"I think you're projecting here." Mike popped the last of the profiterole into his mouth and took a long sip of coffee. "I seem to recall just last year someone lying under oath about the veracity of an arrest and using that testimony to elicit Victoria's help in tracking down a drug dealer, which put her on a murderer's radar. So if we're talking scandals, wouldn't that make you the reigning king?"

"For someone who's supposed to report the facts, you sure know how to misrepresent a situation," Ashton roared.

"Enough," I hissed. "Either sit down and play nice, or leave."

I plopped into my chair and made no indication which man had earned the ultimatum. At this point, they could both get lost, so I could enjoy my scones and tea in solitude.

Mike cleared his throat and moved to sit in the chair offered to him.

Ashton picked up the fleece jacket draped on the back of his seat and looked down at me with regret etched across his brow. "I'll text you about lunch on Friday. I just got my truck out of the shop, so I can pick you up at the courthouse. Maybe we can try for a meal at the dockside restaurant by the ferry?" He reached out and squeezed my shoulder. "Or if you're up to it, we could try to get you out there on the water to work on your aquaphobia. We could drive onto the ferry and stay in the salon or the food court the whole time to ease you into the idea of being on the bay. The food and drink might help take your mind off the setting."

I put my hand on top of his and squeezed back. His tone was so sweet, and

I knew he meant well. But the mere idea of setting foot on the ferry gave me chills, and I didn't have the heart to tell him his big-wheeled wannabe monster truck probably exceeded the vessel's height restrictions.

When I didn't respond, he sighed and glared at Mike before shuffling to the door, where Ma and Jillian watched in confusion.

"Someone's in a bad mood." Mike settled deeper into his chair and crossed his legs like he didn't have a care in the world.

"Really, Mike?" I flapped my arms in exasperation.

"You know, I've never really been in here before," he rubbed a hand along the lush suede of his chair and looked around, "but I see the appeal."

"I'm serious. You can't play nice for one second?"

"What? He chose to leave. How's that my fault?"

"You knew exactly what you were doing."

"C'mon, I came in here to warm up on the mayor's invite. I wasn't expecting him—or you, for that matter."

"Well, you've overstayed your welcome." Ma approached the table with Jillian at her side. "Consider the invitation withdrawn. I'd like to discuss the day's events with my little Angel in private."

Jillian stepped toward Mike's chair and raised a sinewy arm toward the entrance. When he took the hint and rose, she followed him to the front of the café and locked the door behind him.

Ma settled into the chair left unoccupied by Mike and examined me with a hint of melancholy in her eyes.

"Talk to me, Angel. What is going on with you? I hear rumors about a gun. I can't get you on the phone. And now that I have you, you're so quick to brush everything aside." Her voice emitted a slight hitch, the kind that precedes a good cry. "After everything that's happened in this town over the last six months. I would think you'd take your safety more seriously."

Although I'd railed against Mike's depictions of our town's misdeeds, there was some truth to the corruption, and my mother had been one of the many casualties of the fallout. She'd lost her best friend in the slew of people killed during the last courthouse scandal—and she'd almost lost me, her only child and companion. Sure, I was adopted as a baby from a drug-addicted teen, but in Ma's mind, that's what made me all the more special. It's also why she called me 'her Angel,' the unexpected miracle who'd overcome the odds and lit up her solitary life. So it only made sense that she'd find the day's series of improprieties a threat to those she loved.

However, I wasn't in the mood to be coddled.

"I'm capable of weighing risk just like everyone else," I sighed, "but you have to learn to trust me as well as my judgement—all of you do." I spread my hands toward Jillian, who'd gone back to count cash at the register, but I meant the men who had left, too.

I'd never be able to make a future if everyone kept me living in the past.

Chapter Seven

"It's official, people," Candace Fontaine held up a copy of *The Bickerton Bugle's* Friday edition and shook out the folds so that we could read the headline: "President Judge Bans Bailiffs' Guns Statewide After PD Prank Goes Bust!"

Candi was the lead stenographer for our courthouse, mainly because at fifty-three she'd worked for the state longer than any of us, but the position was well-deserved in that she was a cockeyed optimist with a knack for diplomacy. So as she stood before us, her wire-rimmed glasses perched on the end of her flat nose and her strawberry blonde hair pulled back in a bun, she shunned the negativity of the press.

"Nobody expected them to move so swiftly with this," she pronounced from the pulpit of her desk, "but we can't let the missteps of our colleague—or these changes—discourage us from doing our jobs." She folded the paper and tossed it aside. "Now, President Judge Yaris will be arriving from upstate this morning to conduct a staff meeting about the decision and inform everyone what this will mean for security around the courthouse."

I tried not to roll my eyes. The judge's unprecedented visit was just another unwelcome headache for our staff. Most of our court's employees had already heard the rumor of the gun ban when the decision was first proposed on Tuesday, the day after the Ignacio Cardoza verdict. Three additional days of gossip had only led to the consensus that the decision was a big step backward that left us all vulnerable, considering there'd been a murder in our courthouse less than six months ago.

Garrett Yaris, the chief magistrate who oversaw the Superior Court system's entire judiciary, sent the decree down from his office in Wilmington along with a scathing admonishment to Arnold that had our judge's secretaries dying to spread the news. However, now that the Friday morning paper had informed the whole town, Candi wanted to warn us that we were in for one more roller coaster ride at the end of what was already a tumultuous week.

"Shame," she concluded. "Arnold will now have to carry the blame for this ban on top of everything else."

My fellow court reporters, James and Ed, nodded their heads. Personally, I wasn't sure this was such a bad thing since I'd recently been at the receiving end of the bailiff's gun.

"When's he getting reinstated?" asked James. The twenty-one-years-young milky-skinned red head sat closest to Candi but was third in rank behind me. Ed, who was almost twice as old as us both, was new having joined our office four months prior.

"Who knows? The investigation is still pending. We'll just have to hope for the best." Candi bit her lip as she sank into her seat.

Pretty tough to put a positive spin on that hard piece of reality.

"Should we send Arnold a note to let him know we're thinking about him?" asked Ed.

Ed's hiring came in conjunction with the new judge who had been transferred from upstate to replace my dear friend, The Honorable Frederica Scott Wannamaker, who'd been brutally murdered during our last big courthouse scandal. As the new guy, Ed had been working hard to get everything right—from his perfectly coiffed gray comb over to his faded but crisply pressed two-piece suit. Thus, his supportive response to a questionable situation that happened to someone he barely knew was odd but understandable.

I turned my back on them because I was a realist. Arnold's ongoing investigation was just a slow boat toward the same fate that had befallen Johnny Erving, who was outright fired from the Public Defender's Office. However, Arnold and the gun prank was the last thing on my mind. I'd been in a sour mood for days because the week's events had made Mom and Ashton more protective than ever—a dubious combo since she didn't trust him, and he couldn't or wouldn't stay away. While Candi droned on, I peeked at my phone to find a text from Mike.

Friday 8:45 AM
MIKE: Wanna do lunch today?

I typed a quick reply and hoped he was still around to answer.

Friday 9:03 AM
VICTORIA: Can't. Meeting Ashton to celebrate his first real job interview.
Friday 9:03 AM
MIKE: Pleeaasse! Consider this an olive branch for my behavior during trial.
Friday 9:04 AM
VICTORIA: Thanks. No worries. You're forgiven. You were doing what you thought was right.
Friday 9:04 AM
MIKE: Appreciate it. Is there anything I can do to change your mind? I'll even brave some of those scones you love so much!
Friday 9:05 AM
VICTORIA: Tempting, but Ashton needs my support today. Rain check?
Friday 9:05 AM
MIKE: I don't think you should hang with that guy.
Friday 9:06 AM
VICTORIA: Your concerns about Ashton have been duly noted. I trust him, and so should you.

I swiped the app closed and tucked the phone deep into my purse despite the rapid series of alerts that followed. I was tired of the complaints each man brought up when the other was mentioned. Life was too precious for such petty gripes. Tension crept up my neck when I realized I'd probably have to reveal all the details about the bailiff's new gun policy during my lunch with Ashton. I pined for the days when I could take such frustrations to Freddie Wannamaker. She was the one person at work—heck, in my life, I could turn to for advice when the world treated me like a helpless child.

"Anyhoo," Candi's high-pitched sigh cut through my reverie, "we should probably divide today's calendar. Does anyone have a preference? Who wants to sit in with Judge Bragg?"

James swiveled his chair to face the credenza behind him and fiddled with the cord on his printer while Ed looked down and straightened his tie. Candi was being diplomatic by posing the question to the room, but the truth was she was talking to me.

Because Fridays were reserved for civil matters, all three judges had full dockets. Therefore, the choice at hand was less about the work involved and more about the personalities we'd face in the courtroom. One could roll with the maverick known as Judge Maddox or rise to the occasion with the no-nonsense Navy man, Judge Radnor.

But Judge Bragg, the fast-talking ultra conservative, had managed to rub everyone the wrong way, especially me, since he'd replaced my trusted confidant and our county's only African American female judge. Today was Candi's turn to opt out of court and cover the office phones while I was at the bottom of the rotation and therefore stuck with the worst pick. Thus, she'd cast her question to the others in hopes of sparing me from the inevitable.

Unfortunately, my colleagues weren't taking the bait.

"I guess that would be me." I slouched in my chair and spoke the reply to the floor.

"Maddox," Ed chirped as he reached for the earbuds he used to block us out while he scoped his transcripts.

"Radnor it is," James muttered this mostly to himself since his assignment was obvious.

With the day's daily meeting over, we turned to our respective desks. I could already hear the faint chords of Bach's No. 1 Prelude in C Major seeping through Ed's headphones when a sharp knock rang from the wooden entryway and the keycard entry system sounded.

The door opened a crack and, to my surprise, Judge Bragg stuck his head inside. He didn't say anything. He simply stared at us with blank hazel eyes and an expression of disgust contorting the sunburnt arcs of his pudgy cheeks.

I stood with the expectation that he needed me for court, but he flapped a hand at me.

"Sit, girl." He then looked over his shoulder and said a few words I couldn't hear.

The door opened wider, and a squat white man appeared. He had a Charlie Chaplin mustache gone completely gray and a Caesar haircut dyed a color best described as mud. I immediately recognized him from one of the many photographs lining the walls of chambers.

We'd been graced with the presence of President Judge Garrett R. Yaris.

"And this is the court reporters' office." Judge Bragg jabbed a thumb in our direction. "Here we have…four folks who…I guess you could say…"

Didn't take a genius to figure out he didn't know our names. I would have let him stammer around all day. But Candi, always the team player, jumped to her feet.

"I'm Candance Fontaine. That's James Brandenkamp. She's Victoria Justice, and we have Edgar Marconi on the end there."

Judge Yaris stepped inside the room and shook each of our hands in turn as Judge Bragg kept his distance. I found it incredibly rude that he didn't know our names, not because of the invaluable and incredibly difficult service we provided the court, but because of the fits he threw when we placed "Joshua B. Bragg" on our transcript coversheets rather than the preferred "J. Braxton Bragg." Why didn't he use his full name to pull the sting out of the Confederate moniker? I'll never know. But his choice told me exactly where his loyalties lay.

"So, there we have it. Most of the clerks occupy—"

"Not so fast, Braxton." Judge Yaris patted his colleague on the lapel, not quite tall enough to reach the man's shoulder. "I thought I'd introduce myself before the meeting this afternoon and thank you for your dedication to government work. It's so rare that I get to meet anyone, especially outside my own county. I know it's been a tough few months for the team down here, but I hope that every new security measure we put in place helps to build morale."

I plastered on a smile and wondered how someone as brash as Bragg got stuck playing tour guide to his polar opposite. Had the other judges put him up to it as the new guy on the bench, or had he hoped the move would win him some political points?

"A pleasure meeting you all." Yaris walked backward toward the door. "I look forward to any questions you may have during our meeting this afternoon."

When they'd departed and the door closed gently behind them, Candi cleared her throat as if eager to start a new discussion.

"I've never had the pleasure of meeting Judge Yaris," she clasped her hands and leaned forward on her desk, "but did you know that at fifty-nine, he is the youngest President Judge in the history of the state?"

"Is that so?" Ed was clearly feigning interest since his earbuds were already back in his hand.

James didn't even bother to respond. Instead, he pulled a cellphone from his pocket and scrolled through TikTok.

"I never would have guessed." That was all I could offer.

As gracious as Yaris had been and as nice as it was to meet what many would consider a local celebrity, I had become accustomed to meeting judges and politicians. So, I left Candi to her thoughts, opened my laptop, and immersed myself into putting the finishing touches on the Ignacio Cardoza trial transcripts.

About a half hour later, the office phone rang. As our fearless leader, Candi was in charge of answering calls, so I didn't pay much attention to the conversation until I heard her squeal.

"Did you say bomb?" Candi sputtered into the receiver. Her face had gone from its usual rosy glow to a bright fuchsia.

I spun toward her and shot out my arm. "Don't hang up." The words punctuated my movement just as she pulled the receiver away from her ear and pointed it toward the phone's cradle. "Keep them talking."

Her eyes widened behind her spectacles, and I could tell her instincts were pulling her in the opposite direction as her free hand whipped haphazardly through the air in a show of her confusion.

James, who sat at the station between Candi and me, looked up from his smartphone, dumbfounded. I hopped out of my seat, reached across his desk, and snapped my fingers in his face.

"Get off that thing." I fought the urge to slap it out of his hand. "If there's a bomb in the building, we don't know what kind of signal could set it off. Go to the clerk's office and call 911 from their landline extension. Then find someone from Capitol Police and bring them back here. Go. Now!"

James poked out his lips in a show of unhappiness about the sharpness of my tone, but he jumped up and flew out the door.

"Try to get more information." I hissed at Candi, who had miraculously returned the phone to her ear, but she'd yet to form new words. "And be polite."

Not that I needed to add that second part. If there was one person in the courthouse who'd be able to keep their cheer even in the face of imminent death, it was Candi.

"I'll talk you through it." I eased around the corner of my desk and stopped in front of her.

With that, she pressed her lips together and let her head bounce once in a stiff nod. A small shimmer of sweat emerged along her brow.

"I-I-I'm sorry." Her voice was shaky but perky. "Could you say that once again, please?"

I grabbed a sticky notepad and two pens from her desk, one of which I tossed at Ed's head. Up to this point, he'd been oblivious to the office commotion because he still had in earbuds that blasted Bach. He glanced over at me, his mouth open to protest, but I held up an index finger and waved it in a frantic arc between him and his steno machine and back again. Ed always kept his mind firmly on his work, but thankfully, he seemed to understand exactly what I wanted. With one swift motion, he yanked the earbuds from his ears, swiveled his chair, and pulled his steno machine from its corner hideaway so that he sat behind it at attention—just as he would have at the start of a typical day in court.

I circled around behind Candi's desk chair and hit the red button marked "speaker." I then mimed the universal phone signal so she'd keep the receiver next to her ear. I didn't want her putting down the phone and somehow disconnecting the call.

"You know you heard me." The scratchy tones of the caller's voice scrambler made the speakers pop. "There's a bomb in the courthouse. People are going to die today."

I pointed at Ed so he'd capture the words in steno, and I prayed his machine was mic'd like mine so we'd have a recording too. The voice sounded like a man, but it had been disguised with some kind of auto-tuner. No matter. Authorities could still benefit from the audio, and between the three of us, we might be able to recognize something the caller wasn't expecting.

My lips curled upward. Gotcha sucker. You called the wrong office.

"I meant, where is the bomb?" Candi managed. "Nobody has to die."

I put my thumb and forefinger together, giving her an "okay" sign as I looked up at the clock by the door and jotted down the time.

"That's not your decision, is it?" The voice barked, which caused Candi to jerk in her chair. "Just like what you all did to me wasn't mine."

"Sorry. So sorry. I was just—"

"Apologies won't help you now. Time for payback. Time to suffer the same fate my life and career suffered in those very halls. Your office is just the first of three—"

"My-my-my office? The court reporters' office? But what did we—"

I held up both of my arms and crossed them back and forth in front of Candi's face. She needed to stop talking. I looked over at Ed, whose nostrils flared at the caller's grave news, but he held fast at his post.

My hand zipped across the sticky pad as I scribbled a note to Candi in tall block letters:

"Let caller explain. Don't prompt."

I didn't have time to get all of my thoughts onto the page, and with the speakerphone on, I couldn't tell Candi exactly what was on my mind, but

I held the message in front of her face and hoped she understood. I didn't want her finishing the caller's sentences and giving away information. They might not have known what office they'd called, and now she'd just given away our location. The more she calmed down and let them talk on their own terms, the more information we'd have about how much they knew about the courthouse's layout, which might help to assess their identity and the authenticity of the threat.

Her eyes worked furiously behind her glasses as she read both lines of my note. When she finished, she exhaled on a staccato breath that sounded half like a whimper, half like "Mmm-hmm."

My own breathing slowed as we waited for the caller to respond. And that's when I heard a faint musical sound in the background like a calliope, the jingle of wind chimes, or a slide whistle, and the rumble of a sousaphone. All familiar sounds, but their placement remained on the fringe of my consciousness.

"Are you starting to feel it? The fear? The anxiety? The pressure?" The deep, discordant tones of the voice scrambler gave the caller's voice a sardonic edge. "You've all played your role in destroying lives. This call is merely a courtesy. Don't bother checking your surveillance system. The bombs are set. You have three minutes to escape."

"There's more than one bomb?" Candi cried. "Where? We need more time."

"There's no stopping the inevitable."

CLICK.

The sound caused Candi to yelp and jerk her face away from the phone. I put my hand on her shoulder and leaned into her field of vision.

I silently mouthed, "Don't hang up."

"Why?" She mouthed back and tapped her wrist. "We need to go."

Time was definitely of the essence, but we couldn't afford to make any mistakes. I pressed the "speaker" button and mimed for Candi to keep the phone to her ear. She squirmed in her chair but complied, and I waited for the red light of the speakerphone to go out before I spoke aloud.

"The click you heard might be a ploy. The caller may still be on the line.

Wait for the error tone while I get the information on your display." I pointed to the phone's digital screen, which was about the length and width of a pack of gum. Even with the bomber potentially off the line, the caller ID had picked up a number for display as well as the duration of the call.

"Ed," I called to him as I wrote down the number, "grab your steno machine and get out of here. We'll be right behind you."

"I hear the tone," Candi squeaked. She slammed the phone onto its cradle and bolted for the door.

I scribbled the call's end time on my notepad: 9:48 a.m. Then I grabbed my purse and followed Candi.

Ed, steno machine in one hand, held the door open with the other. As we rushed through the threshold, James sprinted down the hall toward us with his arms flailing.

"The State Police are coming with a bomb squad. Somebody found a suspicious knapsack in the lobby."

The call clearly hadn't been a prank…

…which meant our three minutes were nearly up.

"Run!"

Chapter Eight

I'd worked at the courthouse for six years, one as an intern and five as a court reporter, and never had I experienced a situation where the entire building required evacuation.

The endeavor must have been one of Herculean effort as it required both the safe removal of employees and civilians. I would imagine the only fortuitous aspect of it all was that there were no criminal trials on Fridays, so there were no incarcerated individuals and no jurors to contend with as people poured from the structure onto the pavement like swarms of bees.

Even though no flames or explosions had yet to unfold, the horns and sirens of the approaching fire department filled the air around us with a piercing and persistent squawk that intermittently swelled beyond what our ears could tolerate.

Since the four of us had fled from our office rather than the courtroom, we were able to slip out the back of the building through the employee entrance, which spilled onto the staff parking lot. As we hurried across the expanse of asphalt away from the structure, we found ourselves glommed in among a number of clerks and other court administrative staff who knew even less about the situation than we did.

The judiciary had a separate point of egress, but they too would end up behind the courthouse in the staff parking lot that ran parallel to the building and bordered Merchant Street. Once Candi had determined we were a safe distance away from the threat, I spotted two of our three judges, the trio of women who made up our judiciary's secretarial pool, and President Judge Yaris. All of them stood at the opposite end of the parking lot's rear, near the side of the courthouse that flanked the County Administration Building.

I didn't see any of the bailiffs in the immediate vicinity, nor the Capitol Police, the law enforcement body that oversaw security for all the state facilities. I supposed most of them were either making sure the building was completely evacuated or wrangling the civilians who had assuredly been ushered out front onto Oceanside Drive. I did, however, see a few Bickerton Police about a hundred meters away attempting to stop Merchant Street traffic from turning onto York Road, which flanked the opposite side of the courthouse. York Road was empty at present, and I assumed that similar efforts were taking place at the other end where the road intersected Oceanside Drive.

We'd been lucky this occurred on a temperate morning with the sun hanging high in a cloudless sky, so my standard uniform of a satin blouse under a cotton pantsuit seemed sufficient to keep me warm. Yet, I still desperately wanted to sneak away to Cake & Kettle for some hot tea. Candi quickly vetoed any separation because she thought it best we all stick together to keep an eye out for a law enforcement authority who might benefit from the information we'd gathered—and I imagined the café's proximity to the courthouse's façade probably put the business in jeopardy as well.

However, not everyone shared Candi's logic of staying put. It wasn't long before the noisy growl of what sounded like a diesel engine competed with the mass of sirens emanating from the roadways as scads of police cruisers and firetrucks joined the scene. I craned my neck for the source of this new sound. Two rows from the rear of the courthouse, a huge hunter green dual-cab Ford F-150 pulled forward from the line and crept slowly down one of the empty aisles that led to the back of the parking lot and its exit onto Merchant Street.

I envied the person leaving, wishing I could do the same. The vehicle was too far away for me to clearly see the occupant's facial features, but I could identify the unmistakable dye job of President Judge Yaris. He hunched over the wheel and stared straight ahead, probably to mind the ridiculous series of speed bumps that lined the lot to keep people from careening around the tightly packed space.

Under the circumstances, it was frustrating to see him go since his corrective efforts had been disrupted by another act of corruption, and I was somewhat curious what else he thought could be done to make the courthouse safer. We'd had new cameras installed and our keycard system upgraded after last year's murders, but now that the bailiffs were no longer allowed to carry guns, I didn't know if I felt more or less safe.

A small sigh parted my lips at the thought, but nobody heard it because as Judge Yaris's truck passed over the first speed bump with a thunderous *thunk*, his entire vehicle exploded into flames.

Chapter Nine

Friday 10:13 AM

MOM: They're evacuating town hall. Are they evacuating the courthouse?

Friday 10:23 AM

MOM: Why aren't you answering?

Friday 10:28 AM

MOM: CALL ME NOW!!! PEOPLE ARE TALKING ABOUT A CAR BOMB!

Friday 10:51 AM

ASHTON: Just got out of my interview. News alert on my phone says explosion in courthouse parking lot? Is it true? You okay?

Friday 10:56 AM

ASHTON: V, talk to me.

Friday 10:57 AM

ASHTON: Call me as soon as you get this.

I shook my head at the handful of visible texts that stood out from the dozens stacked up and down the lock screen of my cell. Several hours had passed since the blast, and the madness that followed had left little opportunity to check the device that had been tucked away in my purse. Now that I had the chance, I could barely concentrate on the words for all of the horrific images that lingered on the edge of my consciousness.

Screams erupted amidst flying debris and clouds of putrid gray smoke.

Sirens competed with the crackle of bright orange flames. Shouts echoed and receded as firefighters in grossly optimistic yellow jackets tackled the blaze. Booted footsteps smashed against the pavement while the boys in blue attempted to wrangle the chaos of the increasingly frenetic crowd.

As tactical vehicles descended on the horrific scene, several voices from bullhorns demanded we clear the perimeter of the Trident County Superior Courthouse as well as the nearby portions of Bickerton's center known as The Quad. Police units stationed themselves at the area's boundaries, and sniffer dogs roamed the parking lots and nearby streets in search of additional incendiary devices.

My three coworkers and I, along with the other courthouse employees, took shelter in Bickerton's community firehall two blocks over, which the police had designated as both a command center and a holding area. As we settled in place, Candi let the authorities know we'd made initial contact with the bomber via telephone and that we had a recording of the conversation.

For that reason, our group had been separated for questioning. So, I now sat alone in the firehall's kitchen where I'd been asked to give a detective my version of the morning's events. My coworkers, having played a more vital role, had given their accounts first, privately one by one, and had subsequently gone home—although Candi insisted we reconvene for lunch the next day to dissect the steno and audio Ed promised to email us.

As I waited for the detective to return from conferring with his cohorts, I considered calling Mom and Ashton to quell their fears. They had every right to be concerned, but I only had it in me to be interrogated once. So, I sent an *I'm safe in police custody* text and abandoned the phone in favor of staring at the black-and-white clock that hung on the dingy mint green wall of the musty stationhouse kitchen. The hands hugged two and six while my stomach growled, and I pined for one of Jillian's cottage pies.

The kitchen's swinging door soon burst open to reveal Detective Connor Daniels of the Delaware State Police Homicide Division. He froze for a moment and examined me with what I interpreted as exasperation in his droopy bloodshot eyes. This, unfortunately, wasn't the first time we'd met. He'd worked the murder case of my friend and mentor, The Honorable

Frederica Scott Wannamaker, and I'd given him nothing but grief over his substandard handling of the process.

He tugged at the lapel of his worn sports jacket and recovered with a nod over his shoulder to the uniformed man who followed. "Ms. Justice, have you met Capitol Police Chief Jim Strickland during your dealings at the courthouse?"

"Not formally."

"He oversees the statewide law enforcement agency responsible for the security of our state's government facilities, and he's going to join me for this interview."

Strickland removed his peaked service cap to reveal a perfectly shaved head. He then gave me a fleeting, closed-mouth smile as the two men settled onto the stools located across the kitchen's island. Together, their visages looked like the definition of solemnity—one with the taut mahogany lines of a seasoned officer, the other with the haggard, leathery folds of a detective who has seen too much.

"Let's keep this simple, Ms. Justice." Daniels cleared his throat and pressed the red button on his mini-recorder, which he slid to the center of the butcher block countertop. "We've reviewed the audio and transcript provided by your coworker with regard to the bomb threat called into your office. Did you recognize the voice or speech patterns of the person on the line?"

"No, sir. I couldn't even give you a gender based on the autotuning device they used."

"Then what made you think to engage the caller and record the interaction?" asked Strickland. He sat straight as a poker with his hands clasped against the edge of the island and his cap tucked under his arm. The question came out rapid fire, but he barely moved his lips as he spoke. "Had you considered that further action could have agitated the caller and precipitated retaliation?"

"I—I guess I didn't think about that." My mouth went dry, but I bit my lip determined not to apologize for my actions. "Maybe saying nothing or getting up to leave was the logical move, but taking down the verbatim record of criminal proceedings is what we do. The habit just kicked in, and

I figured preserving the moment would not only protect the courthouse but also buy us some time. If we kept the person on the line, maybe they'd give up or screw up and say something we could use."

Small crinkles formed around the corners of Strickland's eyes and mouth. If my name were Tyra Banks, I would have sworn he was smizing. Had my brazen efforts garnered me some respect?

"That's all fine and good." Daniels drummed his fingertips on the wood as if impatient by the sudden mutual admiration party. "But is there anything you can tell us about the call that we may not have gotten from the recording?"

I squinted at him while I thought, but he took my silence as a "no" and continued with a new question.

"You're the one who took down the caller's number, correct? Did you by chance recognize it?"

"Why would I? Nobody memorizes numbers anymore. That's what your cellphone is for. I wouldn't even know what to do if I lost mine."

"Fair enough." Daniels flared his nostrils either at the glib nature of my answer or because the dank odor of the room had finally hit him. "But did anything stand out about the number or the call? Anything unusual? Or familiar for that—"

And that's when it hit me. I knew exactly what I would do if I lost my cellphone, and so did our culprit. I don't know why I didn't put the connection together sooner, since anyone with a decent smartphone and half a brain could successfully cloak a number. The caller, however, didn't mask the number because they couldn't...due to their location, which they'd inadvertently made obvious by staying on the line too long with a bunch of savvy court reporters.

I hadn't recognized the clues earlier because the sweet sounds were normally associated with the innocence of childhood. And in the moment, the distant rumble of a sousaphone, wind chimes, slide whistle, and calliope had ominously underscored the caller's final threat in a manner that accentuated the odious deed. The truth, however, was laughable.

"Candy Kitchen." I shifted my gaze between the two men and smiled so wide my cheeks hurt. Not everyone shared my love of sweets, but surely they knew what I was talking about. "It may have been too faint to hear on the recording, but the Candy Kitchen jingle came through during the call."

The two men glanced at each other as if to share a silent communique. Daniels's thin lips disappeared as he pressed them together. Strickland inclined his bald head toward the detective, who sighed and reached over to turn off the recorder.

Strickland leaned forward so that his broad features were in line with mine. "What would you say if I told you that the number you took from the caller ID can be traced to a pay phone by the boardwalk?"

The statement nearly knocked the wind out of me, not for its profound nature as I'd figured as much the second I recognized the noises for what they were, but hearing him confirm the obvious forced me to connect some unwanted dots. Mike had been the last person I'd seen use that bank of pay phones. But why would he want to blow up the courthouse or kill Judge Yaris? The concept didn't compute, and I hoped the confusion didn't show on my face because I wasn't sure I was willing or able to share my realization with the detectives. At least not yet. Pay phones were public. There had to be a better explanation.

"The caller mentioned our office was the first of three." I kept my gaze locked on Strickland, who still sat hunched in my direction and seemed more likely to indulge my curiosity than Daniels. "And yet, the only explosion that occurred happened outside. Did anyone else in the courthouse receive a threatening call?"

"No such other calls were received today to our knowledge," Strickland offered. "The backpack found in the lobby was a decoy."

Daniels's olive skin flushed red, and his eyes widened. He slowly pivoted on his stool to examine his colleague, whose cleft chin jutted forward defiantly. The two matched stares for a tense second, which I seized to do some quick mental math.

A decoy? Either the caller lied about the number of targets, or there was more trouble on the horizon. Regardless, both scenarios pointed to my office as a pawn in a larger game. Maybe the same was true of Mike? The caller had to have known the authorities would check the history of incoming calls, whether someone had taken down the number or not. Perhaps the culprit had seen me and Mike together by the phone and considered the interaction the perfect opportunity for a misdirect: Have a court reporter cast a finger at a non-sequitur suspect, thus leading to an immediate dead end. Of course, that was a theory with a lot of moving parts.

But the more I thought about it, the more it made sense. Someone had seen us by the pay phones—or at least run into me by them—former Controlled Substance Lab Director Phyllis Dodd. She despised me and my mother and had a true grudge with the state over her dismissal and conviction. She also knew Judge Yaris and could probably make a bomb with her eyes closed thanks to her advanced degrees in chemistry.

"Let us ask the questions, Ms. Justice," Daniels growled once he broke eye contact with Strickland. "With all that you now know," he cast one last bit of side eye at his colleague, "is there anything else about the call that seemed familiar?"

The detective resumed the recording, and I tallied up what I should say, considering I had no discernible proof.

"Nothing about the call itself." I paused to brush a swath of curls from my eyes. I wanted them to have no doubts as to my sincerity. "But you should know, former State Chemist Phyllis Dodd works near the area where the call originated, and she fits the profile of someone who'd have an interest in disrupting the inner workings of the courthouse."

"I see," said Daniels. He knew the story behind Phyllis, as she had been tangled up as a suspect in the murder case of my mentor. But rather than inquire about my motive for the statement, he rocked back on the legs of his stool and took a beat to survey me with his hound dog eyes. He probably feared I was on the verge of concocting some wild theory he'd have to fend off in front of his colleague. Strickland merely resumed his perfect posture and let his face fall into a hard mask of indiscernible lines.

Daniels eventually put a hand to his mouth and stroked the hairs of his graying mustache as he asked his next question. "The caller specifically mentioned payback and revenge as it pertained to your office, have you or your coworkers received any threats like that before?"

"No, not by phone." I got along with everyone at work, save for Judge Bragg, but that was more him than me. "But as you know, Phyllis Dodd once conspired with an oxy dealer to throw me into a dumpster to cover up the fact she'd given civilians access to the drug lab. And I saw her on Monday before the verdict while the Cardoza jury was viewing—"

"Ms. Justice, please." Daniels wrapped his knuckles against the counter like a judge would have a gavel. "While I understand the correlation you're making, that's an issue from a case that has successfully been resolved and doesn't need to be rehashed unless you can offer some new evidence." He glanced at Strickland, who merely shrugged. "Our time and resources here are limited, so I will rephrase the question. In the last six months, have you or your coworkers received any indication that someone may want to exact revenge or payback *on your office or the courthouse?*"

With everything that had happened today, I couldn't understand why Daniels wasn't more amenable to taking past misdeeds into account. Maybe his reluctance had to do with the constraints of a joint agency effort, or maybe they already had a prime suspect. But his question certainly brought to mind Johnny Erving's recent firing from the public defender's office as well as the investigation into Arnold Knight's conduct. Granted, both punishments fit the crime, and neither was quite reason enough for either of them to target me or the court reporters for revenge. But was it enough for one or both of them to target the courthouse in general and Judge Yaris in particular?

"I don't think most people know us court reporters exist." My instincts told me it was best to take the modest approach under Daniels's current mood. "That's the magic of our profession. We're known for our words, not our deeds. But there were some recent reprimands in the legal and law enforcement communities that could result in a desire for retribution."

"We're aware." Strickland held up a hand and waved away my words. "I take it you're referring to the parties in the gun prank."

"Correct." I snapped and dropped my head so that several coarse brown ringlets obscured my face. My tolerance for this whole we-know-what-you're-going-to-say-so-don't-bother line of questioning was wearing thin, and I dug my heels into the legs of the stool to keep myself from saying as much.

"The follow-up to that case is part of the reason I'm sitting in on these interviews." Strickland readjusted the cap tucked under his arm. "Let's move on to how you knew the deceased."

"I didn't really, Chief Strickland. Much like you, Judge Yaris is someone I was familiar with in name only. Today was my first time meeting him, and then only briefly."

"What was the nature of your conversation?"

"Friendly. He stopped by the office to say hello before a meeting we had scheduled today."

Strickland nodded, apparently satisfied.

Daniels piped up to take over. "Who was set to attend this meeting?"

"The entire courthouse staff."

"And what was the meeting for?"

"To cover the new provisions for bailiffs and how that would affect safety procedures around the courthouse."

The detective raised an eyebrow. "Had you shared your knowledge of this meeting with anyone outside the courthouse?"

"Or do you know of anyone who might have?" added Strickland.

"No on both accounts."

"Has anyone ever expressed to you their desire to hurt Judge Yaris?" asked Daniels.

"No, but again we have Phyllis—"

"Please, Ms. Justice." Daniels's weathered skin twisted into a sarcastic smile. "Let's stay focused on current facts. A simple 'yes' or 'no' will do." He slapped his palm against the countertop. "Do you have any concrete knowledge or substantial evidence as to who may have done this?"

"None."

"Did you see any suspicious persons hanging around the courthouse or The Quad?"

"No."

The two men turned to face each other for another taciturn chat. What was with these guys? The wall clock tick-tocked for eight seconds before I couldn't stand it anymore.

"Why? Is there someone I should have seen?"

Daniels ignored me and held out his hand toward Strickland in an "after you" gesture. Strickland pursed his lips and proceeded.

"Were you the only stenographer who covered the Ignacio Cardoza trial?

"Yes, but what does that have to do with this?"

"I never said it did." Strickland stood and slid his service cap on by the brim with a closed-mouth smile. "Just a simple question. Both our offices would like copies of the transcripts for the full proceedings."

He dropped a navy blue and gold business card onto the center of the island and walked out of the kitchen.

Daniels picked up his recorder, tossed his own card into the mix, and followed Strickland without a word of thanks.

I set my elbows atop the slightly sticky countertop and held my head in my hands. The two officers had done nothing to ease my fears or answer my questions about the lingering threat. But on top of it all, Strickland had the nerve to nonchalantly add Ignacio Cardoza's name to the mix—not that the revelation made a bit of sense since the man just won his case. What vengeance could he possibly need?

The caller, turned bomber, claimed there was more chaos to come within the courthouse walls without being specific about who was next on the payback list. So the real question wasn't who did it, but why had Yaris been the first and only person killed? He didn't even work in our county, so why would Ignacio or anyone else in Bickerton consider the President Judge a target? And how did the killer know Yaris was in town…unless that person was somehow privy to our staff meeting?

As much as it pained me to consider, Arnold Knight and Johnny Erving had a solid revenge motive. They also probably still had enough courthouse connections to learn about the meeting and make their move. And yet, Phyllis Dodd's criminal past suggested she had the strongest skillset and temperament to pull off something as intricate as a bombing.

The possibilities made my head hurt, but not as much as the prospect of how I was going to explain all of this to Ashton and my mother.

67

Chapter Ten

lthough it took an additional half-hour of waiting around the community firehall to get clearance from the bomb squad to pull my car from the courthouse parking lot, I was able to make it home through Friday afternoon traffic without any added holdups. On the trip, I listened to all of my neglected voice messages and discovered that Ashton insisted we meet for dinner since the tragedy had preempted our lunchtime meetup. Despite being tired and frustrated and wary of his desire to discuss the day's events, I sent a voice-to-text message to confirm because I wanted to be supportive of his job search.

I powered my Mustang up our raked driveway to find Ma in the front yard of our two-story colonial. She crouched on her hands and knees by the front step, a trowel in her gloved hand and a batch of seedlings at her side. We lived in the part of Bickerton farthest from the beach, about a mile and a half inland from where the bombing had taken place, so it was no surprise to see that she had been evacuated from the Mayor's Office downtown and had beaten me home.

However, the scenario struck me as strange even for my notoriously eccentric mother.

For one, the weather wasn't conducive to yardwork. The air remained warm, but the wind had picked up during the late afternoon, and the sky had clouded over with the threat of a muggy April shower. Ma was nothing if not fastidious about her hair and makeup, both of which were in imminent danger under such conditions. But more tellingly, she'd never shown any interest in lawn maintenance—especially since we both chipped in good money to have a professional gardener maintain our stubby little plot of land year-round.

I parked in front of the garage and climbed out of the vehicle. "Who are you, and what have you done with my mother?"

She glanced up from the hole she'd dug. A smear of dirt decorated her cheek, and a floppy straw hat covered her tawny pageboy despite the absence of spring sunshine. She gave me a forced smile—the thin one that was more lips than teeth, the one she typically offered her constituents.

Something was bothering her.

"I thought the house could use a little sprucing up." She tossed a seedling into the dirt and stood. "Come give me a hug."

I hiked up the cuffs of my pant legs to avoid the muddy clots of earth that had accumulated on the sidewalk, then fell into her embrace. Being home had never felt so good.

She squeezed me tight and spoke through a muffled sob. "Don't you ever scare me like that again."

Rather than respond with my customary sass, I put my lips to her ear and whispered the mantra that had become our bond over the years. "I am yours, you are mine, and together we'll be fine."

Ma coined the phrase after elementary school when I discovered I was adopted. It was her way of saying that even though all we had was each other, it was all either of us ever needed. She'd never give up on me because she'd chosen me despite the odds, and that meant our connection was greater than blood. But today, I used the words differently because I was wrong for failing to call her. Today, I offered them as an apology.

When she pulled away from me, her eyes brimmed with fat tears. "Are you sure you're okay?"

I nodded and brushed the moisture from her cheek.

"I want so much for you," she sniffed. "And with that analytical mind of yours, you're capable of so much more. I've never understood why you insist upon working in a place that traffics in miscreants, misdeeds, and mayhem. What happened to grad school?"

"Come on, Ma. Those were your dreams for me, not mine."

"Well," she squeezed my shoulders, "you should at least make an attempt to get out of this town for once in your life. Experience what it's like—"

"Could we not start with this again?" The wind whipped through us then, and I longed to take our conversation inside. "I could use some Oreos—several in fact."

"Not so fast. Come help me finish. This way I can keep an eye on you." She plucked a pack of seeds from the ground and tossed them to me.

I stepped aside and watched them float by. "Seriously?" My gaze met her primitive work with suspicion. "What are you even doing?"

Ma picked up a plastic carton of sprouted bulbs and crouched beside the barren flowerbed to resume planting. The knees of her jeans and the sleeves of her flannel shirt grew filthy with grass and mulch as she used the trowel to flip new dirt hither and yon.

"Some gladioluses and dahlias will do this yard some good. Add a pop of color and a hint of sweetness."

Was she serious?

"Since when do you even know the difference between a gladiolus and a Glad bag?" I retreated to the top step of the porch and watched her work, confused by the whole display. "Ma, what is going on? Talk to me. Since when do you have time to plant flowers that don't have something to do with raising money for the Town of Bickerton?"

Ma jammed the trowel into the ground on a loud huff. I'd disturbed her attempts at domesticity, and now I was going to get an earful. She wiped her brow with the crook of her elbow and rested her butt on her heels.

"Haven't you ever seen someone blow off steam? I couldn't sit inside and watch any more of that skewed news coverage. Between the Ignacio Cardoza case, the car bomb, and the gun prank to which my own daughter was a victim," she threw her hands in the air at this, "everybody has something to say about public safety, but no one wants to do a doggone thing about it." She pulled off her work gloves and threw them to the ground. "And that stupid website they've been pushing on everybody instead of publishing an evening edition of *The Bugle*—like they used to in the good old days—had six different articles criticizing safety regulations today alone. *Six!*"

The shrill screech of her final words rang in my ears.

"You want me to talk to Mike?" I rummaged in my bag for the phone and scrolled to the text-messaging screen. "Maybe he'd be willing to do an interview with you and the council. You could make an appeal to the community. Outline your ideas. Give specific calls to action."

She tilted her head to the side, eyes narrowed slightly. One hand pressed to her temple. The meditative pose of a woman on the verge of combustion. I'd seen it hundreds of times. She had decided I wasn't listening and that I didn't care. I'd do better to let her complain uninterrupted.

"Fine, Ma." I shifted on the edge of the step and crossed my arms. "What did you have in mind? Is there something you'd like me to—"

"Yes." Her eyes sprang open, and she clasped her hands together. Ready to dictate.

My mother, the master manipulator, with her, there was always a catch. Always.

"I need you to limit people's access to the Cardoza transcripts—"

"Ma, you know I can't do that. Those transcripts are public record."

"Not forever. Just a few days."

"You don't—"

"Just hold off on releasing anything new. Let us get in front of this thing." She held up a finger. "I'm not saying ignore your requests. Just slow down the turnaround time. Allow the council an opportunity to come up with a decent response to the complaints about the verdict. People are already making correlations between Cardoza's attack on our historic district and the car bomb. This may be our only chance to get in front of things."

"No, Ma. That's ridiculous. First, it's not ethical. The transcripts are public record. Second, none of that makes sense. Ignacio won his case. Why would he want to kill a judge and put himself in jeopardy? And even if he got away with his previous crime, why would that mean he'd immediately commit another? Bombs weren't part of his M.O. His criminal record showed he only ever lit things with matches."

"Exactly my point." She scrambled to her feet and crossed to stand in front of me. "He has a criminal record and a history of this."

"You're thinking about this all wrong. The bomber is a cutthroat professional seeking revenge, not some small-town arsonist."

"And how exactly do you know that?" She placed her hands on her hips.

Curses. She'd tricked me into saying more than I'd intended, but I was savvy enough to know that discussing further details about the bombing would do nothing but send her into a whirlwind of worry about my safety. So, I pivoted.

"You should talk to the editors at *The Bugle*. I can text Mike right now. I'm sure he'd be willing to mediate so that you could tell your side of the story and clarify the county's position on the issues." I point-clicked a short message, and the phone sent it off with a whoosh. "Please don't put me in the middle of all this. Manipulating the system by limiting people's access to the facts will only make things worse, then the media will have a real reason to drag you over the coals."

"Oh, that's rich. You can keep secrets from me, but you won't slow the release of information for the greater good?"

"What are you talking about?" I jerked my head back in shock.

"The whole town knows your office received the bomb threat. When were you going to tell me?"

"I didn't want to say anything because I knew you'd assume I was the target of some conspiracy." I raised my voice and looked her square in the eye. "Mine was an omission of necessity, not some self-serving whim."

Ma's face crumpled at my outburst, and her bottom lip quivered.

Dang it. In my defense, the anger and insults weren't about her comparing the two situations; it was about my refusal to admit she was right. Sometimes we need to shield those we love from the truth.

My tone softened. "I'm sorry. That was out of line. I'm just trying to protect you because I know how worried—"

"Worry is part of my job." She stepped forward and nudged me over so that she could squeeze beside me on the porch's top step. "And I'm not talking about being mayor. I'm talking about being your mother. I'm the one who is supposed to protect *you*, but I can't do that if you're not honest with me. I let this whole rebellious tough girl act go when it came to that gun fiasco with Johnny Erving because nobody got hurt, but today's bombing took a life. Don't you trust me? All I want is the truth."

I turned away and stared across the street at the neighbor's overgrown lawn, steeling myself for the worst.

"We fielded a bomb threat from someone who the cops have confirmed was calling from the beach using one of the payphones. The person's voice was disguised, but they let it slip that the court reporter's office was the first of three targets."

"*Three?*" Ma's eyes widened. "Did they say where? You don't think they were talking about the Mayor's Office, do you?"

"I don't know," my hand instinctively reached over to clutch hers, "but I think it's safe to theorize that the caller is focused on the courthouse or those who work within, since the voice alluded to exacting revenge for mistreatment within our halls."

"So, the caller could be anyone?"

"Exactly. Anyone from a disgruntled employee to a bitter defendant. In fact, with that line of reasoning, it's a good chance the caller's next target could be someone at the Department of Justice—"

"Because their prosecutors botched the Cardoza verdict?"

"C'mon, Ma. Would you let that go and listen? I'm trying to tell you. This isn't about the firebug trial, it's about Phyllis Dodd."

Ma inclined her head with a furrowed brow.

"I can all but guarantee the call wasn't from some idiot protesting the verdict, and it doesn't make sense for it to be Ignacio seeking revenge for a case he already won. My gut is telling me the caller was Phyllis Dodd plotting payback on everyone who helped to put her behind bars—my office, the President Judge, and the Department of Justice."

"How can you be so sure?" Ma gripped my hand as if willing me to take it all back. "Couldn't the caller have been Johnny Erving trying to scare you into keeping your mouth shut about the gun incident?"

"Possibly. But that story's been out there for nearly a week, and he knows I had nothing to do with telling the judge how things went down." Or at least I hoped he did. "And that would make more sense if the call had gone to my direct extension rather than the main line, but you're not letting me get to the point." I raised a hand before she could interrupt me again. "I saw Phyllis at the boardwalk on Monday during the jury view, and she works right where the payphones—"

"Phyllis has been released?" Ma tugged at a strand of her tawny hair. "That's not possible. She was sentenced to a full year in prison."

"Yeah, well, she said she got out early for good behavior. I assumed you knew."

Ma rose from the step and stumbled toward the front door.

Confused by the silent departure, I sat still for a moment and watched the rapidly darkening sky break open into a hearty downpour. The open-air porch protected me from the onslaught, but not the sense of unease that lurked at the pit of my belly. I didn't know if it was the weather's eerie timing or my mother's reaction to the news—or both. I glanced around the neighborhood, wanting to ground myself with the familiar sights of my childhood home, but the moldy odor of water against overturned earth and the feeling of being on display drove me inside.

When I walked into the family room, I found my mother scanning the built-in bookshelves along the wall of the fireplace. Her hand trembled as she pulled out a thin tome that looked like a yearbook.

"You know I'm not fond of you playing detective, but if you suspect Phyllis, I suppose I should give you some insight about what she was like before the Controlled Substance Lab." She beckoned me toward the sectional and opened the text to reveal its contents as the history of the Kappa Mu sorority, where she presided over the local chapter.

I nestled beside her as she flipped through the book and located a page with a membership photo that dated back over twenty years. In the center of about thirty women stood Phyllis holding a plaque; her posture was ramrod straight, and her hair was pulled in a tight bun per usual. She looked almost unchanged, except she wore a broad smile that radiated through her eyes and lit up her angular face. Her arms were linked with the woman next to her, my mother.

"We were so young." Ma traced her finger along the faces in the photo.

"Phyllis had only been president a few months before the news broke of her arrest in connection with a car crash that killed a 22-year-old boy. It was an accident, of course, but I knew that Phyllis had been drinking. And even though she was able to get the blood alcohol results thrown out because they weren't obtained within the legal time limit, I knew it wasn't just an isolated incident…she had an addiction—whether she cared to admit it or not." Ma bit her lip and sighed. "I loved her like a sister, but ignoring it would have just been enabling her like I had for years. So, I petitioned the board to revoke her membership."

She snapped the book shut and tossed it onto the coffee table like she'd resolved to leave the emotion of the memory behind.

"You'd think a silly sorority would have been the least of her worries under the circumstances, but she was livid and held me personally responsible despite the unanimous vote. Once her charges were dropped, she started following me around town, screaming at me whenever she could catch me alone. She even slashed my tires once."

"What did you do? How'd you get her off your back?"

"Staged an intervention where I threatened to go to her employer if she didn't deal with her sobriety—that pretty much put a stop to it, and she eventually got enough help to turn things around. Now, I'm not proud of weaponizing someone's illness, but I'll do anything to protect myself and my family." She wrapped an arm around my shoulders and pulled me into a hug. "Phyllis would love people to believe I turned the world against her, but the truth is that she pushed me away, then used that to justify her bad behavior. Stay clear of her, you hear?"

"Yes, ma'am." I was a little freaked out by the conversation's dark turn and surprised that my normally skittish mother had taken a stand.

"And promise me you'll talk to your supervisor about working from home next week?"

I leaned back, breaking the embrace. We were on the verge of another lecture, and I needed a shiny object to pull Ma's focus. Who better than her favorite punching bag?

Diversion time in three, two, one…

"I'm going out to dinner tonight. Ashton is going to cook for me. He thinks he may have found a job."

Ma sat silent for a long, hard moment.

Too long.

Dang it, not good.

"You have nothing to gain from hanging around that…that…perjurer." She spat out her words as if their formation caused her physical pain. "He'll forever be remembered for starting a chain of events that led this town down the road to disaster. No public servant should put his personal agenda over the greater good."

Ah, the irony.

"I know you're grown and determined to do what you please," she continued, "but I think you're damaging the strength of your character and putting your reputation at risk every moment you spend with him."

"Ma, he pled guilty. He paid his price."

"Probation? Community service? Ha!" She ripped off her floppy hat and leaned in, determined to display her displeasure. "He has some nerve continuing to show his face around this town. That man is like a tea bag, his lies will float to the surface the moment he hits a little hot water."

"Seriously, Ma?" I couldn't help but laugh.

Her homespun advice was legendary, but she'd wrapped this one in a famous quote. Perhaps to see if I'd take the bait. Call her on her misstep. Politics and debate fueled me as a kid, and she knew the slightest hint of history would take me back to those happier times when the only thing the two of us argued about was which book to read next.

"You're misquoting an Irish Proverb." I looked over and gave her a sly grin. "Often attributed, falsely I might add, to Eleanor Roosevelt and, more recently, Hillary Clinton. The saying goes—a woman is like a tea bag, you never know how strong she is until she gets in hot water."

"Well, my dearest, Angel," she wrapped her arm around my shoulders and gave me a squeeze, "the point here is, you should do everything in your power to keep your teabag out of his hot water."

Chapter Eleven

I held my breath as I knocked and waited for Ashton to open the door. His house was on the beach side of town, where the temperature had grown crisp, and the bitter essence of sand and saline lingered in the air. Knowing it would be cooler, I'd changed out my work suit into a pair of sailor slacks, a long-sleeved scoop-neck tee, and a heavy wool cardigan, which I pulled tightly around me—protective armor against the uneasiness that gnawed at my chest.

Although Ashton and I hung out on a regular basis—mostly on Sunday mornings when we'd visit the Cape May-Lewes Ferry Terminal to work on my phobia—the thought of us being alone in his home made me shiver...even if it was hard to pinpoint why. After all, we'd grabbed coffee or had lunch together before. We texted almost every day, and he'd picked me up from my house dozens of times.

Granted, I'd never been to his...and therein lay the rub.

Not that this was something I was afraid to do. On the contrary, unlike Ma, I trusted Ashton. We'd had our doubts in the past, but he'd saved my life enough times for me to know that his intentions ran pure.

Even still, going to his apartment after work, as the light of day dwindled into dusk, smacked of subtext. Was I ready for subtext?

I exhaled.

Good gosh, girl. Get a grip.

Why was this even an issue? It's a measly visit, right? I mean, sure, part of me considered Ashton someone with the potential for more. A potential that, if I was honest with myself, I couldn't realistically explore because of my living situation. A situation that started with my overprotective mother and ended with her overall distrust of Ashton. She blamed him for almost getting me killed—never mind the fact that we'd saved each other in the end.

I knocked once again, self-conscious that I'd been standing on the raised step a little too long. Was he watching me through the peephole and having second thoughts? I shook my head, encouraging my curls to conceal me from unseen eyes.

Seconds later, Ashton ripped open the door on a gasp of breath as if he'd been running or doing last-minute cleaning. His already picture-perfect grin widened at the sight of me, and I greeted him with a burst of anxious laughter. I couldn't help it. His normally tame crew cut had devolved into a wild mass of spiky copper and blond tangles, slightly wet from the perspiration on his brow.

"Great. You made it—what's so funny?" He pulled at the lapel of his tan blazer. "Is it the suit? It's the suit, isn't it?"

Guess I wasn't the only one grappling with nerves.

I bit my lip to extinguish the laugh. Sure, his getup looked slightly dated due to the dark leather patches on the elbow, but the crisp white Oxford shirt he sported underneath spoke to a man determined to make a good impression.

"Don't mind me." I stepped into the apartment. Happy to see him. Subtext and all. "You look handsome."

His mouth widened into a grateful smile. "It's what I wore to the interview. Got home hours ago, but I couldn't get myself to take it off. Been a while since I've worn anything but a uniform." He took a self-conscious look down at his attire. "Anyway, welcome. I've been listening to the news since I got back, but I'm still trying to wrap my mind around everything. It makes it feel like we haven't seen each other in ages. I was starting to miss you."

He grasped my elbow and pulled me toward him as his face came down to meet mine. A light Parisian-style air kiss brushed my cheek. He smelled bright and breezy like lavender in the noonday sun.

I froze. That was new.

Is this a date?

"Uh, yeah, missed you too?" I pulled away and blinked up at him. "Sorry I didn't answer any of your messages. Things were so hectic for a while there. I lost track of time."

"Don't worry about it. Plenty of time to talk over dinner, and Jillian sent a cake for dessert." He loosened his tie and closed the door behind me. A large hand grazed the small of my back and shepherded me toward a linen sectional overstuffed with teal pillows. "I might not be the best cook, but what I lack in presentation, I make up for in effort. Would you like a drink?"

"Pardon?" The tangy aroma of basil and fresh tomatoes filled my nostrils as I nestled into the cushions of the couch, but my mind clung to the greeting... the oddly warm, oddly soft, oddly affectionate greeting.

Stop overthinking.

Relax.

That's a perfectly acceptable greeting for two friends.

"Oh, uh." I scrambled to get back on track. "Nothing for now. Thanks. I'll wait until dinner. What are we having?"

"Hopefully, stuffed shells and sauce," he remained standing and cast a nervous glance behind him at a door I assumed led to the kitchen, "but I'm having a little trouble with time management. It's been a while since I've made anything more complicated than a steak."

"Where did you learn to cook?"

"Don't think I have really. Just picked up a couple of dishes during my travels with the football team in college—speaking of football, Del State wants me to start next week."

"You got the job?" I bounced in place, unable to escape the gravitational pull of the couch cushions.

"Assistant coach." He beamed.

"That's awesome. Congrats." I gave him a mini round of applause. "So I take it you're not worried about that forty-five-minute commute to Dover?"

"Oh, it'll be worth it because there are perks—" A buzzer sounded beyond the kitchen door. "Hold that thought. We should be able to eat and chat in ten." He pointed to an archway on my right. "Bathroom's the middle door on that hall if you need it."

I waved him on his way and looked around. The living area didn't contain much furniture. In fact, the decadent sectional and a huge bay window dominated most of the room. From there, he'd arranged a coffee table, a television, and a couple of bookshelves around a plush area rug. But he needn't have done even that. The strong bones of the fifties-era architecture spoke for themselves—the authentic hardwood floors stained a deep mahogany to match the crown molding turned the otherwise forgettable space into a homey nook.

"Your place is lovely," I called to Ashton.

A loud crash came back in reply along with a couple of expletives. I stumbled to my feet and debated peeking into the kitchen.

"Need a hand?"

"No, no. I've got it." He stuck his head through the doorway. "Pan hot. Use oven mitt. Some lessons you just can't learn in school. You. Sit. Make yourself at home. Won't be but a minute. You were saying."

I pressed my lips together to stifle a laugh.

"Beautiful place. Love the natural wood and that bay window," I gestured to the wall of faded light across from the sectional, "you must get a ton of sun in the morning."

"Yeah. This place was a mess when I moved in. Did all the renovations myself." He sniffed at the air, which had grown slightly acrid with the smell of burnt bread. "Uh, give me a minute."

"Sure."

I retreated to the forest of fluffy couch cushions and found my purse vibrating. A quick excavation produced my cell. Mike Slocum had answered the message from earlier and recently sent another. I tapped my phone screen and scrolled through our latest text chain.

Friday 5:04 PM

VICTORIA: What's with all the negative coverage? Ma wants to do interview on town safety. Diffuse panic over recent events.

Friday 5:19 PM

MIKE: Not my call. Editor goes with what sells. People's right to

know. Yada, yada. Can't guarantee anything but will relay message.
Friday 7:37 PM
MIKE: E-mailed editor. She says it's a go, but I can't do the interview because I have to chase a lead on the courthouse bomber. Whoever they assign will contact the Mayor's Office. Tell your mom to expect a call next week.

I cocked an ear toward the kitchen. The clickety-clank of dishes and silverware dominated the airwaves. With my host occupied, I typed a reply.

Friday 7:38 PM
VICTORIA: What kind of lead? Need to know what you have. My gut points to Phyllis Dodd.
Friday 7:38 PM
Mike: What makes you think that?
Friday 7:39 PM
VICTORIA: Bomb threat came to my office from pay phone by the beach. She works there at Readalong. She's not a fan of me. She has bad blood with the courts in general as you know. All too coincidental to be coincidence.
Friday 7:39 PM
MIKE: Interesting!

His single-word reply came as quickly as the previous, but he must have swiped away from the screen or moved on to something else because I didn't get those three dancing dots indicating a more significant response to come.

Friday 7:39 PM
VICTORIA: Does that match what you found? What's your lead?!?!?!

"Hey, you ready?" Ashton leaned in the doorway of the kitchen. He'd taken off the hideous blazer and rolled up the sleeves of his dress shirt. A dishrag over his shoulder. "You look awfully busy over there. We could wait if you need to—"

"Not necessary." I peeked at the phone. My last message hadn't been marked read. Mike must have balked. "I'm ready. Let's eat."

"I should warn you. The kitchen is a disaster. Promise you won't judge."

"Promise."

I left the luxury of the couch and followed him into the kitchen. My cell tucked safely into the pocket of my cardigan in case Mike responded.

"So…" Ashton shuffled his feet as we entered the room. "I hope you weren't craving stuffed shells because I, uh, dropped the pasta."

I covered my mouth, but the laughter escaped in a series of hiccup-like giggles.

"Tipped it really." He waved a palm in the direction of the oven. "Kind of got some sauce in there, but most of it fell on the floor."

"Ashton," I managed between snorts, "you could have asked for help."

What would have been a homemaker's dream, with its farmhouse sink and spacious marble countertops, looked like the site of an eighth-grade food fight. Pots and pans crowded the sink. The herringbone backsplash displayed splotches of goodness knows what. The oven hung open, and the scent of smoke lingered at its perimeter. Crumbs and small puddles of water dotted the checkboard floors. And his outdated blazer lay crumpled by the back door, covered in tomato sauce.

"Yeah, well, I wanted to do this for you—as a thank you for standing by me, believing in me when everyone else turned their back." He gestured to the breakfast nook with a twinkle in his eye. A full table setting awaited me, complete with a red cloth spread and white votive candles. "Have a seat."

"This is sweet." I moved toward the table.

Possibly too sweet. Candles? Really?

"No, sit there," he directed, "by the pink box."

Amidst the table's finery sat a small rectangular-shaped box—the kind one would use to store a necklace or bracelet—with a white bow wrapped around it to keep the two halves closed.

"Ashton, what is this?"

"Just a little something to let you know I appreciate you."

"A gift?" Uh-oh. I sat down on the wooden bench that lined the corner of the nook, confused as to what this could mean. "We should be celebrating you. This new job is huge."

"Success is nothing without someone to share it with." He leaned against the refrigerator, which was one of the few appliances not covered in sauce. "Now, open it so we can eat."

I pulled at the bow until it slipped through its tangles and released. As my hands flipped open the top, half of me prayed for something sparkly while the other half feared the implications of such a gesture.

Inside the box, on a black velvet cushion, sat a large silver pen that was thick throughout, squared off at one end, and rounded with a sharp nub on the other. I gasped in relief, lifted it from the box, and marveled at its weight.

"I guess I should explain." My silent examination must have thrown him because his skin reddened, and he attempted to mask it by ducking his head. "It's a tactical pen—a multitool. You can write with it if you pull off the cap, but it is also a flashlight, a glass breaker, and a small knife." He gestured for me to unscrew the nubby end where I found the blade. "I thought you'd get a kick out of it with your job and all. You know, the pen is mightier than the sword."

"Oh, I love that." My heart melted at the thought he'd put into the gesture. I hugged the pen to my chest, then clipped it to the collar of my cardigan. "I will cherish it always."

"I know it's not much, but maybe it will make up for this disaster of a dinner." Ashton shrugged and moved to open the refrigerator, but I could see his posture straighten at the compliment. "I managed not to drop the salad, and I made some grilled cheese sandwiches out of the pieces of French bread that didn't get ruined. But if you're not feeling this, we can go out."

"Ashton, stop. I came to hear about your interview. That's all that matters."

His jaw relaxed, and he ambled over to the nook, the salad in one hand and a greasy-looking pan filled with charred pieces of gnarled, cheesy bread in the other.

"Tell me about the job. You said something about perks."

"Right." He set down the food and went back to the fridge. "Full-time Del State faculty and staff get free tuition, and I'd be eligible come fall. As much as I love the idea of coaching football, I can't see myself doing it forever." He crossed back to the table with a pitcher of iced tea and a bottle of Ranch dressing. "I figure this would be a great opportunity to go back to school. Get a Master's degree while I work and eventually start teaching, maybe something in criminal justice."

"You'd be happy with that?"

After his dismissal from the State Police, I'd have thought he'd abandon anything to do with the legal side of things.

"I don't know." He squeezed in beside me on the bench. His hulking frame commanded the space and pressed a tickle of warmth against my thigh. "I feel like I've got some unfinished business. I'm not ready to completely give up on law enforcement. I'd still like to play a part if people will let me."

Buzzzzzzzzzzz.

The vibration from my cellphone caused me to jump.

"You okay?" Ashton filled our plates with food.

I nodded and slid the device out of my sweater's pocket with my hands under the table.

Friday 7:59 PM
   Mike: I'm glad you're safe, but I can't reveal my sources.

I glanced up at Ashton. He'd gone through so much trouble. I hated to be rude. But he seemed preoccupied with arranging the food, so I typed.

VICTORIA: Can we meet up to compare notes? No need to share sources. Just want to know what's going on and make sure I'm not crazy.

Three bubbles appeared on the screen. Good. Mike's phone was active. Maybe I'd get a reply before Ashton finished filling our glasses.

MIKE: You're not crazy ☺ We can talk, but it's gotta be tonite.

Dang it, Mike. Everything had to be on Slocum time.

VICTORIA: Ugh. Give me a couple hours.

I lifted my head to find Ashton staring at me. He took a bite of his sandwich. The crunch sent flaky bits of French bread flying. I dropped the phone in my lap and followed suit.

After we'd chewed in silence for several seconds, Ashton asked, "How's your sandwich?"

"Huh?" I licked my lips. My mind still weighed Mike's proposal.

"I know it's just melted cheese and bread, but how is the food?"

"Fine. Thank you."

"I warned you. My talents in the kitchen are limited." He took a large bite and relished in the cheese pull that followed. "Although I think it's fair to say you can't go wrong with grilled cheese. You need anything else? More salad? Or I can open a can of tomato soup?"

"I'm good. This is fine."

"Two fines." Ashton shook his head. "I'm not exactly setting the world on fire with this date."

This is a date?!?!

"What?" My voice cracked.

And there it was again. The subtext. Hanging all out in the open.

"I mean…" I swallowed. "I'm having a great time."

Surprisingly, that was the truth despite the sudden pounding in my chest.

"You're having a great time," Ashton wiped his mouth and smiled, "but the fact that you keep looking at your phone would suggest otherwise."

Busted.

"Oh. Sorry. Work." I brought the device up to table level—a nonverbal mea culpa—and placed it face down to show my dedication to the conversation because I…was on a date.

"Not a problem." He drummed his fingers along the table's edge. "It's just that, between the phone and the 'fine,' I'm not convinced. Those are big blows to a guy's ego when he's trying to make a second first impression." He reached over and took my hand. "I'd much rather you look me in the eye and tell me the truth: Your sandwich is barely adequate, and you could make a much better one yourself." He stroked the back of my palm. "Or better yet, tell me how to salvage this dinner."

I could get used to this. I liked this new Ashton. Open. Honest. Charming. And more debonair than ever now that he'd found a direction for himself. I placed my free hand on the rounded peak of his cheek. His skin was smooth as if he'd shaven just for me—and he probably had.

The likelihood of that made the pounding in my chest skip a beat.

"You're saying you like women who are brutally honest?" I tipped my face upward to bask in the bright blue pools of his eyes.

"Who said anything about women? I like you…just you, and I want you to be honest." He reached out and traced my lips with his fingertips. "Isn't that what we agreed on when we decided to become—"

Buzzzzzzzzzzz.

My phone vibrated and shimmied on the tablecloth.

We both turned to glare at it—our bodies centimeters apart—and I could feel a wave of frustration radiating from Ashton as he processed the interruption.

I tensed. Should I ignore it?

Of course.

My hand still cupped his cheek, and I caressed his jaw—urged the muscles to unclench.

"You were saying?" I inclined my head and fought for his gaze.

He slowly pulled his attention away from the phone. When we locked stares again, his eyes had grown dim.

Buzzzzzzzzzzz.

"You should get that." Ashton's voice was guttural. "You know, since it's for work."

He then cupped my hand and removed it from his cheek.

So much for subtext.

I flipped over the phone to find two texts from Mike on the lock screen.

Tuesday 8:12 PM
MIKE: No worries. Boardwalk pay phones at 10:00?
Tuesday 8:13 PM
MIKE: We on or what?

Geez. Why couldn't he have waited for me to set the time…and the place?

Ashton stood up, walked over to the oven, and slammed the door closed.

"I knew I was probably moving too fast with all this." He gestured broadly at the room and leaned on the messy stovetop, his face in profile. "But is there somewhere else you need to be?"

"Oh, no, Ashton, please. This is perfect." I rose, unsure if I should go over to him or keep my distance. "It's Mike Slocum. I had no idea he'd get in touch, but he has a lead on what happened today." I fiddled with the new pen that suddenly felt cold against the flesh of my neck. "My office fielded the bomber's call, and I'm convinced it might have been Phyllis Dodd."

His head snapped toward me, and I held up a hand. Ashton had been a big part of why Phyllis's mismanagement of the drug lab had been exposed, so he was all too familiar with her caustic nature.

"I'd planned to tell you everything, but you kind of kissed me when I walked in, and that threw me. Then, a moment ago, we almost—"

"Don't. Don't do that. Don't try to put this on me. I just asked you to be honest. Our whole deal is about being honest." He took a step toward me, then stopped and shoved his hands in his pockets. "If someone who has hurt you before is possibly plotting to hurt you again, why not tell me? Why tell Mike? What does he have to do with this? I thought I was the one you could confide in no matter what."

"You are. This isn't about that." The pounding in my chest had grown so loud I could barely think. "This is about the bombing. The caller talked about revenge and said there were three targets. No specific places were outlined, but I figure it has to be the Court Reporter's Office, the Judiciary, and the Department of Justice if someone like Phyllis Dodd is behind this."

I gripped the edge of the table to steady my nerve. "The cops didn't want to hear me on Phyllis because they're probably looking at Johnny Erving, Arnold Knight, and Ignacio Cardoza. But if Mike has even the smallest lead on who it could be, I'd like to know for the sake of my coworkers and myself."

"What?" His neck muscles bulged. "This is exactly what I'm talking about. Why wouldn't you have started by confiding your fears to me?"

"I didn't tell you because I don't have any proof other than a random sighting and a hunch. Don't you get it? I didn't say anything because I wanted to avoid this kind of reaction."

"But I'm your…"

"My what?"

He couldn't finish the sentence, and neither could I. No one had ever exchanged romantic labels with me before.

"Ashton, if I've hurt you, I'm sorry." I picked up the phone and held it out to him. "Mike says he's willing to share his information, but only if I meet him tonight."

Ashton didn't reach for the phone. He didn't speak. He barely seemed to breathe.

After several seconds, I dropped my arm and pleaded with him. I needed him to understand.

"This is not some kind of attempt to push you away. I—I wanted this night as much as you did…" My brow prickled in a series of hot flashes, and I closed my eyes against the embarrassment. "…maybe even more, but I can't miss this opportunity."

Silence.

When I opened my eyes, Ashton had filled the space between us. He wrapped me in his bear-like embrace. "Well, if you're going to flee into the night toward the arms of another man, you better believe I'm going to be right by your side."

Chapter Twelve

I'd never been to the boardwalk after dark despite having lived in Bickerton my entire life. The seaside tourist destination, with its colorful neon signage and carnival-inspired confections, stirred up a general uneasiness that had less to do with the fun-filled facades and more to do with my anxiety about the ocean that lay beyond. Arriving at night, when the water was cloaked in darkness, did nothing to quell the fear that lurked at the edge of my subconscious or the dread that gripped my lungs. But with effort, my rational mind held fast to the goal of learning more about who could have set the bomb that killed Judge Yaris.

What helped was knowing Ashton was by my side. I had to admit that a six-foot-four-inch ex-cop with muscle to spare wasn't a bad accessory to have when exploring a semi-deserted area after ten o'clock at night. During the tourist season, the main drag would have been packed with music, merriment, and myriads of beachgoers, but the first week of April meant that most of the shops had already closed their doors for the night.

As we walked toward the beach from the western portion of Oceanside Drive, I could see Mike's lanky form standing by the pay phones outside the dark and eerily silent Candy Kitchen. Beyond him, about twenty yards, the floodlights that illuminated Readalong Bookstore's awning were still on, and I wondered if Phyllis was inside. The thought gave me goosebumps.

"You're late," Mike grumbled once we'd reached his orbit, "and this was meant to be a one-on-one conversation." He glared at my companion.

"Nice to see you too, Slocum," Ashton grunted through gritted teeth. "Now, get over yourself. We don't have all night."

The reporter snorted at the comment as if to dismiss it.

"He's right, Mike." I clutched the collar of the cardigan so that it covered my exposed neck. The salty air had gone frigid and not just from the tension between the two men. "With everything going on in town, it wouldn't have been wise for me to come here alone."

"Yeah, bright guy." Ashton crossed his arms and leaned against the bank of pay phones. "If you weren't going to pick a decent time, why not pick a decent place? What's with the cloak and dagger routine?"

"Location, like the company one keeps," Mike's tone rumbled low and fierce, "should be chosen with care. This spot seemed apropos, considering Victoria mentioned it as the site of the bomber's call."

Ashton's neck muscles bulged and stiffened. He looked down at me with his eyebrows raised. Dang it. That was one more thing I'd neglected to tell him. Fortunately, he recovered quickly.

"Courtesy, as exercised by true gentlemen," Ashton mimicked Mike's earlier mocking, "takes a person's phobias into consideration before organizing a late-night meetup."

Mike's gaze drifted over to me. Ah, the awkward moment when mention of my phobia puts a wrench in everything. These days, all of my friends and coworkers were aware of the near-drowning incident that made me fearful of large bodies of water, but it never ceased to bring me a sense of shame because it always meant people pitied me rather than viewed me for what I had overcome.

My already anxious mood curdled into annoyance.

The positive side effect was that Ashton's snipe put a damper on their desire to gripe at each other.

"Guys, could we focus for once?" I stepped between them with a warning finger raised in each man's direction. "Regardless of how it happened, we all made it here. Let's work together." I tipped my head toward Mike. "We'd be grateful for anything you're willing to share. It's possible the bomber could strike again."

Mike emitted another snort, but he seemed mollified. Keeping a wary eye on Ashton, the reporter dug a cellphone from his jeans pocket and slid his thumb across the screen. The glow of the device bathed his broad features in light as he began to read.

"The State Police confirmed that the backpack found in the courthouse lobby contained a defunct decoy mechanism, which they believed was a ploy to get people outside for the real event."

"The car bomb," I supplied.

"Exactly." Mike scrolled through his notes. "According to my sources on the Bomb Squad, the explosion was detonated using a tilt fuse."

"What's that?" I asked.

"Think of it as a switch." Ashton weighed in, probably eager to justify his presence. "But the mechanism works on movement rather than a trigger. It's usually a glass or plastic tube filled with mercury on one end, while the other is wired to an open circuit on an electrical firing system. When the fuse is tilted or jerked, the mercury flows to the top of the tube, closes the circuit, and triggers the incendiary device." He stuck his hands in his pockets and shrugged. "That way, the killer doesn't have to be there for the bomb to explode. All that's needed is a way to secure the item under the car. When I worked at the troop, the boys on the EOD dreaded coming up against one of those because their canines can't detect them."

"EOD?" I asked.

"Explosive Ordnance Disposal Team."

"So that explains why the bomb didn't blow until Yaris's truck ran over the speed bumps in the parking lot, and that sounds like exactly the kind of trickery Phyllis would come up with."

"Not so fast, Victoria." Mike held up a hand and pointed at the screen. "There are reports that Ignacio Cardoza was seen in and around the courthouse at the time of the incident. Surveillance doesn't show him with a backpack—in fact, there was so much traffic in the lobby, it was unclear how and when the decoy got there—but the police have taken his presence into consideration, and he's become a person of interest."

"But that doesn't make any sense." I paced the width of the sidewalk. "If Ignacio was hanging around the courthouse, he couldn't have been the same person who made the call."

"Maybe he's working with someone," Ashton offered.

I scowled at him and his desire for a quick solution. "A tilt fuse sounds far more sophisticated than anything Ignacio Cardoza could have come up with."

"I don't know." Mike shook his head and slipped his phone back into his jeans. "My research shows he has a long history of setting fires. Who knows what he's capable of."

I stared down the vacant street toward the unseen ocean whose crashing waves underscored our conversation with a soft hiss and the occasional cry of a gull. Goosepimples prickled my flesh at the mere thought of what lay beyond, so I concentrated on Ignacio. Sure, he'd served time for arson long before the destruction of the Rainbow Sands Hotel. But in both the past and present instances, he'd been accused of lighting small fires with common combustibles then abandoning them so they'd grow out of control.

"I don't buy it." My gaze returned to my companions, who'd both turned to study me. "No one has ever mentioned him using accelerants like gasoline or fancy mechanisms like mercury triggers."

"There's a first time for everything." Ashton inclined his head. "Why are you defending him?"

"Why not?" Ignacio probably didn't deserve it, but the idea just didn't sit right with me. As with the darkness that lay beyond, there had to be more to this than I could see. "He's got no motive. The person who called my office talked about revenge for a ruined career, and it's been less than a week since his acquittal. Why would Ignacio target anyone in the courthouse, particularly a judge from another county?"

Mike shifted from foot to foot as if searching for an answer, but it was Ashton who spoke again.

"Maybe it's vengeance over being falsely accused. Maybe Ignacio and Yaris have a history."

"Maybe everybody in this town is still so sore about Monday's verdict that they're more interested in getting a second crack at the same nut than they are in examining the facts." I cut Ashton a razor-thin stare that I hoped conveyed my desire for him to shut up and let me think. "What about Phyllis?

What are the authorities saying about her?"

"Not much," Mike wiped a hand across his mouth, "but she has been approached for questioning as have Johnny Erving and Arnold Knight."

"Any reports about those three being here at the beach or around the courthouse?"

"Not to my knowledge—and believe me, I've inquired." Mike anchored his hands on his hips. "The minute we heard about the blast this morning, our whole staff ran down to the scene. The streets were utter chaos. I don't know how anyone could have made a positive ID."

"That was my experience as well." I wrung my hands together, unsure what to ask next.

"Maybe that's the problem." Ashton squared his shoulders and asserted himself again. "You all are looking for one sensible solution when there could be many unrelated ones. Johnny is the one who got fired from his job. A career ruined. And while the sophistication of the tilt fuse may speak to Phyllis, what the device really could point to is someone smart enough to state their true intentions aloud while their actions cast suspicions on someone else entirely."

"You mean like Johnny or Arnold framing Ignacio or Phyllis to take the fall?"

"Yeah," Ashton nodded, "maybe the failed attorney and the disgraced bailiff are working together."

"You sure would know a lot about failure and framing someone," Mike muttered the sarcastic remark under his breath just loud enough for Ashton to hear.

"That's it, Slocum." Ashton took a step toward the reporter with his fists clenched. "If you've got something to say, be a man. Say it out loud. Get it off your chest today, right now, because I'm not going anywhere. Victoria could be a target, so she needs our support. I'm trying to help her come up with answers."

"I'm just saying if we're talking about past behaviors and motives here," Mike puffed out his chest even though he was the smaller man, "I think we should ask where you were when all this went down."

"I had an interview at Del State that can be documented and verified. How about you? Were you at work all day? And how do we even know that any of this stuff you're telling us is true?"

While the two men continued their squabbling, the headlights of a black Mercedes washed over us as it passed on the far side of the road and made a U-turn in the street so that it could park on our side of Oceanside Drive in front of the bookstore. Seconds later, the front door of the establishment opened to reveal Phyllis Dodd. She wore a long-sleeved white silk blouse tucked into a tight black pencil skirt. She made a beeline for the vehicle and walked with a clutch in her hand and a trench coat draped over her forearm.

I broke rank from my group's huddle and dashed toward her in hopes of reaching the car before she disappeared inside. Her hand was on the door's lever as I arrived breathless and desperate. I had no idea what I was going to say or even if I had a right to do so without proof, but I was close enough to catch a hint of her lilac perfume, so I wasn't about to squander the opportunity.

"Ms. Dodd, do you know anything about the bombing at the courthouse today?"

She looked down at me with a dark expression. But when recognition of who I was dawned on her, she laughed—a deep belly laugh that made her freckled face light up.

Still, I persisted.

"What about tilt fuses?"

Her laughter fizzled at the question, but she ignored me and pulled up on the lever to gain entry to the vehicle. As she folded forward to take a seat inside, the driver's door opened, and a balding but distinguished man with heavy jowls appeared.

Beauregard Munroe Harriston, Esquire.

He was one of our town's premier private defense attorneys, best known for his impeccable win record. I'd been a court reporter on cases with him in the past, so I was quite familiar with his flamboyant style.

Once Phyllis closed her door and imprisoned herself behind the tinted glass, Harriston adjusted one of the cuff links on his designer suit and spoke in his Foghorn Leghorn-like drawl. "My client does not wish to talk to law enforcement or the press without the advice of her counsel. And as her counsel, I politely submit 'no comment.'"

With that, he slipped back into his seat and piloted the Mercedes away from the curb. By that time, Mike and Ashton had gotten their heads out of their butts long enough to join me. But as far as I was concerned, the damage was already done.

Harriston never took a case he couldn't win, plea out, or make vanish. So if I was right about Phyllis playing a role in the bombing…she already had an airtight plan to get away with it.

Chapter Thirteen

I agreed to meet my coworkers for a late Saturday afternoon lunch so we could discuss the previous day's bombing and subsequent fallout. My hope had been that we'd convene at Cake & Kettle, but The Quad was still closed and most of the buildings in the vicinity remained evacuated while the police conducted their investigation. Candi suggested we meet at Cooper's around 2:00 p.m., which would put us there after the noonday regulars but before the rowdy happy hour crowd and swinging singles night set.

Cooper's was the most popular dive bar in Delaware, best known for its fried fish and crab cake sandwiches as well as a dizzying array of alcohol, but it didn't have much of a formal dining area since it also doubled as a karaoke lounge. Therefore, the timing of our arrival was key. The joint's owner, ex-NASCAR driver Ian Cooper, didn't believe in reservations and held no mercy for his customers. His all-fried seafood and poultry menu was a prime example, as it had a strict no substitutions policy—no baked, no boiled, no salads—and he was notorious for tossing people out who saw fit to challenge him.

The bar itself sat off Route 1 in what was once a Howard Johnson's restaurant. Although the signage had changed, the building still sported the chain's signature orange roof and bright blue weathervane-topped spire. I admired the aging A-frame façade as I climbed the short flight of steps to the entrance, where I found Candi in a snit.

"Thank God," she exclaimed the moment I crossed through the bar's glass antechamber. "Cooper wanted us to wait until you got here, even though all eight tables are empty."

"Sorry," I shouted over the howl of laughter coming from a pack of bearded men standing on the opposite side of the entrance. "Where are James and Edgar?"

"Grabbing drinks at the bar," Candi called over her shoulder as she pushed through the surprisingly large crowd to the rear of the joint, where Cooper had restored several booths with blood orange velvet seats and matching tabletop jukeboxes. She picked the largest table in the far corner, probably because its curved banquette faced outward and allowed us to spot our coworkers upon their return.

"Did you get Edgar's email with the transcript and audio?" she asked once we were settled beside each other.

I bobbed my head in confirmation and tried to ignore the fetid aroma of hot grease and stale beer.

"I couldn't bear to open the message." She tweaked her wire-rimmed glasses and stared toward the distant bar as if replaying the event. "Geez, I don't even know how I got through the call. What if that maniac strikes again?" She shuddered. "As far as I've been told, we're all expected to go back to work on Monday, but I don't know if I can do it." She fell silent for a long beat, then turned to face me. "How are you making it out?"

The question seemed to bring her back to the present and return her to the pragmatic leader I had come to know over the years.

"I don't know. Confused? Curious? Defeated?" I placed my hand over the one she'd rested on the table. We were in this together. "Thank you for setting this up. I have a thousand theories in my head, and I'm really looking forward to working through them with everyone."

"You made it." Ed's excited holler pierced our bubble as he glided up to the table with a beverage in each hand.

James dawdled behind him with two drinks of his own, but the sullen expression on his pale face was almost comical in comparison.

"Candi said you don't drink," Edgar set a pint glass in front of me with a flourish, "so I got you a lemonade."

He snapped a finger at James, who flopped down beside me and slid a curvy glass across the table.

"And a strawberry daiquiri for the boss," James added without much gusto.

"Don't worry, ladies, it's on me." Ed took a sip from his tumbler of brown liquid and scooched onto the end of the banquette beside Candi.

"Now that we're all here," James whined while he cracked open his Red Bull. "Let's get this over with before someone convinces Cooper to fire up the karaoke machine."

"Nah," Edgar said, "you can't beg, bribe, or bully that man into starting the karaoke machine before five. And even then, he needs a couple of shots before he'll comply because, and I quote: 'Ain't nobody fittin' to listen to a bunch of hippie idiots squawk all the live-long day.'"

Candi raised her glass at the spot-on impression of the gravelly-voiced grump.

I couldn't help but widen my eyes in amazement at the newcomer's familiarity with our local juke joint—even James whipped his curly red head around in disbelief.

"What?" Ed shrugged, "I've been dropping by on Wednesdays with the clerks in the criminal unit. Those gals know how to party. Last week, they gave me a standing ovation for my rendition of 'Born to be Wild.'"

I covered my mouth to suppress a giggle since the sweater vest and khakis he donned hardly spoke of a motorcycle man ready to hit the road looking for adventure.

"Whatever." James rolled his eyes as if he was already sick of having to deal with us old heads. "I say it's pointless for us to waste time hashing over something we can't change."

"Perhaps," Candi conceded, "but if there's any chance one of us could be next, we owe it to ourselves to take a second look at what we know. Protect each other. Maybe we can prevent the worst from happening again."

"She's right," said Ed, "we need to at least acknowledge we're in this together. Aren't you worried?"

James didn't answer, so I spoke up to fill them in on what I learned from Mike and the police about the lobby backpack acting as a decoy, the bomber's call originating from the beach pay phone, Ignacio's person of interest status, the tilt fuse used in the explosion, and my suspicions about Phyllis.

"But that's ridiculous," James laughed and took a long sip of his Red Bull, "why would Phyllis do something so stupid if, as you claim, she has a hidden history of vehicular manslaughter *and* she's still on probation for opening up the Controlled Substance Lab to a drug dealer? She'd be a fool to risk her freedom. Nope. No dice. My money is on one of the judges."

I squinted at him. "Why would one of our judges want to kill the President Judge? And why with such flash? Why not something quick and inconspicuous like…poison?" I gestured to the frosty glass of lemonade before me. "Remember, our suspects need to align with *how* the crime was done in terms of a bomb set and a call placed. Besides, the judges were all in the courthouse as best we know and couldn't have made the threatening call from the pay phone outside Candy Kitchen unless they had an accomplice."

"Were they *all* in the courthouse?" James leaned into my personal space and teased me with the words in a song-song manner. "We didn't hear anything from Maddox *or* Radnor that day. Instead, the newest and least seasoned judge was tasked with ushering around a high-profile magistrate. Seems fishy to me."

"That does appear a little strange in hindsight," I shot back, "but I remember seeing all the judges outside after the evacuation…except Bragg, so it just doesn't fit."

"Then maybe the events aren't related," Ed said. "What if the call was simply a prank by a miffed defendant, and the car bomb happened on the same day by coincidence—a totally unrelated situation?"

"Why wouldn't we assume the two are related?" James squawked. "Your logic only works if the car bomb was a con for some other crime, like in *Die Hard,* when they pretend to be terrorists, but they're really international thieves."

Ed gave the young man a withering look. "What you're saying makes no sense."

"My point is, even though the caller didn't exactly blow up the courthouse like they said, we have to assume every move was coordinated for a specific reason to get a specific result."

"In that case," I held up a hand, "forget whodunit for a second. Let's talk about why the deed was done. Why kill Judge Yaris? Why not Maddox, Bragg, or Radnor?"

"Maybe the killer is from the judge's home turf upstate." James blurted things out rapid fire as if the energy drink had kicked in. "Maybe the killer got it wrong or one of the other judges was a hater."

"Envy." Candi leaned forward and wagged her finger at James. "Now that's a possibility. I mean, God forbid we have a killer in our midst, but if we're talking in terms of jealous judges, Maddox has been on the bench longer than any Delaware judge, and he has always aspired to a higher political office. Perhaps—and I hate to allege anything about someone I respect—but if we're looking for motives, his could be an eye on the title of President Judge."

"See." James elbowed me in the ribs like he'd been vindicated.

"The cops would need more than that." I scowled at his scattershot approach and rubbed my side. "Besides, there are more realistic possibilities when it comes to a jealousy motive. Remember, the caller talked about getting revenge, which could very well point to Arnold or Johnny. Plus, very few people other than Phyllis had the opportunity to make the call as well as the skills and motive to make a car bomb with a tilt fuse set to detonate at the slightest jostle."

"Well, that's not quite true." Candi downed the bottom half of her drink and passed the empty glass to Ed, who hopped up to get her another. "Haven't you two ever read the biographies for our judges?"

James merely grunted, and I shook my head.

"Again," Candi continued, "this is all conjecture based on his Naval experience, but the bio for Judge Radnor on the state's website lists him as having served as an EOD technician."

"Explosive Ordnance Disposal," I gasped. The phrase Ashton had used the night before hit me like a brick.

"Of course, that doesn't necessarily mean he knows how to make a bomb, but he has to know more about them than the average citizen."

I frowned at Candi as she finished her speech, then turned to face James, the dummy who started it all. "So you guys seriously want us to put our judges—Maddox and Radnor—

back on the suspect list?"

James crushed his can of Red Bull with one hand and pointed at our boss with the other. "She's the one who said we owe it to ourselves to look at all the options."

Ed slid back into the booth and handed Candi her drink. "What did I miss? Did we get to how Yaris and Radnor hate each other?"

We all stared at him. The discordant sounds of the bar's distant revelry filled our silence.

Ed fidgeted with his collar. "The clerks were talking about it on Wednesday during karaoke after word had hit that Yaris was paying our county a visit. Apparently, they had some major rift over policy a few years back, and something strange went down between them. I didn't get all the details, but Radnor hates his guts. I thought everyone knew."

"Why would we?" James threw up his hands as if finally pushed to the brink. "What did I care about the President Judge? Until yesterday, I'd never even met the guy."

"I try to stay away from gossip," replied Candi, who seemed lost in thought as she slowly stirred her daiquiri with its straw.

I racked my brain for a follow-up question as this new information made my calculations about the crime more complicated, but my thoughts were shattered by a gravely bark.

"Order up, or get up. Diners get dibs on tables."

"Coop, sweetheart," Candi batted her eyelashes behind her glasses. "We were just waiting for Victoria to get here and get settled, remember?"

"I ain't senile." He snapped, but his normal Dirty Harry glare softened ever so slightly as he took in the low V-neck of her pink cashmere sweater. "What'll it be?"

"Clam fry feast for me and Ed," she gestured at our khaki-clad coworker, who gave a brief salute. "And an assortment of wings for the table. Chef's choice on the glaze." She winked.

I cringed. Even for someone as gracious as Candi, it took guts to flirt with our town's camo-wearing cowboy.

Cooper turned to me.

"Crab cake sandwich." The words tumbled out fast. I wanted no trouble. "I'll take the up charge for extra fries."

James reached for the laminated menu card stuck in the condiment caddy by the mini juke box, and Cooper growled like a feral wolf. Everyone at the table averted their eyes and suddenly became quite fascinated by the contents of their drinks.

"Ain't nobody got time for you to go pecking through the menu." Coop hollered. "Food's been the same for twenty years. You either know what you want or you eat at home."

"Crab cake sandwich?" James ducked his head.

"You doggone right." Coop spun on his heel and stormed off.

"That man is a hoot." Ed chuckled as he swirled the last sip of liquid in his glass.

"Shut up." James had gone from his normal pallor to a bright pink.

"Relax." Candi reached across me to nudge his shoulder. "You're among friends. Happens to the best of us."

"Man up" is what she really should have said. Odds were that James would do nothing but pout for the rest of the evening, and I needed everyone focused on sorting out means and motives.

I propped my elbows on the table so I could sit a little taller and seize the reins of the conversation. "Even if we run with the idea that Maddox has intent based on ambition or that Radnor knows bombs and hates Yaris, that doesn't explain the phone call. That whole conversation was about revenge."

Candi shuddered at the reference to her ordeal.

"This is lame." James rose from the booth.

I placed a hand on his forearm to stop him. "Forget Cooper. Your judge theory wasn't terrible. There's just more to consider. Let's see this through."

He chewed at his bottom lip for a moment, probably hoping I'd beg or apologize, but he eventually sat back down. "What about Bragg?"

"He was with Yaris," Ed countered, "so he couldn't have made the call."

"Says who?" James regained his signature slacker snark. "How long was it between when the two of them left and when we got the call?"

"Half hour," I recalled, "give or take."

"Plenty of time to get to the beach." James crossed his arms, like that explained everything.

"So?" I prompted.

"So, maybe all the judges are in it together like *Strangers on a Train*."

"You mean *Murder on the Orient Express*," sighed Ed.

I shot him a look that would slice glass. We didn't need to antagonize the one person willing to brainstorm.

"Whatever." James fired back. "Bragg could be the ring leader or the pied piper who led the rat to his death."

Ed scratched his receding hairline at that one while Candi entered the conversation with a boozy wave of her hand. "I'll bite. Why would Bragg want in on a wild scheme involving bombs and murder?"

"Not sure," James shrugged, "but he is the lone Republican on our bench. He could have clashed with Yaris on some political issue."

Part of me wanted to buy into this since Bragg proudly wore the controversial scars of the confederacy—from his name to the battle flag on the bumper of his Suburban—but it was clear we were reaching.

I took a large gulp of my lemonade and hoped the icy, bittersweet liquid would wash away my bias. "Let's be logical here. This has to boil down to someone who wanted revenge like Phyllis, Arnold, or Johnny."

"Arnold Knight would never hurt a soul." Candi's words slurred together. "I remember when he used to go to the harness races on his lunch break and share any money he won with the other bailiffs. Last I heard, he was so broken up about all this, he'd taken to drowning his sorrows in dollar slots and booze." She stared at her own glass and shrugged. "He has always been a kind man."

"True," Ed drained his drink. "But he's under investigation, and he's the cause for all the bailiffs statewide losing their guns. That's a lot of weight for one man to carry. How do we know he didn't succumb to the pressure and do something rash like take revenge on Yaris, a man who had a direct hand in part of his punishment?"

"Sounds plausible," I traced the rim of my glass as I considered the idea, "but Arnold would need to have known when Yaris was going to be at the courthouse."

"Wasn't it in the paper?" James asked.

"No," I pursed my lips at the logistical snag, "the new gun ban policy was in the paper. The visit announcement was an internal memo, but maybe that doesn't make much difference. There are other ways to get that kind of information—and if Arnold has been hanging at the casino, that's close to the payphones at the beach."

"Well, what about Johnny Erving?" Candi slid Ed her second empty glass. "He was fired. Shouldn't that make him public enemy number one?"

"You'd think so," Cooper strolled up to the table with a large platter of hot wings in hand and several baskets of seafood laid across his arms, "but that boy's got more lives than a crawfish has legs."

He set the plate on the table and expertly maneuvered the baskets along his arms until he could slide them onto the surface as well. The smoky, zesty aroma of Old Bay and Tabasco engulfed us. "Shame he got canned. He's a real good tipper. I suppose he thought his uncle would swoop in to help him or something. But he'll survive, especially if he can hang onto his license."

"Uncle?" Candi asked as she shooed Ed toward the bar to fetch her drink.

Cooper pulled a long, grubby dish rag from his waistband and mopped his brow. "You know, the fella that got blowed up."

"Judge Garrett Yaris?" I sputtered.

"That's him."

I reached for my basket of food. "How's that possible?"

"The way I hear it, Yaris married one of Johnny's aunts some years back."

"So not a blood relation?"

"Did I stutter?" Cooper braced his hands on his hips. "I'm not a mathematician. I done told you what I know."

I shut my mouth, and he sauntered away.

When I turned my attention back to the table, I found that my coworkers hadn't seemed to register the news. James chewed happily on his sandwich, and Candi had started dunking clam strips into her coleslaw. My mind, however, was whirling. If Johnny and Yaris were really relatives by marriage, did that make the attorney more or less of a suspect? Is it possible the attorney asked his uncle to exercise some influence over the gun prank's disciplinary process, and when the judge failed or refused to deliver, Johnny sought vengeance—and did so in a way that implicated his recently vindicated client?

The mental gymnastics of it all made my head hurt, so I grabbed the tiny Dixie cup of tartar sauce from my basket and squeezed the contents onto the golden brown peak of the massive crab cake. Satisfied with my work, I placed the potato roll gently on top. Cooper refused to invest in the fancier brioche buns most restaurants used because he believed they were too sugary and overwhelmed the delicate flavor of the crab meat. I lifted the heavenly monstrosity toward my mouth and bit into the crisp outer layer of the cake. Tangy dill melted into the fluffy folds that encompassed the center of the salty-sweet orb.

When Ed returned with Candi's third daiquiri, I shared my thoughts about Cooper's bombshell with the group. "Now, Ed, you clearly spend more time here than the rest of us. Have you heard anything that could confirm such a theory?"

"Nothing specific." Ed sucked the meat from a hot wing. "I hadn't heard about the uncle thing, but I know a lot of the clerks are pretty sweet on him and at least one came to karaoke bragging about how she finally *climbed that mountain.*" Ed's olive skin flushed red as the words passed his lips. "So by my account, he probably still has an inside track on all of the gossip floating around the courthouse, like the Yaris visit, even after getting fired."

"And," I offered, "if he has no compunction about pulling a gun on some of his coworkers, what's to stop him from blowing a few others?"

"I-I-I don't know." Candi mused a bit too loudly. "Nobody's really heard anything about him since the Cardoza trial. It all seems so surreal."

"It is surreal," James muttered through a mouthful of french fries. "Which means, we could be looking in the wrong direction entirely. For all we know, Grant Wells is behind the whole thing."

"Come on, James." Ed bowed his head and ran a hand across his brow.

"Enough with the conspiracy theories. Don't you think that's going too far? There's no way the state's prosecutor could have done this."

"Why not?" James pushed away his empty food basket. "To me, this sounds like the perfect way for Wells to get back at Johnny and Arnold for that crazy gun prank. Wells is smart enough to know that if the motive for all this has been defined as revenge, everybody is going to immediately blame the PD and the bailiff."

"That's sick." Candi pressed her hands against her eyes as if trying to block it all out. "A man died."

"I don't make the rules." James slouched in his seat unfazed.

The three of them continued to argue and eat, but I'd lost my appetite. I'd gone into this so sure about Phyllis's guilt. Now, I didn't know what to think.

* * *

An hour later, our group stood on the top step outside of Cooper's and exchanged hugs.

"Are you going to make it?" I asked Candi who had grown quite tipsy by meal's end. I released her from our embrace but kept hold of her elbow as she swayed lightly with the late afternoon breeze. "Do you need a ride?"

"Oh, you all are so good to me," Candi shouted with her arms open wide like she was Eva Peron addressing her nation. "Even you, Opie." She patted James on the back.

His features fell into the limp formation of befuddlement.

I shielded my eyes against the setting sun and nodded toward his scarlet curls. "Really? You know all those old movies, but don't get a reference to *The Andy Griffith Show*."

"Sorry, guys, this is my fault." Ed stood on the opposite side and watched me struggle to keep Candi from running her hands through James's hair. "I should have cut her off after the first one. She mentioned being a lightweight."

"No kidding." James dodged from Candi's grasp. "I know we all need to blow off some steam, but geez."

"So colorful," she cooed. "So pretty in this light, the flashy, flashy light."

"Whatever. I'm outta here." James groaned and trotted down the steps. "What the—"

A loud wail erupted from two police cars that raced down Route 1 and screeched to a halt in front of the apartment building across the street from Cooper's.

"Look!" Candi clapped her hands together in merriment. "More lights!"

The units joined a large collection of other law enforcement vehicles whose blue and red turret flashers I had failed to notice in my efforts to keep Candi steady.

Ed gripped my shoulder and pointed beyond the crowd of uniformed officers, toward the entrance of the complex. "Is that Ignacio Cardoza?"

Sure enough, I recognized the gaunt, sallow-skinned young man. He was dressed modestly in sweatpants and a tank top. State Police troopers flanked him on each side, both with a hand wrapped around his upper arm as they guided him down the steps of the apartment building. As the trio moved toward one of the police cars, I could see that Ignacio had his hands cuffed behind his back and that he wasn't wearing shoes.

Clearly, the arrest had been sudden and unexpected.

But why?

"What's changed in the last twenty-four hours?" I looked over at Ed, whose furrowed brow and open mouth mirrored my own confusion.

The sirens started up again once Ignacio had folded himself into the back of a vehicle and the officers had shut the door. Once the car peeled away, several troopers stormed into the building while others milled around the perimeter talking into their radios.

"What'd I tell you?" James flapped his arms and looked up at the three of us from the bottom step. "We spent two hours of a perfectly good Saturday rehashing something we have no power to change." He jabbed a thumb toward the commotion across the road. "Case closed."

But was it?

I wasn't so sure. The four of us had come up with a compelling, albeit far-fetched, motive for nearly everyone in town—from our three judges to Johnny Erving, Arnold Knight, Phyllis Dodd, and DAG Wells—but not once did any of us seriously consider Ignacio Cardoza.

Why?

Because the idea just didn't fit. Why would this young man want to jeopardize his freedom when he'd just won it back?

I handed Candi over to Ed, who guided her down the steps while I rummaged through the side pocket of my purse, where I'd stuck my car keys.

But before I could find them, my cellphone rang. I dug the device from my jacket pocket to discover a local number I didn't recognize. With a tap of the screen, the digits disappeared and the call engaged.

"Ms. Justice?" A stoic female voice buzzed from the speaker against my ear. "This is Henrietta Price from the Trident County Medical Center. Our records show you listed as the emergency contact for a Mr. Ashton North. I am calling to inform you he's just been admitted to the ICU."

Chapter Fourteen

I squeezed Ashton's unresponsive hand and rested my head on his forearm, the one that didn't have an IV plunged deep into the pale folds of his skin.

I'd sat at his bedside all Saturday night into Sunday morning, praying that he'd wake up. My body was exhausted from the effort, but I couldn't fall asleep even if I tried. The constant bleep of his heart monitor and the subtle sourness of the antiseptic air made it impossible to forget the seriousness of my surroundings. But most of all, I resented the feeling of unseen eyes watching my heartache, so I shielded my face against the muted glow of the tiny overhead safety light and counted the minutes until the top of the hour when yet another nurse would enter to check his vital signs.

As best as I could piece together from their brief updates and the rushed report from the ER doc earlier that evening, Ashton had lost control of his truck on the highway and crashed full speed into the embankment that separated the north and south lanes. The accident had caused a severe concussion and a ruptured spleen that they were successfully able to remove upon his admittance to the hospital. Ashton was stable now but needed to be closely monitored due to brain swelling they feared might deprive the organ of proper oxygen.

I wished I could do something more productive for him than wait.

My cellphone buzzed on the rolling table I'd pushed aside to make room for the plastic chair I'd pulled up to the bed. I glanced over at the screen to see a text from Ma, asking for the millionth time when I was coming home. I grabbed the device and point-clicked a reply.

"That better not be Mike again." A raspy but deep voice engulfed me. "I'd hate to have to meet him like this."

I looked up to find Ashton staring at me through the dim half-light. His head was still reclined, and his usually bright blue eyes were a bit watery, but his expression was semi-alert, and his chapped lips held a loose smile.

"I thought I'd lost you." I abandoned the phone and leaned in so he wouldn't have to raise his voice. "Do you need some water?"

"No, I'm fine—or at least I will be." His eyelids fluttered for a moment like he was taking an internal assessment. "I'm just glad you're here."

"I couldn't imagine being anywhere else right now."

He opened his palm, and I placed my hand inside. A rush of warm relief rippled across my chest when his fingers actively wrapped around mine. I would have been content to sit like that forever, but the obvious question gnawed at the back of my mind.

"Ashton, I know it's late…" I glanced at the large digital clock mounted on the wall by the modest flat screen television and noted it was nearing 5:00 a.m. "…or rather early, but if you're up to it, I wanted to ask you about—"

"About our Sunday sunrise ritual by the bay?" He raised his eyebrows and turned his head toward the lone window overlooking the dark parking lot. "Looks like I'll be taking a rain check today, but I promise to make it up to you in any way you'd like." He gave me a slow wink.

"Nice try, Romeo." I chuckled. "But you're facing some serious injuries that have me and the doctors worried. Now, I don't want to push you if you're not ready, but can we talk about what happened?"

His brow furrowed, and his lips tightened. He took a deep breath, but he didn't speak.

"Do you remember?" My words came out as a whisper, and a sharp sting erupted in the corner of each eye as I feared the worst for his brain.

He squeezed my hand. "I remember, but I don't want you to worry."

"Too late." I wiped my eyes with the back of my free hand. "Worry is my middle name."

"I know." He turned his gaze away from me toward the open door. For what seemed like an eternity, his focus remained on the bright strip of fluorescent light that seeped in from beyond the threshold. "Promise me you won't overreact to what I'm going to say—"

"That's a tall order from the King of Overreactions himself." I joked then steeled myself for his reply. "Just say it already."

"That's what I love to see." A broad-shouldered female nurse with wild brown hair and a thick Irish brogue appeared in the doorway. "How long has he been awake?"

"About five minutes," I answered for Ashton, who had already begun to poke and prod.

I sat quietly while she checked his vital signs and asked him a few general questions to test his orientation and concentration. She also did some finger exercises to test his motor skills and asked him if he was feeling nauseous or experiencing blurred vision. Once she took his temperature, she picked up his chart and ticked off a few things.

"He'll make it through." She proclaimed loudly in my direction. "Just don't get him too riled up."

If she only knew. Ashton was the one on the verge of dropping a bomb, and it was taking everything in my power not to explode in anticipation.

"You were saying?" I prompted once the nurse left.

"I think someone sabotaged my truck."

My breath caught for several seconds as I waited for him to continue. "Sabotaged how?"

"I can't be sure until the police come back with the accident report, but I think someone may have cut one or two of my brake lines."

"What do you mean? Is that even possible?"

"You'd be surprised how easy it is if you have the right tools. The tubing is pretty thick, but the cutter needed for the job is sold at any automotive store." He cleared his throat and closed his eyes for a moment. "With a lifted truck like mine, anybody can slip underneath and snip the lines in a matter of minutes. I'm ninety-five percent certain that's why I lost control of the vehicle, because I remember getting inside and thinking that the brake pedal felt a little mushy."

"Mushy?"

"Soft. Flat." He bit his lip and seemed to search for words. "You know, when you press the brake to start the car, the pedal is stiff until you ignite the engine. Once the motor is running, the pedal releases but still offers resistance as you thrust down on it. That way, you can regulate how slowly or quickly you stop. Mine wasn't like that."

"Okay. I've never really thought about it, but I think I know what you're talking about. You're saying you think someone messed with the brakes because the pedal wasn't acting normally?"

"Right. The firmness wasn't quite there when I started the truck, but I ignored it since I'd just gotten my baby out of the shop."

Under any other circumstances, I would have snickered at this last comment. His "baby" was an overgrown dual-cab Ford F-150 decked out in camo green. Ashton had even gone the extra mile to outfit the truck with wheels so gargantuan that I'd taken to calling the stupid thing a monster truck behind his back.

"Well," I sighed, "how do you know this wasn't some kind of mix-up with the repair?"

"Doubtful." He wrinkled his nose. "She went in for a fuel filter. They shouldn't have touched the brakes, and I haven't had a single issue or red flag since I drove home from the shop on Monday. Saturday afternoon was the only instance this week that gave me pause."

"You think somebody deliberately planned this?" I pressed both my palms against my eyes. I didn't like where this was going.

"This was no accident." His bed creaked, and the rhythmic bleep of his heart monitor increased as he reached over and tugged at my hands until I met his gaze. "It wasn't until I got out on the highway that I realized I couldn't slow down—but by then it was too late. I was going too fast, and there were too many cars around. I did my best to avoid a crash, but I eventually had no choice but to throw the transmission into park to stop my momentum. Of course, all that did was put me into a skid that spun me off the road and slammed me into the retaining wall."

"I believe you, Ashton, but…" I shook my head and let my curls fall forward like a curtain. I wanted to retreat. I needed to think. "Why would anyone want to sabotage your truck?"

"A week ago? I would have said nobody…except maybe your mother." He cracked a weak smile at the lame joke meant to ease my growing concern. "But considering Judge Garrett Yaris was killed in a truck of the same make and model with an eerily similar color, I'd say this may have been the work of our courthouse bomber."

My mouth dropped open, but not a single word came out. It was as if the entire universe had stopped on a dime and folded itself into that one nanosecond of realization. Had the killer followed through with his promise of a second attack? But why Ashton? He didn't work at the courthouse, and he no longer had any official role in law enforcement. Targeting Ashton didn't fit the revenge plot or the courthouse employee angle unless…the cops arrested the wrong person.

"Phyllis Dodd." My mind snapped back to reality at the sound of my own voice, which had become high-pitched and rapid. "Why did I let myself get talked out of something so obvious?"

My hands shot out to clutch his shoulders, but I stopped myself at the sight of the wires sticking out through the top of his hospital gown.

"We've got to call someone." I stooped over, grabbed my purse from the floor, and rummaged through the various pockets for the business cards given to me by Detective Daniels and Chief Strickland. "I should have known the second I saw her lawyered up with Beauregard Harriston. Phyllis is the only person in town with a means, motive, and opportunity that intersects with you and Judge Yaris."

"Victoria, wait." Ashton croaked. "We need to be strategic about this. So far, all we have is a coincidence and speculation. Let's wait until I get out of here, and we have the police report."

His words droned on and morphed into a full-blown lecture, but my mind was already made up. I was sharing Ashton's theory with the authorities first thing Monday morning.

Chapter Fifteen

"We looked into Ashton North's accident report like you asked," Detective Daniels scratched at his graying mustache and sighed, "and while you were indeed correct about his brakes being cut, it's still unclear how that correlates to our investigation into the death of Judge Yaris."

I gripped the edge of the small oval conference table, where I sat across from Detective Daniels and Chief Strickland, and tried not to scream in frustration. Instead, I reminded myself to be grateful that they were open to my suggestion for a second meeting and that they'd been gracious enough to meet me at 8:00 a.m. on a Monday morning in one of the courthouse's attorney-client interview rooms so that I wouldn't be late for work. Such facts merited patience on my part even as I worried that Ashton's health and the safety of my coworkers hung in the balance.

"Seriously?" I asked in hushed tones to mask my sarcasm. "The connection between the vehicles is obvious."

"That's not what he meant." Strickland's voice rumbled even though he barely moved his lips. "What we're asking is this: Why do you insist upon attributing the act to Phyllis Dodd?"

"Because, like Judge Yaris and most of the people in the courthouse, Ashton played a role in exposing her corrupt use of the Controlled Substance Lab. I can personally attest to her threatening him back when he was a state trooper, right outside the courthouse, less than a year ago. Now, you've gone and arrested the wrong man when it is so obvious—"

"We haven't made any arrests in the Yaris case." Daniels's perpetually baggy eyes narrowed.

"But what about Ignacio Cardoza? I saw him arrested on Saturday afternoon outside his apartment building."

The men exchanged a glance that left Strickland pursing his lips.

"Ms. Justice," Daniels leaned back in his chair, "I don't know what you think you saw, but it has been widely reported that Mr. Cardoza was arrested for a violation of the probation he was serving prior to his most recent trial."

"A probation violation?" I had to admit I'd missed quite a bit of news, spending Saturday evening and all of Sunday tending to Ashton at his bedside, but the detective's depiction didn't pass the smell test.

"Do you usually send half a dozen State Troopers to arrest probationers or just the ones who are a person of interest in a murder?"

Daniels didn't flinch, nor did he answer.

We would have sat in tense silence forever if Strickland hadn't leaned over to the detective, placed his service cap in front of their mouths, and whispered a few words. When the chief finished, Daniels ran a hand through his hair and spoke with reluctance.

"Ignacio Cardoza resisted arrest and refused to leave his apartment when the probation officer confronted him about the violation. The troopers were called in for backup. While I can neither confirm nor deny whether Mr. Cardoza is a person of interest in the Yaris case, I can assure you the two matters are unrelated." He clenched his jaw and added. "And I would hope that it is not your intention to obstruct our investigation by wasting our time with accusations, misinformation, and unfounded claims."

I dropped my head and stared at the cheap Formica tabletop as I silently counted down from ten. The urge to scream had returned with a vengeance, and the tiny walk-in closet-sized interview room suddenly felt claustrophobic, a blank inhumane void where opinion and progressive thought were consumed and replaced with the status quo. These men thought I couldn't see through their ruse—clearly, the only reason Ignacio was arrested was to put pressure on him about the murder case—a dangerously ironic prospect when one considered Ignacio's trial acquittal only occurred because jurors were wary of our law enforcement's deceptive interpretation of justice.

"You're saying that no one has officially been arrested for the bombing at this time?"

"Correct," Daniels growled, "but we do have several suspects under investigation."

"Including Phyllis Dodd?" I asked.

The pair stared at each other again. Daniels bared his teeth as if to put a note of finality on the matter, but Strickland licked his plump lips and turned to face me.

"Ms. Justice, we appreciate your desire to help us with this investigation, but the insistence on pointing fingers at Ms. Dodd is unacceptable. She has come in for questioning and indicated through store surveillance footage that she was working at the time of the phone call and initial bombing incident—"

"But that doesn't mean anything. She didn't need to be there. The explosion was triggered with a tilt fuse—"

"And," Strickland held up a hand as he continued to talk over me. "Ms. Dodd and her attorney were meeting with Detective Daniels at the estimated time of Mr. North's collision."

"So? Like the placement of the tilt fuse, those brakes could have been cut any time—or that just means she has an accomplice."

"With all due respect," Strickland returned the peaked service cap to his shiny bald head and frowned, "we appreciate the work you've done on this so far with recording the bomber's call. That's why we were willing to entertain you today, and Daniels has explained to me that you've provided insight in the past on another murder that took place in this very courthouse. But this is an entirely different scenario, and we can't afford to act on instinct and emotion. We're happy that you brought the similarities between the trucks to our attention. There is definitely something there, but I think we can all agree it is far too soon to pin this on any particular person."

I'd heard this song before, so I got up without a word, opened the door, and slammed it behind me as hard as I could. Ma would have been appalled at my behavior, especially since I was at work. She'd raised me to be courteous and compassionate, but she'd also taught me that a woman never has to worry about getting things done if she tackles them herself—and that's exactly what I'd do to make sure Ashton and my coworkers didn't fall prey to a killer.

I checked my watch to find that I still had about thirty-five minutes before I had to return to my office for the usual 9:00 a.m. morning briefing. That didn't leave time to drive to the beach and track Phyllis down at work, but maybe I could do the next best thing. Her attorney's office was within walking distance of the courthouse, along the area of town, known as The Quad, which was less than three minutes away. Without a second thought, I worked my way to the front of the courthouse and strolled down Oceanside Drive to Beauregard Harriston's law practice.

When I opened the door, I was greeted by his administrative assistant, Margaret Swinson. I knew her from the days when she worked at the courthouse in the Prothonotary's Office as a criminal trial clerk. Maggie was a busty Southern Belle with a sky-high blond bouffant. One might call her a Dolly Parton type, but I wouldn't dare insult the beloved Queen of Nashville. Whereas Dolly was the height of hospitality and graciousness, Maggie was petty and narcissistic.

"What are you doing here?" she asked.

Maggie wasn't my biggest fan, so she made no effort to mask her dismay. The last time we'd spoken, I called her out on her penchant for adultery…and got slapped for it.

"I need to talk to Harriston."

"Not without an appointment." She pointed one of her talons at the majestic grandfather clock that sat at the end of the small but lavish sitting room that acted as their lobby. "And you should know better than anyone that he doesn't conduct any business until after 9:00 a.m. So why don't you tell me what this is about, and we'll set you up with an appointment two days from next *never*."

"Cute, Maggs. I just want to ask a few questions about Phyllis Dodd."

"Oh, come on now, Victoria." She rocked back in her swivel chair and chuckled. "You're smarter than that. Ain't you ever heard of attorney-client privilege?"

I crossed my arms with my hip cocked. "Humor me."

"Ugggh." She tilted her head back and let out a loud groan of exaggerated exasperation. "Oh, my God. Why are you always so full of yourself? Fine. I will. Just for the pleasure of seeing you fail."

She rose from her desk and knocked on the ornately paneled set of French doors that sat directly across from her reception area.

After a few seconds, Harriston bellowed from the confines of his office. "This better be important, Maggie. I'm trying to prepare a motion."

"Yes, sir," she called in response. Then opened the door and shoved me inside.

Harriston sat in the middle of the room at a wide mahogany desk that dominated the space. The surface was strewn with so many papers that it gave the illusion of being crème and manila. He had a laptop open to his right, but his attention was focused on a legal pad where he was feverishly crossing out notes. I stood there for a moment while he finished. When he looked up and caught sight of me, his heavy jowls quivered for a moment, and the nostrils of his bulbous nose flared.

"I should have known you'd come a calling."

"Why represent Phyllis Dodd when you know she's—"

"Now, before you say another word," he removed his reading glasses, then brandished his pen at me, "let me save you a heck of a lot of trouble by giving you a nickel's worth of free legal advice. If you keep going around town spreading rumors and falsely accusing people of crimes they didn't commit, you could be hit with a defamation suit or charged with falsely reporting an incident."

I stood my ground. Even if I couldn't get anything out of him, I wanted him to know that I knew there was more to this. "You can try to intimidate me all you want, but everyone knows what she's capable of, and she wouldn't need a lawyer if there wasn't something to hide."

"Ms. Justice, this is not some childish game. People's lives are on the line. I don't know what you expected to accomplish by walking in here unannounced, but I told you last week that neither I nor my client has any comment at this time. Now, I suggest you align yourself with the law that you so lovingly serve by remembering that everyone is entitled to legal counsel…even the innocent." He raised a hand toward the door. "Now, if you would kindly follow my assistant, I'm sure she'd be happy to escort you out."

I turned to find Maggie leaning against the door of his office with a glint in her eye and the sticky-sweet smile of a child who just got everything she ever wanted for Christmas.

* * *

When I finally returned to the court reporter's office, I found Candi standing at the front of our shared office space chattering about the antiquing she'd done the day after our gathering at Cooper's despite the worst hangover she'd had in her life. Ed listened attentively while James covertly fiddled with his phone under the desk.

I slumped in my chair and stewed over the information I'd gathered in the last hour. If Phyllis's whereabouts were accounted for during both crimes, maybe there was a solid argument to be made for Ignacio as a suspect. His arrest time left room for him to sabotage Ashton's brakes, and Mike mentioned during our late-night meetup that surveillance cameras had Ignacio in the courthouse around the time of the bombing. But then, who made the call from the boardwalk pay phone? And why would Ignacio sabotage Ashton, a person he's presumably never met?

I just didn't see how the Ignacio theory could hold.

And yet, it didn't sound like the police were willing to let it go, which begged the question: How low would law enforcement stoop to find a suspect? Or conversely, how badly could the judicial system have destroyed Ignacio's life for him to risk his recently earned freedom for revenge? I guess that same question could be posed for Phyllis, especially since her alibis seemed too perfect. Plus, I wasn't willing to let her off the hook as easily as him. I just wish there was a way I could talk to her or Ignacio to root out the truth.

"Victoria, they're requesting you in chambers." A sharp version of Candi's normally chipper voice snapped me back to reality.

I'd chosen to work on an evidentiary hearing with The Honorable Charles Wayne Radnor, but he must have decided to first address an issue or some motion with the attorneys in his office. I grabbed my steno machine by its tripod along with a copy of the day's docket, in case I needed to make notes or check the spelling of an attorney's name, and headed to the judges' suite.

Small compared to the other judges' offices, but probably the neatest of the three, Radnor's private space sat at the rear of the suite and overlooked The Quad from tall windows that loomed behind his desk. As a Navy man, Radnor was a minimalist. A massive oak desk and matching bookshelves was all he needed. No clutter adorned the space. The papers on his desk sat stacked neatly, and if he had a laptop, he'd stored it away.

"Good morning." Radnor stood as I entered with the lawyers in tow. The judge was broad and big-bellied, but not in the way one would call fat. He was simply larger than life, standing at a good six foot six, despite being in his early seventies. His full batch of wavy hair was another element that seemed to defy his age. I could tell that he was quite the looker in his day because he still held the air of a 1950s movie star, even when he wasn't wearing his prestigious black robe.

I liked Radnor for his attention to detail and efficiency. Unlike the other judges, he kept a comfy high-back chair next to his desk for court reporters and thought idle chit-chat was for the birds.

"What's on your mind, gentlemen?" Radnor inquired as he pointed to me to get started. I noted the time and double-stroked the simple finger combination STA*RT/STA*RT to insert the pre-designated parenthetical phrase used at the opening of every transcript destined to become part of the official record.

"Your Honor, the State requests we postpone this hearing since our medical expert has failed to show."

Radnor inclined his massive head in disbelief. Uh-oh. Never a good sign when the prosecution shows up unprepared on the day of the hearing. This was going to be a contentious one, so I let my eyes wander around the room.

Radnor's utilitarianism left very little to admire—a pair of diplomas from Cornell, a framed photo of what looked like a fish that one of his grandkids must have drawn, a family portrait of his wife and three adult boys, and an eight-by-ten of him shaking hands with Judge Yaris.

My eyes widened as I remembered what Ed told us about Radnor's contentious relationship with the President Judge. While it was unthinkable that a distinguished jurist would kill a man in broad daylight, Radnor knew both the deceased and Ashton from his days as an arresting officer attending court to testify on cases. So if the two crimes were connected, the judge had just as many means and motives to kill as anyone else. I hated to even consider such a notion since questioning Radnor would be tough, but I was determined to leave no stone unturned.

After thirty minutes of bickering between the attorneys, my window of opportunity opened. Usually, I hopped up to leave first. This was not only a gesture of respect, in case the judge wanted to have a private chat with an attorney, but also a practical solution for getting my steno machine out of everyone's way once people got to their feet. Today, however, I pretended to fiddle with the screen and forced the attorneys to squeeze past me as they departed.

Alone, I looked over at the judge. "I'm sorry for your loss. Were you and Yaris close?"

He met my gaze, slightly startled, since he had already busied himself with signing documents.

I gestured toward the photo on the opposite wall. "I can't imagine watching a friend lose his life—at least not under such horrific circumstances."

"You'd be surprised what you can get used to when you've seen as much as I have."

"Did you witness many deaths like this during your time in the Navy? Candi mentioned you were an EOD technician."

"What is this all about?" He set his papers aside and steepled his hands in front of his long nose.

"Nothing, Your Honor." I fidgeted in my chair, knowing one wrong word meant expulsion. "I assumed you knew Judge Yaris better than most and could provide some insight into his death."

"I don't know any more than you do. Naturally, I don't wish for anyone to experience such a gruesome end, but I don't have much time to worry about it either. Talk to Maddox, he's the one fixated on Yaris and life upstate."

"You don't care that everyone is saying this was an act of revenge against our judiciary and that the bomber may strike again?"

"If it is my time, it is my time." He turned back to his documents.

"That philosophy may work well on a personal level, but what about the rest of us? Your insights could save somebody's life."

A low grumble emanated from his throat, but he didn't speak. It was as if he was content to wait me out. I decided to share the information I learned from Mike about the bombing.

"Investigators say the explosion was triggered by a tilt fuse and that the judge's vehicle was the only one rigged with such a device—although there has been other suspicious activity since that initial incident." My chest constricted a little for Ashton, who was still confined to a hospital bed.

Radnor raised his eyebrows at my statement, and I mimicked him to show that I'd registered his reaction.

"If the explosion was really triggered with a tilt fuse," he sighed, "the perpetrator only knew enough to get the job done. A mechanism like that, though relatively undetectable and easy to make, is unstable and unpredictable. Anyone with trained expertise would have used a blasting cap to ensure the bomb went off exactly when and where it was intended."

"Could you have created such a device?"

"Why would I?" He spat in clipped tones. "Did you ask anyone else such a ridiculous question?"

"Rumor has it there was friction between you and the President Judge."

"Ah, I see where this is going." He closed his eyes and rubbed the lids. "Someone has put it in your head that I had something to do with this senseless murder, even though I was the only judge who left the courthouse willingly when the evacuation was announced. Never mind that Maddox initially refused to leave his office, and Bragg was nowhere to be found."

He thrust a thick finger toward me, and I gripped the edge of my seat, bracing for the worst.

"Let me squash that notion right now. Like I told the police, it's no secret that I wasn't fond of Garrett Yaris. He tried to ruin my nomination to the bench by spreading a rumor that my father bribed the governor and key members of the state senate's selection committee. Nothing could have been further from the truth. In fact, it wouldn't surprise me to learn that tactic had been his own path to success."

"Why would he go to such lengths to hurt you?" I whispered so as not to disturb his train of thought.

"We attended law school together, and he—along with a couple of his cronies—took it upon themselves to make my life a living hell because I was an ex-con's kid from the wrong side of the tracks who was beating them at their own game despite the odds. Things didn't change when we entered the real world. Some men remain self-serving no matter how much money or power they amass." His nostrils flared as if he were suppressing a growl. "Garrett may have come out on top, but I haven't forgiven him, and that certainly won't start today."

He slammed his hand on the desk as he said this, causing me to jump. I knew he meant it as my cue to leave, but his candor left me curious.

"Your Honor, I'm so very, very sorry. I—I can't even imagine." My heart poured out to him, so I lowered my voice to avoid further offense. "I didn't— I don't mean to pry, but none of that quite answered my question…could you have created such a device?"

He stared at me, then turned to study the photograph of Judge Yaris. After a long moment, he stood up from behind his desk and crossed over to close the office door. I once again shifted in my seat, unsure what was happening, and wrapped both hands around my steno machine's tripod, ready to use the unit as a weapon should things get ugly.

Thankfully, Radnor held his position by the exit and dropped his head as if deep in thought. "I was diagnosed with Parkinson's disease a little over a decade ago. The early symptoms were barely noticeable—a slight hand tremor, slowed reflexes—but ultimately this is a disease of deterioration. Now, I occasionally lose my balance because my muscles get stiff. Sometimes I have trouble multitasking. Even concentrating on a document for short periods has become a huge challenge. When Garrett announced his visit,

I made a point to keep my distance because I didn't want him to notice my illness. With our history, he'd surely rally his supporters and force my retirement before the end of my term. I have less than two years to go and no desire to give him the satisfaction…even in death. So, the answer to your pathetic question is 'no.' I could not have built that bomb." He opened the door and swept one arm toward the hallway beyond. "I don't know what you're looking for, but you're not going to find it here."

I rose with my steno machine in hand and walked to the door, but I stopped at the threshold. Something didn't make sense.

"Why display a picture of a man you hate?"

"To remind me to keep at it when things get tough since nobody else has faith that I will." He offered a solemn smile and gently closed the door in my face.

I nodded in spite of myself. As a person who'd also suffered under a classmate and overcome the odds, I understood better than most.

Alone in the suite's plush corridor, it hit me that I had the rare opportunity to speak with the other judges, too. After all, each of them probably had a different perspective of the bombing, having exited the building on the other side of the parking lot from the rest of the staff. And surely, at least one of them spoke to Yaris in the moments before his fatal end.

I glanced around the hall to assess who may be watching. About twenty feet from where I stood, the hallway opened into a large common area the judges and their law clerks used as a conference room. Maddox and Bragg had offices that fed off that space, but to visit them, I'd be put in direct view of the secretarial pool and waiting area stationed beyond the enormous conference table.

A person with common sense would have gone to one of those secretaries and made an appointment, but I didn't want to be in a position where I'd be denied or put off for several weeks. So I waited until the coast was clear, tiptoed to the open office door of Judge Maddox, and knocked on the frame before stepping inside.

"Did I call for a court reporter?" he asked from atop the StairMaster located in the corner of his office.

I discreetly pressed a finger to my nostrils as the smell of stale perspiration wafted my way.

"No, Your Honor. I just finished an office conference down the hall where we were talking about the President Judge." I placed my steno machine on the floor beside me. "I figure since you've been on the bench the longest, you'd probably know Yaris best. I hoped to get your thoughts about his death."

"Is this for a sympathy card or something?" Maddox dabbed his forehead with the towel around his neck, but he never stopped his slow climb. He had on track pants and a tank top that revealed a series of gnarly scars on his chest and forearms.

"No. Sorry. I wasn't clear." Asking someone about murderer never was. "I didn't mean to intrude, sir. I was just wondering if you saw anything unusual about Judge Yaris's behavior prior to the bombing?"

"Nope. I was holed up in here writing a legal opinion."

"Is that why you didn't evacuate when they sounded the alarm?"

He hesitated on a step and almost lost his balance. "No."

"But Judge Radnor said you refused to leave."

"Frankly, my dear, I don't think that's any of your business." He looked down his nose at me with a seriousness often reserved for his criminal defendants.

"With all due respect, Your Honor, it isn't my intention to pry." The words had taken on a needy quality that I immediately resented, but old men with power often lived for such suppliance. "Nobody seems to know what happened or why, and I was just hoping for a few reassuring words from someone who'd actually witnessed the event."

"Who could see anything in such chaos?" He huffed and flapped a dismissive hand my way. "Once we were all outside, Garrett kept saying he didn't want to wait around. He couldn't afford to waste his whole day downstate. And if he couldn't do what he came to do, he'd rather hit the golf course. I urged him to stay put, but he slipped away in all the mishegoss—none of the bailiffs were paying much attention to any of us once we were out of the building. Next thing, you know...boom. Hold onto your butts."

"That doesn't upset you."

"Of course it does." He dabbed at his forehead again, but the edges of his dusty blond hair had already turned dark with sweat. "That means yet another appointment our governor will need to fill, and I may very well be saddled with helping him shoulder that burden."

If he'd meant to hide the sly smile lingering behind his faint green eyes, he failed miserably.

"Now, if you'll excuse me." He tapped a few buttons on the machine's console, and the steps gained speed on a low whine. "I have twenty more minutes on this miserable thing, and talking don't helping the walking. Hasta la vista, Ms. Justice. See yourself out."

I picked up my equipment and left the room. Candi had been right about Maddox's ambition, but nothing about the conversation pointed to someone willing and able to kill. I don't know what I had expected to find, but my skin flushed with the realization that I'd perhaps undertaken a fool's endeavor.

"What do you think you're doing?" J. Braxton Bragg stood about ten feet away. He had his coat on like he was about to depart, and his pudgy sunburned face twisted in disgust as he barked at me. "Shouldn't you be in court?"

I bit back the curses that arose in response. The man had a knack for raising my hackles, but I had to be nice if I wanted to get his version of events. Based on what I knew so far, Bragg was the only person in the courthouse who had spent any significant time with Yaris on the day of the bombing. Yet, Judge Radnor said the young confederate wannabe was nowhere to be found when the crime unfolded. Is it possible he left to make that threatening call from the boardwalk?

"What are you gawking at?"

"Nothing, Your Honor. I am simply surprised to see you. I hoped—"

He turned and walked briskly across the vast conference space toward the partition that marked the secretarial pool and reception area. I scurried after him, steno machine brandished in front of me like an Olympic torch.

"Sir, I—"

"Florence," he bellowed as he barreled down the wide aisle toward his assistant. "Push back my 11:00 o'clock with McNally, I'm going to take an early lunch."

Lunch? It was barely 10:00 a.m.

Florence clearly shared my incredulity because when Bragg dropped his gaze to select a butterscotch from the dish nestled on her cluttered desk, she rolled her eyes skyward and shook her head before she picked up the phone.

I seized the lull in conversation as an opportunity.

"Sir, where were you when Judge Yaris died?"

The secretary across the aisle behind us gasped, but I focused on Bragg to gauge his reaction. He never looked up from the candy, which he unwrapped with childish delight.

"I'm not in the habit of answering questions from underlings," he said with a sniff as if I stank, "but I was with Garrett. God rest his soul. You know, it's a miracle I didn't get in that truck with him, but my wife called complaining of labor pains seconds before our departure." He popped the yellow candy in his mouth and rolled it around. "I thank Jesus for my safety, but the state lost a good man that day."

"Too true, sir." I fought to keep my voice neutral even though I knew he was lying. "Do you know why Judge Yaris would have needed to leave amidst all that—"

Bragg sauntered through the empty waiting room like I hadn't said a word and swiped his keycard at the suite's main door, which led to a heavily guarded antechamber that separated their offices from the public areas of the courthouse. I started after him, but Florence cracked her gum with a loud pop that caused me to look back.

"Don't waste your time, honey. An early lunch," she mimed air quotes, "means he's going to the bikini bar. He thinks nobody knows, but he goes every Monday, Wednesday, and Friday morning like clockwork." She snapped her gum again, this time on a large bubble. "I imagine that's where he was the day of the explosion—although you're never going to hear him admit it."

I looked at the other two secretaries who whipped their heads back toward their computer monitors as if they didn't want to get caught up in such sordid gossip.

"Is his wife even pregnant?"

"Yeah, not that he cares." Florence beckoned me closer, the sugary scent of grape gum engulfing us as she whispered. "He's gone all googly-eyes over some gal at the Moxie Fox."

Bingo. The smutty breastaurant sat near the boardwalk and was one of the few beachside attractions whose theme wasn't exactly family-friendly.

"How could you possibly know that?" I set my steno machine down and crouched beside her desk.

"He made the mistake of taking her to Cooper's afterhours once—and Lord knows that crotchety old man can't keep a secret. He was falling all over himself to tell anyone who'd listen. Now, Bragg has reverted to these early lunches so he can meet up with her before the bikini bar opens at noon. You'd think being the new guy, he'd try to show a little decorum rather than running around town like a lovesick school boy, leaving everybody else to pull his slack."

She picked up a thick file from her desk and tossed it onto the credenza behind her. I stared at Florence Hallaway in disbelief. I'd never spent much time talking to her, not because we worked in different offices but because she was that scary older kind of woman who looked like she spent her Saturdays screaming at kids to "get off her lawn." She was a polyester suit-wearing powerhouse with a pointy nose and a set of cat-eared glasses dangling from a chain around her neck. But apparently, I had her all wrong; she was my pint-sized prophet.

"Is it true Bragg wasn't around when you all evacuated the building?"

"One hundred percent."

"What about Maddox? I heard he initially refused to leave his office."

She pressed her lips together and gave me a stiff nod, but directed her words to the two women over my shoulder. "Could one of you cover my phones for a minute? We're going to grab some coffee."

She beckoned me to follow her back through the conference space to the kitchenette located in a large alcove between Radnor's and Maddox's offices.

"How do you take your coffee?"

"No thanks. Too much caffeine." I leaned against the counter and crossed my arms while she fixed herself a cup. "So there's some truth about Maddox's refusal to leave?"

"You betcha. But it's one thing for me to talk trash about my own judge, particularly when he deserves it. It's a whole other thing talking about someone else's judge, especially one as upstanding and dedicated as Maddox. I didn't want to say anything in front of the girls. You understand."

"Of course." I gave her a sage nod to praise her prudence. "Why do you think he was so hesitant?"

"I would have chalked it up to the simple fact that people usually think these things are a false alarm, but Ethel believes it has something to do with those scars of his." Florence gestured to her forearms and shivered. "Ethel has been with Maddox through both of his appointments and remembers him once talking about how he got them in a house fire as a kid. She bets he was having some kind of flashback of being stuck in a burning building. He did seem more freaked out than the average, but who am I to judge how people react to things?"

Florence took a long draw from her mug and settled against the counter across from me.

"How did you react?" I asked.

"I was scared, but I've worked in this building a far cry longer than most." She raised her mug at me. "This wasn't my first rodeo. We've gotten a few of those bomb threats in the past from dummies hoping to get their trial postponed while the police scramble around looking for something that isn't there, so I imagined we'd all be okay once we got out of the building...sucks to be wrong."

"Did you know Yaris at all?"

"Just that he was a rich upstate blowhard who assumed us yokels didn't know how run our own county." She shook her head, which was decked out in a mod-type updo. "Sour most days, but sweet when it came to gladhanding or anything else that put his name in the press." She set her mug down and fiddled with the chain around her neck. "Forgive me. I know most folks don't go around bad mouthing the dead, but I can't see fit but to blame him for bringing his troubles down to bear on us. If somebody wanted to kill him, they could have done it anywhere. Why here?"

A dark silence fell over us. The only way to answer her question was to assume the killer lived or worked in the vicinity, but Radnor and Maddox didn't seem capable of perpetrating such atrocities. Particularly the latter, whose fear of fire might explain why he was so determined to push for a verdict in Ignacio Cardoza's case despite the impropriety of the gun prank.

And yet, since we didn't get the decision everyone expected, is it possible Maddox is one of the many people putting pressure on the police to consider Ignacio for murder? Or worse, did Maddox find a way to frame the firebug while at the same time putting himself in contention for the coveted President Judge seat? All of that was far too complicated and still didn't explain the call from the beach or the connection to Ashton.

However, we still had J. Braxton Bragg. He disappeared at a point when it was logistically possible for him to have made the threatening phone call, and whose alleged whereabouts at that time put him in the boardwalk's vicinity. Unfortunately, Bragg didn't have any connection to Ashton since the judge arrived in our county after Ashton left the force.

No matter how I rearranged the pieces, the full puzzle never came into focus. Perhaps that's because I refused to take the most rational explanation into consideration. If this was truly a crime of revenge, Arnold Knight, Johnny Erving, Phyllis Dodd, or Ignacio Cardoza had to be somewhere at the core of this thing, which gave me an idea.

"Florence, what if I told you the police considered Ignacio Cardoza a person of interest in the Yaris murder?"

"I'm not sure how I'd feel about that." She cupped a hand around her chin. "It makes no sense on the surface, but the guy does have quite a collection of arson convictions. Why? What do you think?"

My thoughts went to Ashton and the near-fatal accident he'd suffered. "I don't know that I buy it because whoever killed Yaris also sabotaged the vehicle of a man I care about, and he isn't someone Ignacio could know."

"This man," Florence leaned forward with a twinkle in her eyes, "is he someone you love?"

"I didn't say all that."

"You didn't have to, honey," she laughed. "You're radiating with it."

"Let's not go there." The heat of humiliation singed my cheeks. "I only brought it up because I don't want to risk being wrong. If there's any chance Ignacio Cardoza could have hurt my…friend, I want to do something about it." I took a deep breath and forged ahead. "I know it's a lot to ask, but do you think you could help me arrange a visitor's pass to the Violation of Probation Center to see Ignacio? I'm not going to threaten him. I just want to ask him a few—"

"Say no more." She made a clicking sound with her tongue. "I wasn't always the dried-up old prune you see before you. I've had my share of whirlwind romances, and I am happy to help. Consider me your champion for love."

I started to correct her, but decided to let it lie. I was getting the access I wanted, and that's all that mattered.

Chapter Sixteen

Since visiting hours for the Trident County Violation of Probation Center were only Friday, Saturday, and Sunday mornings, Florence pushed through an impromptu request for late Monday afternoon by claiming my visit was related to the legal defense for the revocation hearing pending on Ignacio's probation violation. In order to make myself look more lawyerly, I took along a pile of papers that included the transcript from the bomb threat call, pictures of those I believed were involved with the murder, and the transcript from his final day at trial. All of this would prove handy regardless, since I couldn't take my cellphone or any other electronic devices into the facility.

And yet, the legal counsel excuse itself was important because it ensured Ignacio and I would meet privately, face-to-face, rather than through a Plexiglass barrier or the newly instituted video chat. Direct contact was key. Even on the small chance he recognized me from trial, I'd needed alone time, away from law enforcement, to gain his trust.

As I waited in the stark gray room where both the metal table and the two metal chairs that lived opposite each other sat bolted to the floor, my hands grew clammy with sweat. While I should have been nervous about my first time being in any sort of lock-up facility, my nerves were more frazzled over how to make Ignacio talk. What if he refused? Or what if he didn't, but everything he had to say was irrelevant? Although, I suppose neither scenario was as bad as discovering Ignacio had played some role in the judge's death…because that would mean I'd just agreed to lock myself in a dingy, malodorous room with a killer.

As if on cue, the room's only door, a large metal one with thick hinges and a massive deadbolt, creaked open. A barrel-chested white man and a blockheaded black man, both wearing tight blue uniforms, ushered Ignacio into the space. His face was sullen and his cheeks hallow, which made him look gaunter than I remembered. He wore the pale-yellow pajama-like uniform associated with probationers. His hands were cuffed in front of him, and his legs shackled so that he had to shuffle as the officers navigated him toward the seat across from me and shoved him down.

"You want him cuffed?" asked the white guard, who still had one hand on Ignacio's shoulder.

I looked at my new companion, who stared back at me with wide-eyed curiosity. He clearly didn't remember me or suspect my agenda. But more importantly, he didn't protest my presence, so part of me considered having the officer do away with the cuffs as a quick way to gain Ignacio's trust—or was such thinking a road to folly?

"Leave them on," Ignacio answered before I could make up my mind. "I don't want no one else around here accusing me of something I didn't do."

The guards nodded at each other. The barrel-chested one kneeled to clip a short portion of Ignacio's extensive chain to a bolt on the floor so that he was bound and tethered to the ground like an animal.

I averted my eyes. The moment was hard to watch.

Once the chains were attached, the blockheaded guard snapped his fingers at me. "You have thirty minutes to wrap this up, so our little violator here can return to his institutional work assignment."

I glanced up at the standard black and white clockface that had been encased in a metal cage for its protection: 4:01 p.m.

Time to put up or shut up.

When the officers left the room and the metal door slammed, Ignacio's chain clinked and clattered as it slid along its loops. I looked over to find him leaning forward, elbows on the table.

"Who are you, and what do you want?"

"My name is Victoria Justice." I extended my hand in greeting, but thought better of it since his were still cuffed. "I work at the Trident County Superior

Courthouse."

"Oh, you're another one here about that judge. I'll tell you like I told the others. I didn't have nothing to do with that explosion. I don't care who you all send here to threaten me, the story is not going to change. Guard!"

"Wait." My hand shot out to stop him. "What others? And how did they threaten you?"

"That's all I am going to say without a lawyer."

The barrel-chested guard stepped into the room. "Finished already?"

"No, sir." I batted my eyelashes and whipped up my sweetest voice. "We still plan to use the rest of our time. Mr. Cardoza misunderstood my intentions."

Ignacio scowled in a manner that made his unshaven jawline look menacing, but he did not dispute my claim.

When we were alone again, I adopted the approach I'd seen work a million times during trials: *Ingratiate yourself to the witness by taking their side of the argument.*

"I should have finished introducing myself. I work at the courthouse, but I am a stenographer. I'm not a lawyer or a cop. All I do is make trial transcripts. I brought yours from your case last week, and I wanted to say that I think it is unfair that you're being condemned despite having proven your innocence."

Of course, I wasn't sure I believed all of that, but it was a start, and he was listening. I slid the thick stack of papers encompassing the final volume of his trial transcript, the one with the 'not guilty' verdict, across the table toward him. He gazed down at the clear plastic report cover and back up at me with narrowed eyes.

"A lot of people are looking at you for the bomb on the judge's car because they don't believe you were innocent of the hotel fire. And I know you are under no obligation to speak to me, but if I can prove you're not the person the media has made you out to be, maybe I can convince the authorities to start looking elsewhere for viable suspects."

Ignacio blinked but gave no response.

"A friend of mine got hurt, and I firmly believe the person behind that courthouse explosion is the same person who injured my friend. I have a hunch who did it, but that's all it is, a hunch. I'm looking for any information I can get about who did it and why. Again, I'm not with law enforcement, but I could use your help."

Ignacio cleared his throat. "You promise not to twist my words or hold nothing against me?"

"Absolutely." I slid a picture of Judge Yaris across the table. "Do you know this man?"

"I hadn't seen him before in my life until his murder ended up all over the news. Now everybody assumes I fried the guy."

"Did you?"

"No." He held my gaze as if to confirm his innocence.

"Are you aware the police have footage of you hanging around the courthouse the day of the bombing?" I recalled Mike's tip from our late-night meetup. "They say it even shows you walking around inside the building where a suspicious backpack containing a decoy explosive device was found. How do you explain that?"

He was tight-lipped for several seconds. "What's the point? You're not going to believe me."

"Try me."

"What's in it for me?"

Sometimes I was so naïve. I had nothing to bargain with except my goodwill, so I took a gamble by mixing a few truths with a well-intentioned lie.

"I have a friend at *The Bickerton Bugle* who believes your person of interest status on the Yaris case is a sham, and he's willing to publish something about it. Be honest with me about what you know, and I will work to get the truth heard."

Ignacio stuck out his chin as if he'd resolved never to speak again, so I pressed my point.

"Let's be clear here, Ignacio, I'm trying to help you. But if we have to strike a deal over every little point and inquiry, it's going to make me question if I can trust you. And if I can't trust you, then I am just wasting my time. I've already told you I think this whole thing revolves around a culprit the police aren't willing to look at. I'm not asking you to fabricate anything or to implicate a specific person, but if you give me something that shows me it isn't you, I can at least put more faith in my theory."

"Fine." He flared his nostrils. "What do you want to know?"

"Why were you at the courthouse on the day of the explosion?"

"It's complicated," he sighed. "Even before I got charged with burning down the Rainbow Sands, I was on probation for setting a couple fires in an abandoned housing development on the north end of York Road. Losing the hotel trial would have put me in jeopardy of having to do hard time for that crime too. Luckily, I won, making me clear of the hotel but still on probation for the houses." He rubbed his chin. "So I went to the courthouse that Friday because my PO said to meet him there. Something about maintenance going on at the probation office."

"Did you tell the police that when they questioned you about why you were at the courthouse?"

"Yeah. They said my PO couldn't confirm making that call."

"That doesn't make any sense."

"Pssh." He made a frustrated huffing sound with his teeth. "That's because I'm being set up."

"Why do you think that?"

"Wouldn't be the first time."

"Come on. Be serious."

"I am." He shifted in his chair, and the shackles clanked in response. "When I went to the courthouse, nobody showed. I hung around for about a half hour, got ticked, and left."

"Was this before or after the building evacuation?"

"Before. I wasn't even there when all the hoopla about the bomb started. I didn't hear about any of that until the next day."

He paused as if lost in thought, and I circled my hand in the air for him to continue.

"When I left the courthouse, I made sure to call my PO's line. I only got his voicemail, but I told him I was going home and to give me a call if he wanted to reschedule or set up a home visit. Probation and the cops claim that was just a stunt on my part to drum up a plausible alibi because they have no record on the books for a scheduled meeting that day."

"Is that why you're in here?" I gestured to our bleak surroundings.

"Sort of." He frowned. "The problem is that when I got interviewed about the murder, instead of telling the police where I really went after I left the courthouse, I told them I went home. I figured since they couldn't prove otherwise, they'd leave me alone."

It never ceased to amaze me how clueless most people were when it came to the minds of the police, who always found the "home alone" angle suspicious.

"If you weren't at home, where were you?"

"The truth would have been a violation of my probation." He dropped his head and studied his hands. "My grandmother has been sick, and I needed quick money. I couldn't wait for the state to place me in a job, so I took a gig at a distribution center for a computer manufacturer across the line in Maryland. They paid under the table, and I could get there by bus."

"Basically, the police found out the truth and nailed you for leaving the state?"

"Yeah. They had the nerve to say the occupation was a major violation since it's electronics, and I could use the parts to make bombs, even though none of that has nothing to do with my probation since I haven't never made no bomb or been convicted for bombs. My stipulations say to stay away from accelerants and combustibles, so that's what I was doing."

"And on the arrest for the VOP, the cops claim you resisted."

"Yeah, but that's because they put me in here for some technical B.S. that most probation officers look the other way on. It's not like I came out of my place waving a gun. I just refused to leave. They're the ones who overreacted." He shrugged and shook his head. "But what do they expect? I can't be picky about the choices I make. It's not like they're just handing out jobs to ex-cons."

He suddenly yanked hard against his wrist constraints and growled. I jumped back in my chair even though the metal object didn't move with me since it was firmly affixed to the floor.

I searched for a way to bring the conversation back to neutral territory.

"You alluded to being set up before. What did you mean?"

He closed his eyes and muttered to himself in Spanish. "I probably shouldn't say nothing since the trial is over, and I won, but that whole thing with the Rainbow Sands was the owner trying to set me up."

I raised an eyebrow. We'd heard a few hints to this theory in defense counsel's opening statement, but since Ignacio declined to testify and the defense witnesses were so few, the theory all but disappeared by the case's end.

"If that's true, why not press the theory at trial?"

"Nobody would have believed me if I said my footprints were in the basement because I warned management that piling shipments down there like that was a fire hazard. I was trying to do the right thing for once. I'm a convicted felon. I was lucky to get that bellman's job. I would have done anything they said, especially once my grandmother fell ill. I couldn't afford to step out of line and go back to prison. I was trying to help them out. You know, be a star employee, but they used me and my record to make a profit. Burn the place down, cash in their policy, and sell the land to a new developer rather than renovate and bring the joint up to code."

"Of course." I placed a hand across my mouth to mask the shock of my failed realization. The boardwalk was recently declared a historic district, which would have naturally required the original owners to make a bunch of renovations to its façade, electrical system, and a host of other things.

"If I had gotten on the stand to expose the hotel fire as an insurance scam, they would have opened up my full record, picked it apart, and torn me to shreds. No way the jury would have taken pity on me." He stared at his hands and ran a finger across the metal that dug into his wrists. "I freely admit I enjoy watching things burn. Lighting fires was the way I set my frustrations free, but I can't afford to do that and be thrown in here now that my grandmother is relying on me for care."

"If setting fires was how you coped with your anger," I hesitated, "what do you do now?"

"This." He lifted his elbows from the table with a sharp jangle of his chains to expose his inner forearms, where there were a series of small scars lined up like hash marks. "The one good thing about being in here is that we get to see the therapist every day if we want. That helps too."

He didn't say anymore, and I was too ashamed to ask. He had every reason to be frustrated. Whether or not his trip to the VOP Center was justified, there was something fishy about the PO's call and the circumstances leading up to his arrest. Despite his history of wrongdoing, I believed in his innocence for the Yaris murder based on the defeat in his eyes, but how to tackle his story's underlying injustices was the real question.

Like most of us, he was someone trying to survive in a system that had stacked the odds against him. Maybe I was being gullible. Or perhaps, I was still reeling over how honest he'd been about his self-harm. The man was a lot of things—an arsonist, a liar, and a troubled soul—but he wasn't a killer.

Chapter Seventeen

When I got home from the VOP Center, I raced upstairs to my bedroom, tossed my coat on the floor, and locked the door. If Ignacio and Phyllis had alibis, then the only other people with a revenge motive would be Johnny Erving and Arnold Knight. Frustratingly, it was too late to hunt them down, and I didn't want to do so without backup.

I'd give Mike a call a little later to compare notes and see if he'd be game to join me on a fishing expedition. I hadn't talked to him since our clandestine meeting at the beach on Friday, and I was sure he'd have new intel by now. What seemed in order at the moment was a shower. The detention center had reeked of bad B.O. and hot garbage, not to mention that every surface was either sticky or gritty to the touch. My skin bristled at the recollection, and I quickly kicked off my pumps and wriggled out of my pantsuit in favor of a thick, fuzzy red robe.

Once I'd draped the soiled suit across the hamper and stored my purse in the closet, I shuffled over to the nightstand to drop off my phone, but the space was occupied by the laptop I'd recently purchased for my home office.

Odd. I didn't remember placing it there. I tried not to bring court work into my room since most transcripts dealt with druggies, robbers, and murderers, none of whom made great bedfellows. I picked up the laptop, which was folded open, and stared at the screen. The device emitted a soft hum as the internal fan worked to keep the unit cool. It wasn't like me to keep the unit running if I didn't have it plugged up to the docking station located on my desk across the hall.

Maybe mom had borrowed it for a moment to check her email—although even that seemed strange. She had a desktop computer with dual screens in the second spare bedroom across from the master. No real need for her to use my stuff.

I perused the desktop. The file icons that were normally strewn across the screen in jumbled groupings based on the cases I was scoping, aka translating and proofreading, had been rearranged and neatly nestled on the right side of the monitor in orderly rows, but nothing appeared to be missing.

Curious.

I maneuvered the cursor over to the power icon when I noticed the small white light beside the webcam winked on, then off. The blip of color was so minute and fast that I would have missed it had my eyes been focused anywhere other than the monitor.

What the heck?

I plopped down cross-legged on the bed and studied the desktop. Had the camera popped on for a second? I scrolled through the Windows menu to find the webcam. I barely used the dumb thing these days thanks to all the video chat features available on my smartphone, but after a minute or two, I located the icon for the device. As best I could tell, the camera was currently off. But when I checked the storage folder for the software, there was a single file whose 'date modified' stamp matched the current day, Monday, April 8, 5:12 p.m.

I clicked on the icon, and the footage snapped to life. It exposed a full view of my room from the bedside table with the open door and closet in the distance, the rumpled surface of the bed to the right, and crisp sunrays from the window to the left. This went on for several minutes, and I could see that the footage was timed for nearly twenty minutes, so I advanced the scroll bar to the last three minutes of feed only to see myself burst through the door, toss my coat on the floor, and begin to undress.

Oh, God!

I slammed the laptop closed and bit my lip. How was that possible? Was someone watching me? This had to be a glitch, right? I jumped up from the bed and headed to my office across the hall, where I plugged the computer into its dock and rummaged around the desk until I found a Post-it note, which I placed over the camera lens the instant I reopened the PC.

Then I dug through the top drawer of my desk and pulled out a flash drive. I didn't feel comfortable leaving the file on my computer, but I didn't want to lose the proof either. Saving it on a separate device would solve both problems.

Just as I completed the transfer, the floorboards creaked, signaling someone on the staircase. My back stiffened.

"Ma?" I called.

"Hey, Angel." She yelled back. "I brought home a couple pizzas. I hope you don't mind a makeshift dinner."

Perfect timing. I closed the laptop and rushed into the hall to greet her. She carried a pair of stylish heels in one hand and an attaché case in the other. Her dark brown eyes looked red and puffy as she pushed open the double doors to her bedroom suite.

I tightened the fuzzy belt on my robe and followed her inside. "Did you borrow my laptop sometime this afternoon?"

"Please." She set her bag and shoes on the floor by the door. "And risk an unwarranted—and might I add—highly disrespectful speech about the invasion of your privacy, even though this is my house. Hmmm...I think not."

"Well, somebody moved it and messed around with the icons. There's also a video on there that would suggest someone triggered the camera, too."

"Like I'd know about that kind of thing." She loosened her skirt and sat down at the vanity, where she grabbed a couple of moist towelettes to remove her makeup. "That's why I don't bother with those flimsy laptops. You probably left some gizmo on. What's the big deal?"

I clenched my jaw at her obliviousness. "Seriously, Ma. If you didn't move it, and I didn't move it, that means someone has been in here."

She paused with the towelette pressed to her chin as she stared at my reflection in the mirror.

"Oh, Angel, I know these last few days have put a lot of stress on both of us, but don't you think if someone had been in here, they would have *stolen* your laptop?" She turned and pointed at the large flat screen sitting on a

Wharton Esherick-style end table. "Or any other of the other valuables lying around?"

"You're missing the point. This isn't about valuables. I think someone went through my files and might be using the computer to spy on me."

"Could we do this another time?" She abandoned her skin care routine and disappeared into the walk-in closet where she called out to me. "Today has been horrendous. I just got word from Mike's supervising editor that *The Bugle* is going to do that public safety interview on Friday. So now, I've got to prep remarks for that potential minefield while at the same time gather data for all the special regulatory meetings scheduled this—"

"Don't you get it, Ma. What if this attempt to spy on me is all part of the plot attached to the bomber's call?"

"What?" She emerged from the closet wearing a bright orange and yellow kaftan that accented the reddish-browns of her rich complexion, now ruined with the heavy lines of concern. "How do you figure?"

"The caller talked about payback. What if I'm my office's designated mark?"

"No, no." Ma closed the space between us, her arms open wide. "I'm sorry. I'm here. I'm listening. I don't ever want you to think our home is unsafe. We've been over this. I will do everything in my power to protect you." She wrapped me in an embrace, then guided me over to the bed, where we sat hand in hand. "If you feel like you're being targeted, we should get you out of here for a while. Can you take a leave of absence or switch duties with a reporter from another county?"

"Ma, this isn't about turning tail and running. This is about acknowledging that someone has been in our house. What are we going to do about that?"

"I'm doing the best I can here, Angel." She tugged at a tawny strand of her hair and chewed the inside of her jaw. "I just don't understand why a misplaced computer has you so concerned when we both know the real dangers lie inside that courthouse. I've never thought you were safe there, and that's the problem that needs remedying."

"You're right." I patted her hand and rose. No need to start a fight. She didn't get it, and I shouldn't have assumed she would. "I'm going to skip dinner tonight. I have a couple of projects I need to tackle."

Her lips formed a tight pout, but she remained silent as I crossed to the door. The older I got, the more Ma exerted her beliefs, even if it meant ignoring the ideals that were most important to me. This habit obviously came from a well-intentioned place, but that didn't make it easier for either of us to swallow.

I left her alone and walked down the hall to my office, where I was once again confronted with the offending laptop. As far as I was concerned, someone had been in our home, but how did they access my webcam without getting caught on video? A quick Google search indicated that such malware was easy enough to install, or I could have acquired it through any of the emails I received on a daily basis. A virus scrub coupled with a reinforced firewall would rid me of the unwanted intruder, but who would want to spy on me? And why now? Or more specifically, was this breach of privacy really connected to what took place at the courthouse? And if so, how?

Rather than suffocate under the paranoia that each question brought, I decided to share my misery with Ashton, who was hopefully willing to consider the conundrum a distraction from his own tenuous situation. I punched the number to the Trident County Medical Center into the handheld on our landline and waited for the operator to patch me through to his room.

"Hey," I put on my cheeriest voice, "how's my favorite superhero?"

"Out of the ICU and on the mend—although, I'd love to file a complaint about the stitching on this splenectomy incision." The rustling of sheets mingled with a few of his muttered expletives. "I've got enough scars."

"Sounds like you'll live. When are you getting out of there?"

"Wednesday. Maybe."

"Two more days? That's great. What did the doctor say?"

"The last CT scan showed most of the serious brain swelling has subsided. They just want to watch for headaches, vision changes, or memory loss over the next forty-eight hours. But as long as everything in my head keeps gobbling up blood and oxygen, I should be free to go. No major physical activity for the next couple of weeks, of course, but at least I'll be home. What's up with you?"

I filled him in on everything that had happened during the day—my interview with the cops, the confrontation with Maggie and Harriston, my conversation with each of the judges, the visit with Ignacio, and the strange video found on my laptop.

"Okay." He cleared his throat. "Let me get this straight. Now you think the bomber is Johnny, or maybe Arnold Knight, but definitely not Ignacio—although you still haven't given up hope on Phyllis, even though she has an alibi. Yet, whoever the killer is, you think they're watching you through your webcam, and you know this because your laptop moved from your office to your room?"

"Oh, stop it with the snarky commentary. I know how it sounds, but the computer wasn't just moved, it was positioned to get a better view of me and my activities."

"Did you run a virus scan? Check for phishing emails?"

"I'm doing all that now."

"Find anything?"

I leaned my elbows on the desk and glanced at the counter running on the screen. "Not yet. It's only at five percent."

"Look, I agree that you or any one of your office mates could still be in danger when it comes to whatever this bomber has planned—and that pisses me off more than anything because I want to be there for you. However," he said, elongating each syllable in a judgmental manner, "the likelihood that your roaming computer and rogue webcam have anything to do with what's going on at the courthouse seems far-fetched, don't you think? People misplace things all the time, and webcams malfunction."

I pulled the cordless receiver away from my ear and stared at it. I didn't misplace my computer. What was with everyone? Why was this so hard to believe after everything we'd both been through?

"Hey," his tone grew loud and breathy, "you still there?"

"I'm here." I rocked back in my swivel chair and fiddled with the belt on my fuzzy red robe. "I'm just tired. It's been a frustrating day. I should get some rest."

"Wait. What did I say? I was just giving you my honest opinion. That's our thing, right?" His normally deep voice grew high and sharp. "I'm here. I'm listening."

"Sure. You're good. I just have to get ready for dinner, and I still need to call Mike to see what he's got on all this."

"C'mon, Victoria. Don't be like that. You know I am on your side. I was just stating the obvious."

"I said you're good. I've just got to go." I gritted my teeth and hoped he couldn't hear the strain. "You need me to pick you up on Wednesday?"

"Yeah," he sighed. "I'll give you a call as soon as I know for sure. Just remember to pick up if you see a strange number. They still can't find my cell."

We bid each other goodbye, and I tossed the cordless onto the desk. With Ashton out of commission and low on faith, I wasn't sure how I was going to tackle consolidating my theories. He'd always been my sounding board and, dare I say it, protector.

I rose from my desk and trudged across the hall to my room. Ma had her double doors closed, but I could hear her providing *Jeopardy* questions to the host's clues. I debated sticking my head in to say goodnight, but Ma would no doubt want to revisit our conversation. So, I ducked into my room, grabbed my cellphone from the nightstand, and flopped onto the bed.

Although we texted often, I'd only called Mike directly a couple times in the six months I'd known him. However, he didn't disappoint, answering on the first ring.

"Make it fast," he snapped. "I'm on a deadline."

"For the Yaris case?"

"No. Why? You got something for me?"

"Nothing concrete. Just a bunch of theories."

"Hit me with them."

I balked for a moment. My previous confidants scoffed at what I had to say in favor of their own agendas—albeit meaningful agendas, as they both concerned my safety. However, I got the feeling neither of them had really been listening, and I wanted to make sure that this time my voice was heard, so I started with what I knew were facts.

"Ashton is in the hospital after a car crash that I am pretty sure is connected to the courthouse bombing since it turns out he and Judge Yaris have the same color, make, and model vehicle."

Mike fell silent, and the distant voices of his coworkers invaded the line for a moment.

"How's he doing?"

"Turns out he's going to be fine, but that proves the killer can't be Ignacio since he has no connection to Ashton. And when I confronted Ignacio about the bombing this afternoon—"

"You what?" His voice cracked.

"Don't worry. The guy was harmless. In fact, I think he's being framed to take the fall. He said he was only at the courthouse that day because his PO called."

"Okay. That sounds plausible," his voice dripped with sarcasm, "but even if that were true, why are you telling me all this?"

"Because I need someone to believe me. I met with the cops this morning and tried to tell them that if the bombing and Ashton's accident were related, the only logical culprit was Phyllis."

"But she reportedly has an alibi."

"Exactly." I lay back on the bed so that my gaze met the ceiling. "How did you know?"

"I have a source at the department."

"Could you get them to help?"

"Be real."

"Well, do you know who else they're considering at this point?"

"Ignacio Cardoza, obviously. Johnny Erving and Arnold Knight."

"I guess what I'm saying is if they can't pin this on Phyllis or Ignacio, the culprit has to be someone obvious, like Johnny, since he just got fired and would want to get revenge on his uncle for failing to help him keep his job after the gun prank. Or maybe he was just tired of living in his uncle's shadow. Plus, he knows Ashton from his days as a cop."

"Wait a minute. Slow down. You lost me. Uncle?" His voice cracked. "Ashton is his uncle?"

"No." I half chuckled, half shouted. "I thought you were an investigative reporter. Keep up. Yaris was married to one of Johnny's aunts."

"Where'd you hear that?"

"Cooper's."

"Good grief." He snorted. "Gossip aside. Johnny is the logical lead on this. The police should have been looking more closely at him from the very beginning. Not to mention, Arnold Knight, who's been radio silent since becoming the poster boy for misguided gun use and the lone cause for the loss of firearm usage for every bailiff in the state."

"But he doesn't know Ashton."

"Are you sure?"

My mind buzzed. I wasn't.

"And don't forget," I pressed the cell closer to my lips, "there's Judge Bragg."

"Bragg for what? Murder? How are you getting there?"

"Bragg went AWOL around the time the courthouse was evacuated. His secretary believes he was down at the beach meeting up with someone at the Moxie Fox."

"That puts him in the right location to call in the bomb threat, but what's his motive?"

"I don't know. I was hoping you'd tell me."

He huffed. "I haven't dug up anything new over the last few days."

"Well, let's go on the hunt." I punched a fist in the air, hoping the enthusiasm would transfer to my voice.

"Or, we could sit back and let the police do their job."

"Under any other circumstances, I would, but I think I might be on the killer's radar."

The receiver beeped, and Mike's voice got a little louder and a lot more intimate as if he'd taken me off speakerphone. "What makes you say that?"

I took a deep breath to steel myself against potential rejection. "I think someone tried to set up my webcam to watch me, and that they may even have been in the house."

"Are you serious?" He muttered a curse. "How long has this been going on?"

"Just today, as far as I can tell." My words tumbled out in a jumble of excitement at having someone on my side.

"Scrub your computer and reboot your phone if you can." His voice was stern. "I'll help you look into your suspect list, but we've gotta play by my rules, and I can't do anything until Wednesday. I need to meet this deadline first."

"Hold on. Wednesday is no good. Ashton is supposed to get out of the hospital that day, but I don't know when yet."

"We can work around it. Besides, if we're going to look into all of the people you mentioned, you should probably see if you can get the day off."

That would certainly make my mom happy. "Fine. I'll meet you at *The Bugle* at nine o'clock Wednesday morning. We can walk over to the Department of Justice to see if they've received any threatening calls, then go to the Public Defender's Office to ask around about Johnny—"

"Chill. Remember, we're playing by my rules. I'll pick you up at your place at 8:00 a.m. Wait for my text. And be ready, time is money."

And with that, he hung up.

Chapter Eighteen

After the Monday evening webcam conundrum, I passed out on the bed only to be plagued with a series of stress-induced nightmares. I dreamt of being chased by a green-eyed monster who would peek at me from around corners and slowly stalk me down long halls, only for me to open a door and find him already standing there, judging me with calculated scrutiny.

Tuesday was no better. Candi had been kind enough to grant my request to take off the following day. But in the meantime, I got stuck in a high-profile plea hearing with Judge Radnor. Of course, I couldn't concentrate and kept asking the prosecutor to repeat key phrases from his sentencing recommendation to the point where I could have sworn I heard the defendant mutter, "Good grief, can't we just record the whole thing?"

By Wednesday morning, my nerves were fried. The clock read 8:07 a.m., and Mike still hadn't sent a text. I paced the perimeter of my tiny room with phone in hand and tried not to implode with frustration. I needed answers.

"Be well, my Angel."

I whipped around to find Mike's dark, gangly frame standing in the doorway.

"Your mom saw me parked outside and let me in on her way out. She asked me to send you her love." He snorted. "You should see your face. Does your nose always crinkle like that in the morning?"

"What happened to time is money? You're late."

"Barely. Not that it should matter since what I found out about our suspects will blow you away...no pun intended."

"Doubtful." I grabbed my purse and stuffed the now useless cellphone inside.

"I figured out where Arnold Knight's been hiding and why no one's seen him since the Cardoza trial."

My expression softened, and I raised a brow. "How'd you manage that?"

"The less you know, the better. Let's just say most folks are pretty careless about their personal data; anybody who wants that information just has to know where to look."

"Or you could have just asked my boss. Candi mentioned to me a couple days ago he likes to hang out at the casino."

"Geesh," he rested a hip against the doorjamb, "why didn't you say something the other night? That would have saved me a whole afternoon of tailing him around town."

I covered my mouth to mask the laughter. "Any leads on Johnny?"

"You mean you don't know?" He put his hands on both sides of his face like the kid from *Home Alone*.

"Don't be cute. No one likes a sore winner. You got me."

"Well, trust me, it'll make a better impression if I show rather than tell, but let's hit the casino first. Chop, chop." He clapped his hands several times in rapid succession and stepped backward into the hall. "Time is indeed money, and we still have to stop for coffee."

* * *

"Are you sure Arnold was supposed to be here this morning?"

Finding someone in a casino is like trying to thread a needle blindfolded. All we had to go on was that Arnold Knight liked harness racing, which was unfortunately on hiatus for the season, and dollar slots, which we quickly found were interspersed throughout the Bickerton Hotel and Casino. Only the high denominations of fifty dollars or more were grouped together, and since Arnold had recently been put on administrative leave, we assumed he wasn't blowing what little money he had in those high-stakes areas.

"Based on his movements over the last twenty-four hours, he shouldn't have left." Mike stood on his tiptoes to peer over a row of machines. "I talked with the front desk manager last night and discovered Arnold checked in the day after the Cardoza trial. My guess is he must be going home in the evenings, when the casino is busy, to check his mail and stash cash, because I was lucky enough to catch him there yesterday afternoon and tailed him here. He went straight up to his room, and that means he's gotta be playing this morning."

"Or he could have played from midnight to dawn." I placed a hand on my hip. "Did you get a room number?"

"Three Eighteen."

"What are we waiting for? Let's go up and get some answers. We can corner him so he has nowhere to run."

"That's one choice, but you promised to follow my lead." He inclined his head and peered down at me. "I've found you get better results if you let people think the act of sharing is their idea. Running into him accidentally on the casino floor is the best bet. Don't you think he'd be suspicious if a random coworker showed up to a room nobody was supposed to know he had?"

Mike stepped back onto the carpeted path that zig-zagged through the carousels of one-armed bandits, 3D video slots, and behemoth-sized consoles plastered with oversized citrus fruits or the faces of celebrities from popular movies and game shows. The casino floor had more people milling about than one would have expected on a Wednesday morning, but Mike pointed out that mid-April marked the end of tax season and that many folks were willing to throw their refund right back out the window.

Ten minutes into our unsuccessful search, already sick of the stale air, blaring sirens, and flashing lights, I dragged Mike back into the main room where all of the table games stood in uniform rows reminiscent of soldiers on a battlefield. Their less overt assault on the senses made it the perfect place to regroup. I leaned against the wall near an unoccupied ATM and checked my messages for a call from Ashton at the hospital.

"Hold up. Is that him?" Mike gestured with his chin toward a tall, potbellied, rosy-skinned figure who'd entered the space from the opposite archway.

The man sauntered toward the collection of blackjack tables with a drink in each hand despite the earliness of the hour. A tattered white bucket hat sat on his head, and his eyes were obscured with aviator sunglasses, but the figure was definitely Arnold Knight. The outfit was most likely what left Mike baffled. Arnold wore high-top tie-dyed Vans, bright orange swim trunks, and an equally loud Hawaiian shirt. An outfit that was not only weirdly inappropriate for the time of year but also affected the exact middle-aged geezer image he probably hoped the clothes would help him shed.

I rushed forward in Arnold's direction, but Mike grabbed my arm and snapped me back.

"Casinos don't like people sitting at the tables unless they plan to play, so you're not going to be able to just run over there and start asking a bunch of questions. Have you ever played blackjack before?"

"No," I wrenched my arm from his grasp, "but I'm a big girl, and it can't be too hard. Don't go over twenty-one, right?"

"Trust me when I say there's more to it than that. My dad was a librarian, and he taught me a bunch of card games to keep me quiet on the days when I accompanied him to work. One thing he stressed is that card players are expected to adhere to a certain etiquette." Mike pointed at the table's dealer, a stout, button-nosed gentleman in an ill-fitting burgundy vest. "Wait for him to finish the hand in play before you take your seat. You'll then need to buy in and place a bet, but don't hand him anything directly. Got it?"

"Got it. We're playing by your rules."

I approached Arnold from behind. He was sitting at the center of the empty table across from the dealer. I took the seat beside Arnold, and Mike filled in on my other side. Bets were five dollars, so I dug through my purse and tossed a ten on the table. The dealer verified the bill and slid me two red chips. Mike motioned for me to put one inside the circle in front of me.

We'd just started, and this already sucked.

"Oh, my gosh, Arnold Knight, is that you?" I pivoted to face him and plastered on the biggest smile I could muster, which was quite a feat considering he smelled like a rum distillery.

Arnold's features remained neutral as he ignored my inquiry.

The dealer doled out a series of cards in rapid succession. A beat of silence ensued as I sat there and stared at them in hopes they'd inspire a new approach to gain Arnold's attention.

"Excuse me, ma'am," the dealer cleared his throat, "you have seventeen. Would you like to hit or stay?"

"Stay?" Unsure of myself, I glanced at Mike, who nodded.

"I need you to verify with a hand—"

"Wave your hand over your dang cards, Victoria, you're holding up the game." Arnold ripped off his aviators and scowled at me. "Why are you here?"

"Just hanging out with a friend." I signaled the dealer, then pointed at Mike, who gave a curt wave.

"Tell me another tall tale." Arnold tapped the table with his index finger, and the dealer slipped him another card. "I've talked to enough looky-loos this week to know you want something."

"Oh, come on. That's not fair. It's good to see you. How are you doing?"

Arnold stroked his unruly beard. "So you regularly skip work in the middle of the week to play cards?"

"Dealer has twenty." He swiftly cleared the table of our money and cards.

"Aw, Christmas on a cracker." Arnold tossed his hands in the air and bared his teeth at me. "I was on a streak. You're wrecking my mojo. Get out of here."

"Not a chance." I slapped my remaining chip into the betting circle.

"Fine." Arnold slid on his aviators, downed one of his drinks, grabbed the other along with his money, and left the table.

"I'll be back," I called to Mike as I hopped up to follow the former bailiff.

"You can't run forever, Arnold." I trotted beside him as he tried to outpace me. "You're right. I want to talk, but I'm not some looky-loo, and I don't blame you for what happened with Johnny. I'm here as a friend who wants to make sure you haven't put yourself in a bad situation." I reached out and gripped his forearm in an effort to slow him down. "Just tell me what's going on. Why are you here?"

"Where else am I going to go? The investigators decided to give me a six-month unpaid suspension. What's a person supposed to do with that kind of time?" He stopped abruptly and rounded to face me. "So, I came here to drown my sorrows, won $3800 on the *Wheel of Fortune* slots that first day, and met a lady at the buffet. Best time I've had since my divorce three years ago." He knocked back his second drink and shook the plastic cup so the ice cubes clattered against its sides. "When I got home, the old place didn't look so appealing—ground zero for a broken marriage and now a failed career. So I said to heck with it. My life's already a mess, why not live it up? Learn to play some blackjack, poker, baccarat. See where the wind takes me."

"One mistake isn't worth throwing your life away. The state didn't fire you, which means people still believe in you. Why don't you tell me what happened the day of the prank?"

Arnold cocked his head toward the ornately lit ceiling as if searching for answers.

"If we work together," I added, "maybe we can figure out how to make this better."

My peripheral vision showed Mike approaching, so I held out a hand to stop him. If I was going to get Arnold to open up about the gun incident, I'd have to earn his trust; however, that would be tough to do with a stranger in our midst, particularly if Arnold discovered that stranger was the reporter who leaked word of the prank to the world.

"There's nothing to tell." Arnold fed a twenty into a Triple Double Diamond machine and sat down. "The jurors were picking through the construction site, so I was standing on the boardwalk alone, watching over them. Johnny came by to joke for a bit, but my mind was elsewhere. Since Maddox wasn't supposed to encroach on the jury's view of the scene, it fell on me to play both enforcer and host." He pulled the machine's long metal arm, and a series of discordant chimes rang up around us. "I guess you could say I was checked out when Johnny asked me about the gun. He said it was for a prank, and as a fellow Lambda, I trusted him to know what he was doing."

"So he didn't coerce you or threaten you?"

"Nope—though that's probably what I should have said." He emitted a bitter chuckle. "Would have made my life a whole lot easier and kept me from becoming the fall guy for gun use, not that it matters, I don't even think most states allow bailiffs to carry guns anymore…" He shook his head like he'd gotten lost in a memory. "… I mean, between the guards and Capitol Police, everybody around there is packing. I was just a luxury, an old-fashioned throwback to a bygone era."

"Have you talked to anyone from work lately?"

"Uh-uh," he hiccupped, "but if you're going to stand there annoying me with questions, could you flag down a waitress?"

"But you've at least heard about the President Judge's murder, right?"

"I didn't much know the man, but the fact that his business got twiddled up in mine doesn't exactly give me that old loving feeling about his demise."

"What do you mean?" I leaned into his personal space, purposefully blocking his view of the machine's reels.

"The police tracked me down wanting to know if I killed him out of some need for vengeance." He nudged me out of the way.

"Did you?"

Arnold stared at me for a moment, then burped loudly and long, not bothering to cover his mouth. The sour smell of onions, rancid rum, and stale Coke hung in the air between us.

"Well?" I stood my ground amidst the fumes.

"What do you want me to say? When Maddox had me thrown out of the courthouse, sure, I could have blown up the place. I definitely thought about doing something extreme—getting drunk, smashing a window, stealing a gun—but by the time I got home, I realized I had no one to blame but myself, and to do any of that would have made matters worse. Johnny didn't force my hand. I made the choice. Giving him my firearm was stupid, knowing we had innocents in the vicinity."

"That doesn't answer the question. Did you kill Judge Yaris?" My raised voice must have drawn attention because Mike appeared two machines over, slicing his hand through the air in a 'cool it' motion. So I added softly, "Or do you know who did?"

"Leave me alone." Arnold's cheeks turned scarlet, and he bowed his head like he'd suddenly been gripped with the need to vomit. "I've been here all week."

"Can you prove it?"

Arnold pointed at the security cameras above our heads. "That's the beauty of staying in a casino. Every minute of my day is tracked. Nobody can question my movements because they're always in plain sight. And despite getting a little tipsy at eight or nine in the morning, I've been on my best behavior."

"You're claiming you were here during the bombing?"

He nodded. "Gotta be honest, I am not exactly sure when that was, but if it was anytime between getting tossed out of the courthouse and now, I was probably here."

"Where were you on Saturday, April 6, around 4:00 p.m.?" My guesstimate time for Ashton's accident.

Arnold chewed his lip as if unsure what I was asking. "Look, I've been through all this with the police. I'm done talking."

He hit the 'cash out' button and stood up, but Mike's lanky frame was there to block Arnold's path. I pleaded with my now captive audience.

"Arnold, I believe you. I really do. You made one bad choice, but that doesn't mean you're incapable of doing what's right, so help me out here."

I sucked in a lungful of air and thought back to all of the things I learned at the courthouse on Monday. Then I pressed in close and stared up at my old coworker, trying my best to radiate concern while being intimidating—a feat made easier with my backup buddy nearby. "Do you have any reason to believe Johnny or one of the judges may have hurt or killed Judge Yaris?"

"Anything is possible." Arnold lifted one shoulder in a half shrug and swiveled his head between Mike and me. "Is he a cop?"

"Journalist."

"Same difference. I'm outta here."

"Sit down." Mike chest bumped Arnold as he tried to push past, which threw the older man off balance and back into his seat. "We're off the record, and all we want is your opinion."

"Why? Is there something I should know?"

"Arnold, please." I rested a gentle hand on his shoulder. "We're just looking for answers before somebody else gets hurt."

"I really wouldn't know." He sighed. "I didn't spend much time with any single judge, especially Bragg. He never seemed to be around—kind of a knucklehead though—always more concerned about how he could wiggle out of work and blame the other judges for his mistakes." Arnold rubbed a hand across the back of his neck. "Maddox seems more like the type who'd hatch a plan for murder."

"What are you saying?" I narrowed my eyes at him. "Why would Maddox want Yaris dead?"

"He wanted to be President Judge." Arnold pulled off his sunglasses and placed them in his breast pocket. "I remember when the appointment came up four years ago, I think he thought he had it in the bag since he'd been on the bench longer than anyone in the state, but this new fella comes out of nowhere and cinches the job as one of the youngest people to hold the seat."

I froze and considered my own suspicions of Maddox. Nothing concrete tied him or anyone else to the murder, but Arnold had come to the same conclusion as Candi and my coworkers. I went for broke. "Do you think it's possible Judge Maddox could have framed Ignacio Cardoza for Yaris's murder in order to put himself in contention for President Judge?"

"Maddox certainly made it known in chambers during the early part of trial that they should put Ignacio under the jail for what he did." Arnold squinted up at me. "So, sure, I could see it. Long way to skin a cat, but I suppose he'd be putting things in just order—the guy who got away with arson goes down for life, and the seat for the top spot is vacated. Cryptic, but a win-win for him."

"What about Johnny?" Mike piped up suddenly, "You think Johnny could have killed Yaris?"

"Why would he; they're family." Arnold's face fell slack with confusion.

"So you know about the uncle by marriage thing?" I gasped.

"I know it's hard for some people to swallow since I was just a lowly bailiff, but Johnny and I were good friends even before we realized we were fraternity brothers. He might have come off like an arrogant jock to the rest of you guys, but he was a decent fella. Loyal to his friends and his family."

"What if his family and friends betrayed him when he needed them the most?" Mike pressed. "What if he felt like they played a role in him getting fired for that gun prank? Do you think that would be enough for Johnny to kill?"

"I don't know." Arnold stared into the distance, a dark glint in his eye. "This Yaris thing has been bad timing for both of us. I can't speak for what Johnny would do. Yes, the gun prank was an idiotic move, but I don't think that equates to murder."

"Me either." I held up a hand as a signal for Mike to back off. "Do you plan on coming back to work when your suspension is over?"

"Maybe. Maybe not." Arnold stood and inclined his head to Mike, who finally let him pass. When the cowed man had escaped our huddle, he tipped his hat at me and offered a hapless smile. "It's all a roll of the dice."

Chapter Nineteen

"That was about as helpful as an umbrella in a tsunami." Mike flapped his arms in exasperation as we crossed the casino parking lot to his Civic. "Why'd you stop me from asking about Johnny? That could have been the key to everything."

"Did you see the look in his eyes?" I shook my head. "He idolizes the guy. You weren't going to get anything out of him. He was already back on the defensive. Besides, you said you know where Johnny is, so let's just go talk to him."

Mike rolled his eyes and unlocked the doors. We both fell silent when we climbed inside. I assumed he was still pondering the logistics of Johnny's involvement. But for me, out of everything Arnold mentioned, the unsolicited assessment of Maddox's temperament was the most mindboggling. The old maverick was definitely eccentric, but I couldn't imagine him as a murderer. The idea that he'd frame Ignacio to eliminate Yaris seemed plausible in theory, but how could Maddox have accomplished such a feat? Did he have an accomplice? And why would he hatch a scheme that put his own life in jeopardy? With his fear of fire, the smart move would have been to distance himself from the courthouse as Bragg had done—or does that observation in and of itself point to the newer judge as an accomplice? Plus, where did my webcam issue and Ashton's brake failure factor into such a scheme?

I was more confused than ever and disappointed that the conversation with Arnold hadn't generated more intel on Bragg, who'd obviously lied about his intentions to have lunch with Yaris and was probably the last person to see the President Judge alive. A stop by the Moxie Fox was in order, and I made a mental note to have Mike drive us there sometime before lunch. Perhaps catching Bragg in an indiscretion would provide the leverage needed to tease out the truth.

My thoughts were soon overtaken by the soulful sounds of Sam Cooke's R&B classic, "A Change is Gonna Come." Mike had navigated us onto Route 9 toward the beach, and the song's soaring violins were a relaxing accompaniment to the stop-and-go traffic.

"You mentioned earlier that you spent a lot of time in the library with your dad." I shifted in my seat to face him. "Was it just the two of you?"

"Yeah. My mom passed away from a stroke when I was eight, but she was and still is the most courageous person I've ever met." He rubbed his chin. "Although, your stubborn streak—excuse me, independent spirit, reminds me of her."

I punched him playfully in the arm, and he chuckled.

"She worked as a community organizer." He held up a finger. "I know that sounds cliché these days, but she was the real deal. She founded a nonprofit centered on criminal justice reform that helped women newly released from prison find housing and educational opportunities to ease their transition back into society. She was even able to help exonerate a few people who were wrongly accused."

"She sounds like a beautiful soul." I squeezed his forearm. "Who'd have thought brassy young Mike Slocum came from such a civic-minded family?"

"Don't get all mushy on me now. I'm still the smart aleck you've come to know and love, but I'm also a geek at heart, lucky to have parents who instilled in me a love for my community."

"Lucky for us both. Thanks for helping today. And if I forget to say it later, just know I couldn't have done this without you." I patted him on the knee, and he beamed. "Where are we headed?"

"Leisure Land." He winked.

Confused by the answer, I fell silent.

Leisure Land sat on the north end of the boardwalk beyond the new construction in the Rainbow Sands lot. Despite having grown up in

Bickerton, Leisure Land wasn't a place I'd visited recently due to my fear of the ocean. However, Mike's company and the crisp brightness of the warm spring day helped reduce my anxiety. And luckily, thanks to all the rides, arcades, and carnival games that encompassed the family fun park, sightlines to the sea were obscured by a collage of colorful amusements and the sounds of merriment.

But if Mike had told me during our drive that I'd bear witness to Johnny Erving wearing the bright yellow bowling shirt and neckerchief associated with Leisure Land's entertainment team, I would have called him insane. But there Johnny was, a hulking brunette, resplendent in a shade of amber normally reserved for the sun. He sat hunched inside his carnival booth, reading the *Financial Times*. The mic he should have been using to entice people to take their chance on the Wet-n-Wild Balloon Bust sat abandoned on the bone-dry counter.

"Tilt-a-Whirl operator, too complicated a career for you?" Mike shouted at Johnny over an instrumental version of "It's Raining Men," which played on a loop in the background.

The former public defender looked up with a smile that accentuated his dimpled chin, but his heroic features grew sinister once he recognized us.

"You have some nerve showing up here after that stunt you pulled with those photographs." Johnny tossed the *Financial Times* aside and stood up from his stool.

"Me?" Mike placed a hand across his heart and batted his eyelashes in a mock show of disbelief. "Take a look in the mirror, pal. You're the one who pulled a gun on an innocent woman. You're lucky I didn't call the cops or arrest you myself."

"Keep dreaming. You wouldn't last a second. I bench press guys like you for a warmup."

"Try me." Mike squared his jaw and stepped up to the edge of the booth. "Your job won't be the only thing you'll lose. I'll take your license too."

Johnny's nostrils flared and his hands balled into fists, but he didn't say anything. Mike's comments were out of order, yet they had hit their mark. Over the last week, there had been plenty of conversation in the news that

Johnny was on the verge of losing his law license, so the mere mention of the topic was as good as a kick in the groin.

While I shared Mike's disdain for Johnny's misdeeds, the hostile approach did nothing to aid my crusade for answers. So, I rifled through my purse and pulled out a bottle of Advil. Careful to cover the label, I rattled the contents at Mike.

"Hey, could you grab me a bottle of water and a pepperoni slice from Grotto Pizza? I need to take my allergy medicine, and I forgot that it had to be with food."

I put on my most gracious smile. Grotto Pizza was on the opposite end of the boardwalk and probably wouldn't be open before eleven during the off-season, but I hoped the goose chase would leave enough time for me to ask Johnny a few questions in private.

"Sure thing." Mike broke the standoff and looked down at me with concern. "I didn't know you had allergies. Why didn't you say something? I'll be right back." He shot one more dagger-filled glare at Johnny before jogging down the midway.

"You've got him well-trained." Johnny bent down and picked up his crumpled newspaper.

"Not funny." I wagged a finger. "And for the record, he's right. You never apologized for dragging me into your prank."

"I'm sorry." The words were curt, and he avoided my gaze.

"For someone who's hit rock bottom," I gestured to the shelves of stuffed animals and the rows of plastic clowns with wide open mouths ready to receive water from their shooters, "you sure don't act very sorry."

"It's not like those two little words are going to change anything. And for the record," he mimicked my sassy finger wiggle, "it's not what it looks like—I mean, it is, but it's my choice, so lay off."

I held up my hands in surrender. "I didn't come here to fight. But you have to admit that as far as choices go, this is a strange one."

"Clearly, neither one of you is the brains of the operation." He returned to his newspaper and laughed. The brittle sound broke like icy shards as it hit the brisk spring air. "One woman's strange choice is another man's hiding in plain sight. With everyone coming at me about the prank and the trial and the firing, I needed to get out of my condo." He threw a hand in the air as if too exhausted to say more. "My father owns this dump. Good a place as any to work."

"Dump? Wow, that makes me feel safe. I'll keep that in mind next time I'm on the Tilt-a-Whirl."

He emitted his eerie laugh once more as if unimpressed by my sense of humor.

"If it helps," I walked up and leaned on the counter, "you have my sincerest apologies about Mike. He was just being protective. Between the prank, the bomb threat called into my office, and the spyware found on my home computer, he's pretty worried about me—and I'm pretty worried about myself. So, I'm here because I'd be a fool if I didn't flat out ask if you had something to do with any of it."

"Any of what?" He lowered his paper just enough to meet my gaze.

"Let's start with Deputy Attorney General Grant Wells. Have you talked to him lately—perhaps atoned for everything that's happened?"

"Why? He knows as well as you do it was a prank. And it's not like he pressed charges or anything." Johnny repositioned his wilting newspaper with a loud thwap. "I'm the one fighting for my career. He should reach out. Instead, he's run off."

"What do you mean?"

"Guess you haven't been down to the Department of Justice lately."

"Why should I?"

"A couple of my former colleagues claim he hasn't shown up for the past few days."

"Do they suspect foul play?"

"Who are you? Columbo?" He laughed and slapped his knee. "I didn't know real people talked like that."

I stared at him so he'd know I was serious.

"Loosen up, lady. They didn't say why; they just mentioned he's been skipping out. It didn't sound like he got…waxed. Is that how you old timers say it?" He blinked at me twice in an effort to keep a straight face before he doubled over with laughter.

"Real classy. Get yourself together, and tell me about Garrett Yaris. What was your relationship like with him?"

"I don't have a relationship with Judge Yaris. Anything I might know about him has been gleaned from the papers."

"Seriously? You're going to play dumb." I arched an eyebrow. "Everybody knows he's your uncle. Cooper's been spreading it around town, and Arnold confirmed."

"Ah, the young grasshopper uses the master's moves against him by asking questions whose answers she already knows." He rolled his eyes. "Have you ever considered being a lawyer?"

"Spare me the sarcasm." I gestured at the name tag on his megawatt shirt. "Although you're clearly dressed for it, I didn't come here for games."

"Winner, winner. Chicken dinner. She has a little fight in her after all." He smirked and shrugged. "Screw it. It's not like he's a blood relative. Here's the tea: We weren't close. I barely saw him other than the occasional holiday, and professionally, even less so. He lived and worked upstate for Pete's sake. There are probably secretaries who have a better feel for him than I do."

"Why should I believe you?"

"Why should anybody do anything?" He flipped through the pages of his paper. "Nice try. Next question."

I rolled my eyes and tried a new tactic. I should have known what I was getting into trying to question Johnny.

"Where were you when the explosion took place last Friday?"

"At Leisure Land's employment office." His grin grew wide like the Grinch after he stole Christmas. "My dad and his secretary should be able to vouch for me."

"What about Saturday afternoon around four?"

"Training." He made a big show of setting aside his newspaper before waltzing over to the far side of the booth. "Believe it or not, there are rules for running this crappy game."

He pressed a red button mounted on the wall and motioned for me to squeeze the trigger on the plastic purple cannon bolted to the counter beside me. I hesitated, not wanting to get wet, so he did the honors, and a tight stream of water jetted out, leaving a mist of musty droplets in its wake. I jumped back from the counter, surprised and a little disgusted by the toy's power.

"Satisfied." He crossed his arms. "You through with the twenty questions?"

"I told you. People around me are getting hurt, and there's something strange about it. Did you know that the day after the bombing, Ashton North's brakes were cut? He drives the same make and model truck as Yaris, and based on the proximity of the events, I think it's safe to say they're related."

"Or maybe it's somebody he busted, blowing off steam. North's a fool. You of all people should know that after the mockery he made of the Mulligan case and the disgrace he brought to the Delaware State Police. I can't fathom why you think that nitwit has anything to do with me."

"He has everything to do with you if you were the one who did it."

I gritted my teeth to keep from raising my voice. Ashton had paid his dues and made amends for his transgressions. If Johnny had good sense, he'd view Ashton as a model for how he should conduct himself moving forward.

"Screw Ashton North." He spat and hopped over the counter to confront me head-on. "If I wanted to mess with him, I wouldn't waste my time on cowardly tactics."

I shuffled backward, not sure what had set him off or what to do now that the animal was loose from his cage.

"And despite what you and your little news friend might like to think, I still have enough pull to make your lives a living hell."

"Hey," Mike's clipped baritone drifted over to us. "Back off, man. Don't you ever learn? That's not how you treat a woman."

I turned to find Mike holding a bagel and a bottle of water. His plump lips had curled into a snarl. He rushed over, grabbed my elbow, and tugged me away before Johnny could respond.

Once we were a dozen or so strides down the boardwalk, he turned to me. "Are you okay?"

"I'm fine, but the lady doth protest too much, methinks."

"Is that a reference to you, me, or Shakespeare?" He handed me the water and bagel. "Grotto wasn't open."

"Neither. And thanks." I stuffed the items in my purse. "Is it me, or does it feel like we're hitting nothing but dead ends? Johnny was so glib it almost seemed practiced until the end, when it felt like I'd struck a nerve. Overkill on what should have been a simple answer."

"Johnny doth protest too much, youthinks?"

"Precisely." I snapped my fingers and pointed at him. "Particularly, on the issue of Ashton's truck and his connections to Yaris and Arnold. Not only that, Johnny pretty much has the same alibi as Arnold in the sense that they are both making a conspicuous effort to stay out in public so they can't be blamed for anything." I stopped in my tracks and slapped a hand across my forehead just as "Thriller" cued up at the nearby haunted house. "In fact, if I didn't know better, I'd think the two of them were in this together. After all, Johnny is a former PD, so he'd know all the right things to say or do to make them look innocent."

"That thought had crossed my mind, too," Mike rubbed his chin, "seeing as they're both disgruntled employees lumped into the same offense."

"Oh, and I almost forgot to tell you, Johnny said he was at the Leisure Land employment office at the time of the bombing—"

"Which means he was close enough to the set of pay phones over by Candy Kitchen to make the call and run back."

"Right." I pumped my fist and started walking again. "With the tilt fuse already in place, that's all he'd needed to do."

"After having his partner plant the device."

Granted, that still left the issue of my laptop unresolved, since why would Johnny or Arnold want to spy on me? Unless Ashton and Ma were right about the video being some unrelated glitch or hack.

"You wanna stop to eat your bagel?" Mike pointed to a bench. "Or should we find a place to have breakfast while we hash out the rest?"

I checked my cell, 10:16 a.m. Part of me wanted to head back to town and visit the DOJ in order to follow up on Johnny's comment about Wells, but we were hitting the time window where Judge Bragg would be at the Moxie

Fox. The bikini bar was only six blocks away from the boardwalk's main drag, and I couldn't be sure when I'd get another opportunity to catch the judge in his act of deception.

"Hold on, Mike. We've got one more stop to make."

Chapter Twenty

Mike and I dashed down Oceanside Drive away from the boardwalk toward the Moxie Fox. The restaurant occupied a large lot and sat back from the road at a slight elevation that accentuated the massive front deck used for patron seating. This ornate outdoor feature and the rustic but chic hunting lodge facade were probably meant to give the building an air of exclusivity and sophistication, even though it was nothing but the worst kind of bikini bar in the vein of Hooters and Twin Peaks.

We reached the edge of the property just in time to see two men in suits burst through the elaborately carved wood and glass double doors that fed onto the deck. They each had a hand around the other's throat and struggled to maintain their balance while grappling for dominance.

Mike's mouth fell open at the sight. "Is that Judge Bragg and Grant Wells?"

But before I could answer, Bragg's weasely voice rang out and confirmed our suspicions.

"I should have put a stop to this weeks ago, you spineless coward."

He then punctuated the statement with a headbutt to the attorney's nose that sent the young prosecutor tumbling backward into a wrought iron table, where he knocked over several chairs and fell to the ground.

A blood-curdling scream followed the tumble and cut through the calamity, causing Bragg to freeze.

At first, I couldn't pinpoint the origin of the sound. But eventually, a tall, busty, raven-haired beauty with bronze skin stepped across the threshold into the light of the balcony. She surveyed the scene for a moment, then marched up to Bragg and slapped him across the face, which he took with a stunned grunt.

"You have some nerve coming in here claiming ownership over me when you have a wife and a baby on the way." Rather than wait for his response, she spun around and raced over to kneel beside Wells, who still sat on the ground, stunned and bleeding.

Bragg barked a curse at her back. "You're just as bad as him, you lying two-timing floosy."

"You're the hypocrite. Get out of my sight." Her voice was a cold, calm contrast to the river of tears streaking makeup down her face, "and don't darken my doorstep again."

Bragg kicked a nearby metal trash can and sent it flying in their direction. The item went wide, but the couple cowered and shrieked, which seemed to give Bragg the satisfaction he desired before stomping out.

Mike turned to me. "What should we do?"

"Hide!"

We both stood on the sidewalk too far away to intervene but close enough to be seen, and I didn't want the ever-mercurial Bragg to catch us eavesdropping. The street around us only had a smattering of foot traffic since the Moxie Fox and most of its neighbors were themed restaurants or seafood eateries that didn't open until noon during the off-season. However, there were a few cars parked in the angled spaces that lined the curb. I motioned for Mike to duck behind a Ford Fiesta with Maryland plates and prayed we'd remain unnoticed.

Seconds later, Bragg threw open the bar's ground-level entrance and trudged toward his Suburban. His twisted expression radiated a homicidal rage, but that wasn't the sight that intrigued me.

I nudged Mike in the ribs. "Follow me."

When Bragg climbed into the SUV, I sprinted for the entrance with my head ducked low.

The door had started to close, but did so on such a slow arc that if I timed our efforts just right, we could slip inside before it presumably locked shut.

"You sure you want to do this?" Mike hissed as we ran. "Wells probably isn't in the mood to talk, and you can always catch Bragg at work."

"Bragg already lied once. I'm not going to get anything out of him, and there's clearly more to this story."

Twenty feet from the door, a car horn sounded several times in rapid succession. I looked over my shoulder to discover that the now wide-eyed, red-faced Bragg had spotted us and hopped out of the vehicle. Mike pushed me forward, and I hurtled toward the archway just in time to catch a sliver of airspace with my palm. A swift pry and push forced the entrance open, and I stumbled across the jamb.

"Go, Victoria, I'm right—"

I turned to seal the entrance behind Mike, but Bragg grabbed the reporter by the hood of his sweatshirt and yanked him backward onto the ground.

Acting on instinct, I tugged the door closed, but the pneumatic mechanism's pressurized system fought against me, giving Bragg just enough time to lurch toward the glass and hook his fingertips onto the outside handle. His effort forced me into a tug of war that I wasn't sure I could win.

"What do you think you're doing, girl?" He roared as he wedged his foot into the ever-growing hole. "Why don't you mind your own business?"

"Step away from the door." *Click-click.* "Or it'll be the last thing you see."

The menacing sound of a shotgun sliding on its rack, eclipsed the angelic voice that accompanied it. My spine stiffened, and I reached for the sky.

To my surprise, Bragg mirrored my movements.

"Not you, sugar." A tender hand pressed against my shoulder.

I turned to find that the angelic voice belonged to the raven-haired beauty. Her eyes were wild and smeared with makeup from when she'd been crying. She stood with her feet wide and the barrel seated into her shoulder, although the muzzle was angled slightly down. Once I moved out of the way, she pressed her cheek against the stock and set her sight directly on Bragg, who backed away from the glass and allowed the door to close.

Mike scrambled to his feet and followed the judge to his SUV, but the woman didn't drop her guard until the vehicle disappeared. Her tenacity was both to be admired and feared.

"Relax, sugar. It ain't loaded," she lowered the shotgun and slid the forearm into the back position so I could see the empty chamber, "but you can't own a bar like this and not have one around."

"Thank you. I—I didn't mean to intrude. We—me and the guy you saw outside—we were here to…" I didn't want her to feel any shame about what we saw, so I fudged the truth. "Grant Wells asked us to meet him here…to pick up some paperwork."

"Uh-huh, I see." She narrowed her eyes at me, then glanced at the staircase behind her. "He's had a bit of a tumble. I don't know if he'll feel much like talking, Miss?" She held out a manicured hand.

"Justice, Victoria Justice."

"Well, howdy do. I'm Gloria Mae Parker, but my friends call me Glory. And now that we're acquainted, why don't you tell me what you're really doing here and why Joshua was chasing you?"

I hesitated, but she deserved to know. "I recently inquired about his involvement in the Garret Yaris murder and got the runaround, so I tracked him down here to follow up."

"I guess deceit is just like anything else. Some people are just born swimming in it." She pressed her Kewpie doll lips together as if resigned to some unspoken decision. "I was about to run and get some ice from the bar. G.W. is on the deck. You're welcome to go up."

I mounted the stairs to find Grant Wells using the bottom of his tie to staunch a bloody nose. He'd moved to a chair since I'd last seen him and sat slumped with his head back to hasten his recovery.

"Quite a fight you had there." I rounded the table so he could see me. "I take it you and Glory are an item?"

He lifted his head and groaned when I came into view. "What do you know about it?"

"Not much." I pulled out a chair and sat down. "I was hoping you'd be kind enough to get me up to speed. I came here expecting to confront Judge Bragg about the Yaris murder. Instead, I caught a show right out here on the balcony that leaves me unsure what to think." I leaned across the table. "Is Glory the reason you've missed work the past few days?"

For a moment, he jutted out his chin like he was going to deny it, but he eventually bowed his head to hide the Cheshire smile. "Things have gotten pretty serious lately, but I didn't know about Bragg." He returned to pinching his nose and winced. "The man is a jealous psychopath who's been spying on us for weeks."

"Spying on you, how? Where?"

"I don't know. I'm just telling you what he said when he came busting in here."

"But you said he'd been watching you for weeks. Was this the first attack?" I considered the hunch I had earlier about the Department of Justice. "Has he come snooping around your office, or has anyone there gotten any suspicious calls?"

"Not as far as I know. This all came out of left field."

"Hang on then. How long have you and Glory been seeing each other?"

"A little over a month." She stepped onto the balcony with a towel full of ice and gingerly placed the bundle on the bridge of her boyfriend's nose.

I turned to her as she knelt by his chair. "Were you two together anytime last week?"

"Tuesday evening, all of Wednesday and Thursday, and most of Friday."

"You weren't here with Judge Bragg on Friday morning?

"I don't see why it should matter to you," she squared her shoulders, "but no. I broke things off with Joshua as soon as I learned he was spoken for. But apparently, he kept sniffing around."

"My apologies. I'm the intruder here, and you've been nothing but kind." I pressed both hands to my lips in a prayer motion. "I didn't intend that to sound judgmental, it's just that Bragg went missing during the bombing at the courthouse, and I was led to believe he was here."

So where the heck was he?

* * *

By the time I'd bid goodbye to Glory and stepped out of the Moxie Fox, my mind was reeling. I didn't know where to start.

"That was intense." Mike rose from his seat on the steps as I exited the front door. "Well, what did you find out?" He hooked my arm and navigated me away from the building.

I clenched my fists, hoping the action would help me regain my confidence. "If you'd asked me last week who I thought were the main suspects in the Yaris murder, I would have said Arnold Knight, Johnny Erving, Ignacio Cardoza, and Phyllis Dodd."

"But they all appear to have some alibi."

"Right." I nodded as we stepped onto a crosswalk. "Which is odd since each one of them has reason for revenge against Yaris or, at the very least, the court system. Meanwhile, Bragg—someone with no clear motive or connection to the victim—was nowhere to be found during the explosion, according to Grant Wells and his mistress."

Mike's brow furrowed. "I assume you're talking about that broad with the shotgun?"

"Sorry." I waved my hand to dismiss the statement. "Not a fair representation, considering he's not married. Yes, the woman and Wells are dating. Her name is Glory. She was actually Judge Bragg's mistress first, but that's not the point. The point is that Bragg doesn't have an alibi for the Yaris murder, and he's tried to cover up that fact. So, I'm starting to think that means he's somehow involved."

"Okay. But that's a huge leap to take with no real leads. We talked about that the other night."

"I get that, but don't you think he just displayed a temper and capacity for violence that warrants suspicion?"

"No." Mike stopped walking and stared at me. "We basically caught him with his pants down. Rejected by the woman he loves and literally kicked to the curb. I think any man would overreact in a situation like that. And as for his nonexistent alibi, he probably just didn't want to admit he was having an affair."

"Perhaps, but this whole scenario got me thinking about the big picture." I looked around at the light foot traffic and colorful storefronts to make sure Bragg hadn't doubled back and followed us before I made my claim. "Actually—and I hate to admit this—one of my coworkers came up with the wacked out notion a couple days ago, but I couldn't put my head around it until now. What if this was a classic 'criss-cross'?"

"Like the rap group from the nineties?"

"No," I rolled my eyes, "like the Alfred Hitchcock film *Strangers on a Train*, where one man proposes committing murder for the other so that they avoid suspicion for their respective crimes."

"All right." He scratched his head. "I've never seen that one. Let's find a place to sit down and grab a bite so you can explain it." He started walking up Oceanside Drive toward the boardwalk.

"It's simple." I fell into step with him. "What if this was like the movie? Wherein, Bragg agreed to eliminate Yaris to feed Maddox's ambition to become President Judge. Meanwhile, Maddox was tasked to hurt someone unrelated like Ashton or…" I whipped an arm back in the direction of the Moxie Fox "…a mistress stealer like Grant Wells in an effort to complete the ultimate 'criss-cross' murder plot. The issue here being, of course, we're running around town looking for clues when the second half of the deal hasn't been done."

"I don't know that sounds…" he wrung his hands together "…unnecessarily complex. Isn't it just simpler to—"

Ring-Ring!

A notification popped up on my cell with a number that matched the exchange from the hospital.

Ashton!

I placed a hand on Mike's shoulder. "I'll need to take a rain check on brunch. Could you take me back to the house? I promised Ashton I'd pick him up if he got released this afternoon."

"C'mon, now. We were on a roll." Mike threw his hands in the air. "Let's be real. He'd be home much faster if he just took an Uber. No waiting."

"A promise is a promise." I smiled and patted Mike on the cheek. I hated to cut things short, but Ashton needed me, and what was I doing any of this for if not for him?

Chapter Twenty-One

"Let's stop at Redner's on the way back to your place and grab some groceries."

After the long, arduous morning with Mike, I was happy to shift gears and pick Ashton up from the medical center. He'd balked at the wheelchair they'd brought to transport him from his hospital room to my Mustang, but he'd relented and now sat in the passenger seat, challenging my every suggestion in an attempt to regain some of his machismo.

"You haven't been home in almost five days." I continued despite the hand he'd raised in protest. "I bet you at least need fresh milk, and I think a few cuts of meat and veggies would be better than spending the week eating takeout and TV dinners."

"I don't want anyone making a fuss over me, especially you. I can take care of myself." He rubbed a hand across the copper-colored stubble that lined his jaw from the days of being out of commission. "The doctor said I should get a few more days of bed rest; she didn't say I was an invalid."

"I just worry about you, that's all."

I removed a hand from the wheel and reached for his palm. He accepted and placed his other hand on top of mine.

"Speaking of which," he sighed, "the other night when I said your reaction to the webcam thing was far-fetched, I didn't mean it. I'm sorry. I should have taken what you had to say at face value. I worry about you, too, and I want you to know that I'm always here for you.

"Thanks, that's sweet, although…it turns out you were right."

"How so?"

"Well…" I hedged; a quick gut check indicated it was best to avoid the part about Mike's assistance and Bragg's temper. "I went on a bit of a scavenger hunt today, chasing down suspects, and all it proved was that the webcam and this courthouse revenge plot couldn't be more at odds."

"Victoria," he ran a hand through the mussy shag of his crew cut, "didn't I tell you to be careful? What happened to protecting yourself and your coworkers? What if you had gotten hurt? Why didn't you wait for me?"

"Nothing serious happened. I'm fine. It was no big deal. Just one conspiracy theory after another with no merit." I shrugged in resignation. "And that's the point. I should have listened to you." I squeezed his hand and brought his knuckles to my lips for a kiss. His skin tasted salty and smelled of antiseptic soap. "Let the authorities handle the Yaris mess."

He scrunched up his face in a faux exaggeration of disgust like a kid refusing his vitamins. "Don't try to outdo my apology with your lame attempts at schoolyard romance." He brought my knuckles to his lips for a return kiss. "But I'm glad to hear we're on the same page."

A warm flush of satisfaction flittered across my chest, and I fought to keep my eyes on the road when all I could think about was the supple curve of his lips against my flesh.

"Now, if you really wanted to make it up to me," he flashed a sly smile, "you'd honor my wishes on this store thing and skip straight to the part where you tuck me in with a bedtime story."

"Not a chance, Mister. I'm making an executive decision." I sped through the intersection and turned into the supermarket parking lot that lay beyond.

Inside the store, Ashton lost his reluctance for the shopping experience and hovered over the steaks with the exuberance of a man who'd gone years without a good meal.

"You think you might stay for lunch?" He tossed four slabs of meat into the cart without waiting for my answer and beckoned me to follow him to the ground round. "The weather is nice enough that I could whip up something on the grill for us."

I nodded and pushed his now overflowing basket forward until I noticed a woman staring at us from the opposite end of the aisle. Her slim, freckled face flattened into a mask of disgust when I met her gaze, and she zipped away down the produce aisle.

Phyllis Dodd.

"Why don't I grab a couple bags of apples?" I parked the cart by his hip.

"And oranges." He added without looking up from the burgers. "Oh, and grapes, please."

I barely heard his second request as I was already on the move, eager to catch up with Phyllis, even though a guilty part of me noted that I was about to break my promise to abandon conspiracy theories. However, Phyllis had yet to answer for herself, and I had my doubts about there being surveillance footage of her working during the time of the bombing. I'd spent enough time in court to know such evidence could be doctored.

When I rounded the corner, she was picking through a pile of bananas.

"Don't you have anything better to do?" she snapped. "I can't be the only person in this town worth harassing. Harriston told me you broke into his office demanding answers."

"Get off it, Phyllis. You're the only person in Bickerton who'd have the time and the talent to both booby trap the President Judge's vehicle and sabotage Ashton's brakes."

"Get your facts straight, my dear. The police have already cleared me of any wrongdoing in the Yaris case, and I have no clue about—or interest in—that traitor Ashton North."

She turned her back on me and pushed her cart level with the next display case, which contained a variety of berries and cherries.

"Okay then." Undeterred, I ran ahead and blocked her path. "If you're so clearly innocent, why are you afraid of answering a few questions?"

"Because I don't have to prove anything to you." She hissed with a vehemence that turned her face crimson. "I've already paid the price for what I did to destroy the integrity of the Controlled Substance Lab, and I'm well aware of the toll it took on the people of this town. Don't try to blame me for something more horrific just because you don't think the sacrifice I made was steep enough. You didn't do that with your little boyfriend."

She stepped around her cart and seized my elbow. Then she yanked me toward her so that we were only centimeters apart. Her willowy frame towered over me, but she bent down so that I wouldn't miss a whispered word.

"Last year, I lost my dignity, my freedom, my job, and my family. And right now, the only obligation I have is to win back my children's respect by staying out of trouble…and staying away from troublemakers." She met my eyes with a cold, dull stare. "I've never been the type to share my personal problems, but as soon as the police came into Readalong asking if we'd seen any suspicious activity around those payphones, I knew it was only a matter of time before my past came back to haunt me. And the weight of that prospect put a toll on me."

She licked her lips like she was weighing whether to say more.

"I'm not proud to admit I fell back on old habits—a shot of vodka in the morning to take the edge off, a bottle of wine to help me sleep at night." She pulled back the cuff of her blouse to reveal a long vertical bandage that extended well over four inches along her forearm. I didn't need to see the wound to understand what it meant. "My brother reached out to Harriston as a lifeline, and they've been working overtime to keep my struggles private."

She straightened and realigned herself with her cart. Her voice returned to full volume, redoubling in its vitriol.

"As it stands, I've got very little to lose, so back off or I'll take you down with me." She tugged at her sleeve, returning it to its place.

And with that, she turned and headed in the opposite direction. The clickety-clack of her heels against the polished concrete punctuated her effort to steer the cart away as fast as possible. I didn't bother to follow because her confession left me shook.

She was right. I'd come at her expecting a fight, nay, wanting one, but never had I once given her the benefit of the doubt. Why was I so quick to condemn Phyllis for her actions, even though I'd practically made a career out of defending Ashton for his?

The thought haunted me all the way back to his house, where we unloaded my car and settled into the kitchen to put things away.

"I think I'm going to pass on lunch." I leaned against the freshly stocked refrigerator and folded my arms. "I don't quite feel like myself today. Besides, you should probably get some rest."

"You sure? It's no trouble." Ashton put down the paper bag he was folding. "And in case you haven't noticed, I like having you around."

"And I like being around." I managed a lopsided grin, so he'd know he wasn't to blame for my sudden change in mood. "Don't you worry. I'm going to check on you every day, and I want you to call me any time you need me."

"You're the boss." He stood up from the breakfast nook and extended an arm. "Let me walk you out."

We headed into the living room, and I grabbed my purse from the couch while he unlocked the door. When I crossed to the open threshold, he circled a hand around my waist and stared at me with a pensive expression I couldn't quite decipher.

"I know this is probably a lousy time to say something like this, and only a coward would wait until you're on your way out the door to say it. But, you were the only thing that flashed before my eyes when I skidded across that highway, and as weird as it sounds, the experience showed me what I've known since the moment I met you. I love you, Victoria."

Chapter Twenty-Two

Ashton North loved me.

I stared out the window of my Mustang in a daze.

By all accounts, I couldn't remember how I had gotten into the car or how long I had been sitting across the street staring at the front door of Ashton's home, replaying the words in my mind.

I did, however, remember that I'd been too stunned to respond to his declaration. And I could sense that my out-of-body experience hadn't quite worn off, so I continued to stare rather than risk trying to drive.

No one of significance, other than my mother, had ever professed their love before, and I wasn't sure what I was supposed to do or how I was supposed to react.

Ashton had gone back inside at some point after I left—or at least he wasn't standing in the doorway anymore, but I could catch an occasional glimpse of his beautifully broad shoulders through the bay window as he moved about the living room.

I debated going back inside, righting the wrong I'd made in remaining silent, but I couldn't move. All I knew for sure was that my senses had become keener—the sun a little brighter, the air a little fresher—as if time and reality had grown more vivid.

And I suppose it had. I had strong feelings for Ashton.

But why couldn't I articulate that?

The harsh reality of this conundrum brought my soul back to earth, so I exhaled and started the engine. As I prepared to pull away from the curb, I noticed a hooded figure dressed in black streak out from the bushes of the adjoining yard. In rapid succession, the person tossed a large brick, then a wine bottle with a flaming rag through Ashton's bay window. The act only took a second, and the figure disappeared into the neighboring yard as quickly as they appeared.

I slammed on my horn, hoping to draw Ashton's attention—anyone's attention—but it was too late.

The front of the house had already burst into violent flames.

Chapter Twenty-Three

"How did you know the victim?"

The uniformed officer folded over a page on his notepad and stared at me expectantly. I could barely hear the question, let alone concentrate, amidst the rumble of the idling fire engines and the chatter from the gathering crowd. The scene around me looked like a war zone. Ashton's home had burned to the ground. And despite having been dragged away down the street by the arrival of police and medical units, the black hole of acrid smoke and ash mocked me as it sat in garish contrast to the once picturesque April afternoon.

"I'm sorry." I closed my eyes, hoping it would anchor me to the moment. "What was the question?"

"What's the nature of your relationship to the victim?"

Friend? Partner? Lover? I didn't know what to say. Ashton meant everything to me.

"We're dating."

"Do you know of anyone who'd want to hurt him?"

"No."

I didn't know anything for sure, not anymore.

"You saw a single suspect, and that person arrived and departed on foot?"

"Yes." I rested a hand on the officer's squad car to steady myself. "A single figure emerged from the barrier of foliage between yards like they'd been waiting for the right moment to toss the Molotov cocktail into the house. They escaped by running across the yard, where I lost sight of them in the landscaping on the other side."

"Do you recall any distinguishing features about the suspect?"

"Nothing."

My eyes clouded over with tears until warm droplets cascaded down my cheeks. I'd been too wrapped up in my own insecurities to focus on what really mattered.

"Uh, ma'am." The officer shifted his weight from foot to foot.

"I think she's had enough for now." Ashton limped over from the paramedics' vehicle that was parked several yards away. "Give us a minute."

My heart had nearly exploded when I'd first discovered that he had escaped through the back door off the kitchen just as the flames engulfed his living room, but his presence now still seemed like a miracle. Ashton eased in next to me and pulled me to his side so that both our backs were pressed against the police car. Soot covered his face, and sweat beaded his brow. His T-shirt was ripped at the waist where the medical team had cut away the fabric to stitch the splenectomy incision that had reopened during his scramble to outrun the flames. A small patch of blood seeped through the bandage, but if the wound hurt, he didn't show it.

"I know what you're thinking," he nestled his face into my tangled mane so that he could whisper in my ear, "but I don't want you to go running after her."

"How are you not freaking out right now?"

"Promise me." He tipped my chin toward him so our eyes met.

"No. This is the second time you've been attacked in less than a week. I saw her in the grocery store tonight, and she all but threatened me. She must be following you...and she has to be the person who messed around in my room."

"Calm down." He squeezed my hands, which were shaking. "Keeping you safe is my main objective. We have to be strategic about this."

"Why do you keep saying stuff like that? I just spent the day running around town when the answer has been staring us in the face the whole time." I beat my hand against his chest. "Tell me you said something to the police. If you just make a statement, you could end this."

"Victoria, it doesn't matter what I tell them about Phyllis Dodd if we don't have any evidence."

* * *

Since Ashton was injured, with nowhere to go, I convinced Ma to let him stay with us for the night. As repayment, he insisted on doing the dinner dishes.

While he clattered about in the kitchen, I sat with Ma on the couch, trying to keep her from throwing a fit.

"I don't like this." She hissed, lowering her head along with her volume. "I've told you a million times this man is bad news, and now you bring him and his demons into our home? What if the person who tried to kill him comes here?"

"What else should I have done? I couldn't leave him alone on the street. He's hurting. He doesn't have any family nearby—and even if he did, he doesn't have a car."

"He's a grown man. He's not your responsibility, and he's sure enough not mine. My job is to take care of you and me, remember?" She reached for my hands and recited our special mantra. "I am yours, you are mine, and together we'll be fine."

"Ashton isn't going to come between that. I'm just helping a friend in need."

"A friend?" She sucked her teeth and rolled her eyes heavenward. "You might have fooled yourself, but you didn't pull no wool over me. I see how you look at each other. I don't know how far this relationship has gone, but this is where it ends."

"Ma, please, you're over—"

"Every second you're with him, you're putting yourself in danger of becoming collateral damage. What if you had been inside his house during that fire? Don't you have enough on your plate with what's going on at the courthouse?"

"Come on, Ma. Things are just as bad outside the courthouse."

"I think it's time for you to explore other options." She stood and paced the room. "Get away from here, and spread your wings."

"Ma, we've had this conversation before. I'm not leaving my job. I like what I do."

"Just hear me out for once. Aren't GRE and LSAT scores good for five years? You could reconsider graduate school. Tour a few universities. Separate yourself from whatever is happening with him." She jabbed a thumb toward the kitchen and was met by the sound of glass breaking.

"My bad," Ashton called from the other room. "Don't worry, it's just one mug. Everything is fine."

"See!" She threw up her hands like his clumsiness proved her point.

"Ma, I'm not going to just drop everything and go to graduate school."

"I'm not asking you to drop everything. I'm asking you to take a break. Book a vacation, register for a conference, enroll in a yoga retreat. Just get yourself out of the line of fire, and we can talk about something more permanent later." She walked to the closet by the front door and pulled out her purse. "You're all I've got, Angel, and it's my job to protect you." She handed me her credit card. "Go book something now. I mean it. If you don't, I will—and I'll drag you there myself."

Chapter Twenty-Four

The next two days were a slog, acting as referee between my mother and Ashton had worn thin. So per her request, I did some internet digging and found a week-long court reporting seminar in Los Angeles called "Real-Time Stenography—The Software, Accessories, Specs, & Licensing Needed to Succeed." Since the event was work-related and offered continuing education credits toward my Registered Professional Reporter certification, Candi had no problem giving me time off, despite the short notice. She even suggested we have tea after work to discuss tools and advice I could bring back to the team.

"Thank God it's Friday and this crappy week has come to a close." Candi sighed as she sank onto a crème settee on the opposite side of our coffee table, which was filled with finger sandwiches, pink and green macarons, scones, clotted cream and jam, mince pies, trifle, and chamomile tea in an octopus-shaped teapot. "I'm still amazed that everyone is back to business as usual, even though the authorities seem to have no clue what happened to Yaris."

I squirmed in my seat, unsure whether I should reveal that her very sentiment was the cause for my departure.

"You're lucky you were able to find such a comprehensive seminar this time of year." Candi poured herself a cup of tea. "Perfect time to get away. Have you ever been to California?"

I shook my head and picked up a pink macaron. "This trip will be my first visit to the West Coast. I'm really looking forward to the flight tomorrow morning."

"Are you leaving out of Philadelphia or Baltimore?"

"Philly. Ashton is going to drive me up there."

"Really?" Candi laughed. "Are you two an item now?"

"The heck if I know. Like everything around here, it's complicated." I bit into the macaron and savored the tangy raspberry filling. "I think we've both been dancing around how we feel for a while now."

"Everything okay over here, ladies?" Jillian, the café's owner, saddled up to our nook with a couple of cloth napkins on her arm.

"We were just touching upon your favorite subject: Men." Candi patted the empty space on her settee. "Join us. I think Victoria's finally made some progress with that big dreamy zaddy who's always following her around."

"We don't really call him that behind his back, do we?" I cringed.

"Ashton?" Jillian plopped onto the seat. "Do tell. Has he made an indecent lady of you yet?"

"Uh, no," I cut my eyes at Jillian, "but he did tell me he loved me."

"Brilliant." Jillian squealed. "Congratulations. That's huge."

"But," I held up a hand before Candi could comment too, "I've been too scared to say it back because I've never had anyone open themselves up to me like that before. What if it's not real? I mean, we initially met under dire circumstances, and his revelation about the whole thing came right after his car accident—another dire circumstance. I'm just not sure what to think."

"Think?" Jillian snapped one of her napkins at me. "Stop trying to analyze everything. This is a no-brainer."

Candi raised her teacup in agreement. "Take it from an old maid. Love, like life, is fleeting. Reap the benefits of both while you can."

"Maybe, but it's not that simple." I tossed aside my half-eaten macaron. "You heard about the fire at his place, right?"

"No," Jillian replied, sliding forward in her seat. "Is he okay?"

"He's fine, but his home was destroyed. He's stayed with us the past two nights, and things are pretty awkward since Ma doesn't trust him. She's even tried to put a wedge between us by insisting I put too much faith in him. She says having him in my life is reckless because he's reckless." I waved a hand at Candi, who'd grown wide-eyed with concern. "It's a silly notion, or at least I thought it was, but I think he believes I've sided with her because I'm leaving him to go on this trip."

"All the more reason to say something." Jillian hopped up and wrapped an arm around me in a half-hug. "You must set things straight. Forget about your mum for a moment. This is your life. What do you want?" She kissed the top of my head and walked off to check her other tables.

"She's right." Candi nodded, then sipped her tea. "The fact that you're torturing yourself speaks volumes about how you feel. You can't leave with a question mark hanging over the relationship. You don't have to declare your love, but do say something. When it comes to life's troubles, you can't run. You have to stand and fight. And if I were you, I'd set things straight with my mother, too. No one should force your hand when it comes to love."

"Easier said than done. Ma has been in maniacal mayor mode lately." I reached for the teapot. "Criticism has been coming from all sides about public safety. Plus, folks are still protesting the Ignacio Cardoza verdict. She's actually supposed to do an interview with *The Bugle* tonight about the town's fiscal efforts to ramp up safety around the boardwalk." I clenched my jaw, recalling the strain underlying our most recent conversations. "I don't want to get into an argument when she's already stressed."

"I hear you." Candi tweaked her glasses and changed subjects as if sensing my discomfort. "I wish the governor and Capitol Police showed the same level of concern for safety at the courthouse."

"Me too."

"Speaking of our superiors, I noticed you avoided Judge Bragg's courtroom this week. Is everything okay?"

I flashed an obsequious smile and sipped my tea to avoid comment. Candi had already extracted more information from me than I desired. Since I was less than twenty-four hours away from leaving everything behind, it didn't make sense to tell her about Bragg's temperament or our run-in at the beach. Besides, I didn't want the conversation to morph into more speculation about the courthouse bombing. Another evening dissecting people's personalities and motives just seemed not only futile but exhausting.

Maybe Ma was right about the advantages of taking some time off.

* * *

"Hey, Ma. I'm home." I tossed my purse on the couch and headed toward the kitchen. "How was the interview? Candi said to tell you 'hello,' and Jillian sent some of that toffee pudding you love so much."

"She isn't back yet." Ashton stared down at me from the middle of the staircase.

"Oh." I brushed a frizzy strand of hair from my brow. "I thought you'd be out."

"You thought I'd be out, or you were hoping I'd be out?"

"Ashton, please. Don't start. I'm simply surprised to see you because I thought you'd be searching for an apartment or dealing with the repairs on your truck."

"At eight o'clock at night?" He crossed his arms.

"Yeah, well…"

I crossed to the kitchen and put the clear plastic to-go container on the counter. When I returned, I found him at the bottom of the staircase with his foot on the last step.

"Listen, I got a call this morning from the athletic department at Del State. The head coach wants me to come in on Monday so they can get me up to speed on their matrix for spring training." He stuffed his hands in his pockets. "And I've been thinking, with you leaving and me being homeless, this might be a sign that I should look for a permanent place upstate in Dover."

"Why?" I reached for him, but he stepped back. "I'm not leaving forever."

"In some ways, it feels like you already have." He bowed his head and studied the floor. "I see how you've been avoiding me, and I don't know if it's because of your mother or because of what I said, but I'm tired of not knowing."

"Ashton, nothing anybody says will ever change how I feel. You know how much I care for you."

"Do I?" He arched an eyebrow.

"Sure you do." I swallowed hard and searched for the three other words that would make him happy, but I couldn't find them. "You've got to understand,

I've spent my entire life either being bullied or underestimated. Both those things make it difficult for me to open up to people and accept what they say at face value."

"I know, but I'm not someone trying to take advantage of you." He gripped the banister so hard it rattled. "I'm here because I want to be your support system. Don't you trust me?"

"Yes, but putting pressure on me isn't the answer." I bit my lip and fidgeted, unsure where to put my hands. "How do I know you're not just telling me you love me as a way to control me—or as a shield to avoid looking at your own problems? I'm sorry, Ashton, but I'm scared. I need more time. Why turn this into an ultimatum? What happened to just being honest with each other?"

"I am being honest. And the truth is, I can't stand being this close to you, only to watch you drift away."

"It's just one trip to get me out of harm's way. Lest you forget, we have a killer on the loose."

"It's not about the trip. It's about you not seeing in me what I see in you." He turned and trudged up the stairs. "But don't worry, I'll stick around long enough to take you to the airport tomorrow. That's the least I can do for a friend."

He disappeared above the landing, but his final word cut like a knife.

Chapter Twenty-Five

Still haunted by Ashton's words, I awoke the next morning to a brisk spring draft whistling in through my window. Funny. I didn't remember leaving it open, but I was exhausted and irritable and—according to the alarm clock that someone saw fit to turn off rather than waking me—a half-hour behind schedule. Oh, boy. The two-hour drive to the airport was going to be tight. The only silver lining to the already doomed day was that I'd pre-packed my bags, so all I needed to do was to get dressed and grab a bit of Jillian's toffee pudding if there was any left.

When I arrived downstairs, Ashton was standing by the coffeemaker with a steaming mug in his hand. He was wearing a light blue Delaware State University sweatshirt and a sour expression.

"Morning," I said.

He merely nodded in response and averted his eyes. I stared at him for a moment, hoping to resume our conversation from last night, but he remained silent and eerily still.

My heart sank, and I turned toward the counter to find solace in the toffee pudding. The container was exactly where I left it, and the spongy dessert was completely intact.

Odd. Sweets were my mother's weakness as much as they were mine.

"Have you seen Ma this morning?"

Ashton shrugged.

I rolled my eyes at his audacity. "Unbelievable. Is this how it's going to be for the rest of the day?"

I walked out into the living room, growing increasingly annoyed, and hollered up the stairs.

"Ma, it's eight o'clock. We're heading out in a few minutes."

What was weirder than the toffee pudding was that she wasn't the first person up. She had to preside over her monthly Kappa Mu sorority meeting at nine, which was the only reason she hadn't shunned Ashton and agreed to drive me to the airport herself.

"Ma?" I climbed the stairs to her bedroom and knocked on the double doors. She still didn't answer, so I pushed them open and stepped inside. The room was empty, and her bed was made. A quick sweep of the bathroom and walk-in closet returned zero results as well.

I pulled out my phone and dialed her cell.

No answer.

I returned to the kitchen. "Did you hear my mom come home last night?"

Ashton shook his head.

"Could you speak, please. This is important, and I have no idea if you're saying she didn't or that you don't know."

He shrugged his big dumb shoulders.

"You don't know?" I threw up my hands. "Great."

For the next few minutes, I checked the garage and the carport outside. Ma's Buick was nowhere to be found. Logic would suggest that maybe she left early for the sorority meeting. But with everything that had occurred over the past two weeks, I didn't feel comfortable making assumptions.

Ashton was still in the kitchen sipping coffee when I returned.

"Change of plans. Ma's not answering her phone, so I think we should run over to the church to see if she's there. I don't feel comfortable leaving until I get in touch with her."

He snorted and muttered something that sounded like "typical."

"Get over yourself." I snapped. "This is serious. If you don't care, that's fine. I was just informing you as one human being to another. In fact, you know what?" I spun on my heel and headed for the front door. "Stay here. I'll drive myself to the airport when I'm through. Good luck in Dover. Don't forget to lock the door behind you after you finish your precious coffee."

It only took fifteen minutes to get to Wesdale United Methodist Church, where the Kappa Mu's held their monthly meetings. However, the parking lot stood completely empty, so I waited until the meeting started in case Ma had decided to use her morning for shopping or conferring with an out-of-town sorority sister about the agenda.

But to my dismay, nine o'clock came and went without any sign of her or her vehicle.

To make matters worse, no one at the meeting had heard from her.

By noon, the church parking lot was once again empty, and my heart was in my throat.

Desperate. Sweaty. Panicked. Unsure what to do next and unwilling to elicit Ashton's help, I called Mike.

"Ma's missing," I announced without preamble.

"What?" He sounded hungover or half asleep. "Aren't you supposed to be in L.A.? What time is it there?"

"Forget L.A. I can't find my mother. She's not answering her cell."

"Have you called the police?"

"No." My mouth fell open. "Do you think I should?"

"Depends. How long has she been missing?"

"Since last night, I think."

"Did you call her office? Maybe she had an emergency at work."

"Right," I groaned. "Of course. Why didn't I think of that? You're a genius."

"Just keep that in mind next time you need something."

I hung up and dialed the number for Bickerton's Town Hall. The automated voice messaging system indicated they were closed for the weekend, but Mom's extension was busy. That was a good sign. Maybe she was on the line or in a meeting, so I fired up the Mustang and drove over to the east side of The Quad, where the building was located.

To my immense relief, her Buick was parked out front. I pulled in beside it, hopped out, and jogged up the steps to the Town Hall entrance.

The doors were locked.

I called her extension several more times.

Busy signal.

Where could she be? I walked back to the curb and peeked into her car window. Nothing seemed out of place. I examined The Quad. The day was overcast but warm. City maintenance workers had planted a rainbow of perennials around the tree line that guarded the fountain. An occasional car slowly circled the roundabout. Foot traffic was equally light, but it was a Saturday, and most of the buildings directly on The Quad were government entities that didn't have Saturday hours.

I tried the landline at the house, half expecting Ashton to pick up, but all I got was our answering machine. The crisp sound of her melodic falsetto instructing callers to leave a brief message brought me to tears. I leaned against the hood of her Buick and resigned myself to try her cell a couple more times before contacting the police.

Luckily, it only took one ring for me to hear it.

Ring-Ring! / Ring-Ring!

The distant artificial sounds generated by the circuits inside my smartphone were matched by an equally distant ringing in the real world.

Ma's cellphone was somewhere nearby.

I dialed her number again and peered into the window of the car. I didn't see the phone light up inside, so it had to be the trunk.

Hopeful. Anxious. Frantic. I pulled on the door handle.

Of course, her vehicle was locked, so I did the only sensible thing. I opened my own trunk, pulled out the tire iron, and thrashed her driver's side window until the glass splintered, then shattered.

If the act attracted attention, the observers failed to intervene. I soon had the car door open and the trunk release pulled, grateful that the ringing had grown louder.

But what I found when I rounded the vehicle broke my heart.

Crumpled in the fetal position, lay my mother. She wore the same pale blue dress suit that I had seen her leave the house in yesterday—or rather, Friday morning. A thin line of dried blood mirrored her hairline, and a breathable ball gag had been secured on her head. She was blindfolded, bound at the wrists and ankles.

The cellphone lay beside her, still ringing, but her eyes remained closed, oblivious to the sound. I immediately feared the worst, but the slight rise and fall of her chest and the musty odor of perspiration assured me there was hope.

Chapter Twenty-Six

For the second time in a week, I found myself holding vigil at a bedside in the Trident County Medical Center's ICU. Doctors confirmed Ma's vital signs were steady, but the attacker had used such heavy sedatives, the hospital opted to treat the situation as a drug poisoning and monitored her brain for damage via an EEG. This resulted in such a vast array of tubes and wires that I couldn't draw close enough to shower her with the love I'd failed to give in the days prior, so I perched on a nearby chair and bowed my head in fervent prayer.

Remorse and sorrow over every detail of the last two weeks ebbed and flowed through me. Johnny and the gun prank, the Ignacio Cardoza verdict, the Yaris bombing, Ashton's car accident, and the fire at his home, the rogue webcam, and now my mother's attack.

Despite the disparate elements, the events had to be connected.

I could feel it.

And as far as I was concerned, that common denominator was Phyllis Dodd.

I'd seen her in the moments prior to the gun prank and Ashton's house fire—and she was, of course, the one person for whom a revenge plot against the court system, Ashton, and my mother made sense. And yet, I didn't have a shred of tangible or direct evidence.

Maybe there was something I was missing?

I opened my eyes and studied my mother. Her chest expanded and contracted in rhythm with the bleep of the monitors that surrounded her bedside. Seeing her at her most vulnerable solidified our connection and made it clear how much we needed each other. I couldn't let this situation stump me, and I refused to stand down like Ashton would have me do. The police hadn't made an arrest and seemed focused on a seemingly innocent man, but there had to be evidence or proof somewhere to make sense of these crimes.

I elected a different tactic. Forget the culprit. What did each of the victims—Yaris, Ashton, and Ma—have in common? They all worked for the state and had ties to government or law enforcement—well, Ashton not so much anymore, but each victim was attacked either in or around their vehicles. Yaris and Ashton even shared the distinction of having the same vehicle.

Wait. Maybe that was the key. When the bombing initially occurred, the big question on everyone's mind was, "Why Garrett Yaris?" He was a judge from upstate that most people didn't know. Why was he attacked rather than one of our own judges? The question had originally stumped me and my coworkers. But when a person looked at the problem through the lens of knowing that Yaris and Ashton owned the same make and model vehicle in similar colors, a possible answer came to light.

Maybe the killer got it wrong. Maybe Yaris was never the target. Maybe Ashton was the intended victim from the very beginning.

Such a theory would explain the repeated attempts on Ashton's life despite his lack of a current connection to law enforcement. However, it doesn't explain the bomb threat fielded by my office.

I grabbed my purse and dug out my phone. Ed had emailed the transcript and recording of the phone call to each of us.

CALLER: You know you heard me. There's a bomb in the courthouse. People are going to die today.

CANDI: I meant, where is the bomb? Nobody has to die.

CALLER: That's not your decision, is it? Just like what you all did to me wasn't mine.

CANDI: Sorry. So sorry. I was just—

CALLER: Apologies won't you help you now. Time for payback.

Time to suffer the same fate my life and career suffered in those very halls. Your office is just the first of three—

CANDI: My-my-my office? The court reporters' office? But what did we...Mmm-hmm.

CALLER: Are you starting to feel it? The fear? The anxiety? The pressure? You've all played your role in destroying lives. This call is merely a courtesy. Don't bother checking your surveillance system. The bombs are set. You have three minutes to escape.

CANDI: There's more than one bomb? Where? We need more time.

CALLER: There's no stopping the inevitable.

Looking at the words on their own revealed one important distinction. None of the threats outlined came to fruition in the manner described. The call outlined a three-prong plot for revenge against those who worked in the courthouse, but none of the people attacked thus far—Yaris, Ashton, and Ma—actually worked in the building.

Did that matter? I sighed, then clicked my phone closed. The devil on my shoulder pointed out that such a small distinction wouldn't be much use to the police. Unless...the call itself was a decoy, just like the suspicious backpack found in the courthouse lobby.

So if we erased the call from the equation—or rather, considered it another misdirect—and viewed the Yaris murder as a misstep rather than a precursor, then a common thread became absolutely clear.

ME!

The killer called my office, attacked my boyfriend, activated my webcam, and abducted my mother. I was at the heart of all of this. The killer wanted me to suffer.

Did that mean I was next?

Chapter Twenty-Seven

Seventy-two hours passed without my leaving my mother's hospital room.

By Tuesday morning, Ma had fallen into what the doctors considered a comatose state. Jillian, Mike, James, Ed, and Candi had all stopped by that afternoon to express their concern, but I hadn't been able to get in touch with Ashton—although, considering the attitude I'd taken when last we spoke, I didn't blame him for avoiding my calls.

"Ms. Justice," I looked up to find Detective Connor Daniels of the Delaware State Police standing in the doorway. "Do you mind if I speak with you for a moment? We can go in the hallway if you'd like."

"No, here is fine. I don't want to leave her."

"I'm sorry we have to meet under such circumstances." He stepped toward the bed but kept a respectful distance. "I understand from the statement you made to the Bickerton Police officers who assisted you at the scene, you believe the mayor—pardon me, your mother's abduction, is related to the Yaris murder and the fire at the home of Ashton North."

I nodded and stared at the floor with my hands clenched. "But I don't have any proof, if that's why you're here."

"Not exactly." He rubbed his droopy, bloodshot eyes. "I had hoped your mother was awake. I wanted to speak with her about what happened during the attack, see if she could identify the perpetrator."

"Why? Are you about to make an arrest?"

"It appears so." He sighed, his breath thick with the smell of cigarettes and coffee. "The day after your mother's incident, we received a call from a staff member at Readalong Books, saying he'd found some suspicious items among the personal effects Ms. Dodd had stored in their breakroom. He believed they held a connection to the Yaris murder. Upon further investigation, we found that there was indeed cause for concern."

"Concern?" I rose from the bedside and moved toward him. "What did they find?"

"Bottles of propofol, lorazepam, midazolam, lidocaine—"

"Slow down. I don't understand what you're saying. That just sounds like gibberish."

"Basically, they're all hypnotic drugs used during general anesthesia, and your mother's toxicology report indicates that several of them were found in her system."

"Oh, my gosh." I couldn't breathe.

"We also discovered a couple ball gags similar to the one used in your mother's case, along with potassium perchlorate, ethanol, tube cutters, and a variety of mercury switches."

"What does that sound familiar?"

"Well, potassium perchlorate in its powder form is one of the key ingredients in making primers for explosives, and ethanol—"

"No. I meant the term 'mercury switch.' Aren't they the key to making a tilt fuse for an explosive?"

"Correct."

"So you do believe the courthouse bombing and my mother's attack are connected?"

"I can confirm parallels have been made," he said with reluctance, "and we suspect Ms. Dodd may have targeted Ashton North as well. Unfortunately, we weren't able to detain her for questioning. Seems someone tipped her off. I had hoped we could speak to your mother to further solidify the connection while we wait on a warrant to search Ms. Dodd's home."

"What now?" I pressed a hand to my forehead and willed myself not to cry.

"We watch, and we wait." He scratched his graying mustache. "Everyone in the community has taken this attack on the mayor very seriously, so the state has seized jurisdiction of the case. And based on your earlier concerns, we feel the situation may warrant protection. So until we can secure the suspect, we're placing two armed troopers outside her hospital door and sending a patrol unit to monitor your home." He gave a respectful nod toward my mother's motionless form. "You have my card if there is anything I can do for you or you have any other insights."

As Daniels departed, everything came into perspective. I'd spent the last two weeks arguing with Ma and Ashton over my safety when it was really my actions that were putting their lives in danger—the realization ravaged my soul. No two people mattered more, and the time had come for me to stand up for them both.

So with Ma tethered to a series of machines, fighting for her life, and the perpetrator on the run, I started by making amends with a call to Ashton.

"Uh, hey, it's me." I'd gotten his voicemail again. "I'm sure you're sick of these messages by now, but I wanted to see if the police got in contact with you about Phyllis. She's been behind this whole thing. They haven't made the arrest yet, though, so Ma's under protective custody. I hope they did the same for you." My voice cracked. "Could you please call me? Please? I'm sorry. I am. I want to—just let me know you're okay…okay? Ma still hasn't woken up, and I don't know what to do. I could use your help. I promise to listen. I can't afford to lose her…or you."

Chapter Twenty-Eight

By Tuesday night, I was emotionally and physically exhausted. I needed real food, a real shower, and real sleep on a surface that wasn't a chair or a latex hospital mattress. So, I notified one of the officers outside Ma's door that I was going home for a few hours. He kindly radioed the unit at the house and alerted them of my arrival while his partner escorted me to my Mustang, which she inspected before I climbed inside.

When I'd made it safely home, I locked the door and went straight to my bedroom, where I flopped onto the bed and slept for what felt like days. However, when I was awakened by the sound of an incoming call on my cell, I checked the display to discover only three hours had passed.

11:06 p.m., Tuesday, April 16 – Ashton North

Thank God.

"Hello?" I sat up in bed, suddenly wide awake.

"Hello, Victoria. It feels like we haven't talked in ages."

My pulse quickened. The voice on the other end of the line was auto-tuned on the same deep but discordant frequency of the courthouse bomber.

"Phyllis?"

"What?" The voice chuckled. "Expecting someone else?"

"Why do you have Ashton's phone?"

"Oh, I think you know why. But if you're really curious, check your texts. I already left you a hint."

I tapped and scrolled through several screens to find my messages. Sure enough, I had slept through a text from Ashton. When I clicked on his name, a video appeared as the newest item in a chain of old texts. The preview image showed nothing but the ceiling of what appeared to be a relatively small white room, so I clicked on it.

The video shook and lost focus for a few seconds as if someone was fumbling with the settings, then the camera panned down to reveal an empty office—or perhaps, it was a bedroom, where a distressed wheelchair sat centerstage. The occupant of this lone piece of furniture was Ashton. His legs were bound to the leg rests that jutted outward from the front of the chair, and his forearms were lashed to the armrests. His face was grotesquely swollen around the lips and eyes. Dark bruised patches of purple covered his once peachy hue. Splotches of blood and sweat stained the ripped light blue DSU sweatshirt that hung from his bowed frame.

The camera rushed in toward his face, and a gloved hand, holding a knife, became visible. The hand pressed the weapon's tip into Ashton's flesh just enough to cause a nick that drew a fat drop of blood.

"State the date and time." The autotuned voice barked. "Or I won't be so gentle the next round."

"Monday, April 15, 10:39 p.m." Ashton barely lifted his head. His breathing was ragged, so the words escaped as a meek whisper. "Don't come here, Victoria. Save yourself."

Blackout.

I stared at the screen, not quite understanding or perhaps not wanting to piece together the threads, but the caller was patient and didn't speak until I'd returned to the conversation.

"That was yesterday." My lip trembled. "How do I know he is still alive?"

"You don't. That's why you have to come down here and find out."

"If you want me, why not just come and get me?"

"That wouldn't be any fun now, would it? No, no, no. I want you to come to me. You have to want to take part in this little game. Otherwise, what's the point?" The line briefly fuzzed over with static and a faint beeping. "That way, you can play your part if that cop who followed you out of the hospital, or her buddies out in front of your house, try to stop us."

"You've been watching me?" I recalled the webcam from the days prior and wondered if there had been other recording devices. "What do you want?"

"Haven't you figured that out by now?"

Oddly, I hadn't. If Phyllis wanted to kill me, why didn't she just do it rather than torturing those around me? What was with the psychological foreplay?

"Please, don't hurt Ashton. I'll do—"

"Forget about that Neanderthal. He'll get what he deserves. What I want from you, for now, is simple. Ditch the cops, and meet me at the inlet down where Cedar Street ends across from the marina. Midnight. Any effort to call the police or pull some heroic stunt will result in me slitting the tough guy's throat. And if you are thinking about calling my bluff on any of this, then check out my latest video masterpiece for a little incentive. And to be clear, this one was taken today, right before I called."

Ping-Ping!

The alert for a second message popped up on my screen. When I scrolled over to the text chain with Ashton, a new video appeared. This one had a very clear preview of a digital wall clock similar to the ones used in rooms at the hospital.

My heart stopped.

With shaky hands, I clicked the video. The camera came to life and zoomed in on the time for few seconds—11:00 p.m.—before panning across the room and down toward the smooth sienna face of my mother. Her eyes were closed, her face drawn, and her breathing so shallow it almost seemed nonexistent. The monitors around her flashed and beeped as the same gloved hand from the previous video came into view. This time, the hand held a syringe that pressed against Ma's neck before the video went dark.

The implications here were quite clear.

I almost dropped the phone, but the cryptic voice spoke and caused me to fumble for control of the device. How did she get past the state troopers?

"Don't go all soft on me now." The return of the autotuned laughter gave me chills. "I know it's not every day a person sees a syringe full of toxins held against her mother's neck, but I can assure you Corinne Justice's fate is in your hands."

The call ended, and the phone went dark.

Repulsed and terrified by what I'd seen, I dropped my cell like a hot potato. My now empty hands grew clammy, and the room tilted. Nausea crept into my throat, making it hard to breathe. My thoughts were a tangle. Going to the beach alone at night into the clutches of an armed killer had its own dangers, but I wasn't even sure I could make such a journey to the shore on my own. In the past, I'd always had someone with me and never got as close to the water as the town's inlet, where Bickerton's elite docked their boats.

I wrapped both arms around myself and rocked back and forth. I couldn't let Ashton down again, and I definitely couldn't put my mother in any more jeopardy. She had sacrificed so much for me and done everything in her power to protect me both as a child, when I was being bullied, and as a young adult who struggled to find her path in life. Letting fear stand in the way was not an option. I closed my eyes and recited the only words that could give me strength.

I am yours, you are mine, and together we'll be fine.

The phrase became a chant as I dragged myself out of bed, pulled on a clean flannel shirt and jeans, and formulated a plan for getting to the beach without attracting the cops or losing my nerve.

I'd parked my Mustang out front where a couple of State Troopers in an unmarked sedan sat watching the front door, so I ordered an Uber and arranged for pickup at an address on a street parallel to my own. That way, I could sneak out through the backyard and cross over to the next block, assuming there wasn't anyone watching the rear of our home.

I grabbed my house keys and cellphone and stuffed them into the back pocket of my jeans. In an effort to travel light, I abandoned the rest of my purse items and left the bag on the floor. My hope was that the phone went unnoticed so that I could make a covert call for help once Ashton was safe and the threats against my mother ceased. The big question was, how the heck was I going to accomplish such a feat?

As I made my way to the door, I stopped by the closet to grab a jacket and noticed the cardigan I'd worn on my date with Ashton. The tactical pen was still clipped to the collar. My skin prickled with a mixture of sorrow and delight over the shy sweetness with which the item had been given. Going headlong into danger without him was a first, and the thought of potentially losing my partner forever further fueled my anxiety.

I slipped on my favorite leather jacket, grabbed the tiny metal cylinder, and stuck it inside the breast pocket of my shirt, right against my heart. That way, no matter what happened, at least part of him would be with me during my meeting with the killer.

The thought buoyed my spirits enough to propel me down the stairs and into the garage. The space was much cooler than the inside of the house, which cleared my head and helped me remember an important fact. Our home didn't have a door that led directly into the back yard. The closest approximation was an exit on the side of the house that led out from the two-car garage. I crossed the empty space to face the exit and visualized what I would see on the other side. Fortunately, the property line for the neighbors on that side of our home was relatively close, and they didn't have any security lights facing that area. I reached for the wall switch on my right and turned off the decorative sconces that flanked the door on the other side. Then, I prayed the officers out front wouldn't notice the change and decide to come knocking.

After another quick pep talk, reminding myself to breathe, I slowly opened the door. Half of me expected someone to emerge from the shadows, but I was simply met with the inky-black darkness of night.

I closed and locked the door as rapidly as I could, making sure to keep my body pressed close to the side of the house. I wasn't able to see the police sedan that had been parked out front, but I could hear some distant chatter as if they'd left their windows open or stepped outside the car to talk.

My mind ran through potential ways I could send the officers a message, but none of them included how to do it without being seen, and Phyllis had made it crystal clear I was being monitored.

God help me.

I needed to get moving.

Ducking my head to conceal my face, I crept through the backyard as quickly and silently as possible. Fortunately, the space wasn't much longer than a regulation volleyball court, and the moon was low, allowing me to remain cloaked in half light. When I reached the property line, I jumped the small ditch that separated our yard from the neighbor's. My landing resulted in a soft thud that caused a dog to bark territorially. I couldn't locate the source of the sound, and I wasn't in the mood to get bitten, so I broke into a run.

The Uber driver was already waiting as directed in front of the address that I'd calculated using Google Maps. I could sense him getting annoyed when I asked him to repeat his name several times before getting inside, as I double-checked the app. It was ominous enough that his name was "Azrael," known in some Hebrew texts as the angel of death, so I would have been foolish to jump into the car without considering that he might be a part of Phyllis's trap. Luckily, the ride was uneventful until we reached the drop-off point at the end of Cedar Street.

Most would have marveled at the five perfectly manicured wooden docks that jutted into the water for a quarter of a mile. Each one was flanked with dozens of slips containing majestic vessels of various shapes and sizes. My mind, however, betrayed me as my legs grew numb and my throat tightened. All I could see was the onyx mass, known by day as the Delaware Bay, stretched out along the edge of the dead-end road to an unmarked horizon.

"Hey," Azrael barked, bringing me back to the moment, "I can't sit here all night."

Somehow I opened the door and swung my legs around until they made purchase with the ground. Soon after, I found myself staring at the brake lights of Azrael's Cherokee as it faded into the distance. The sudden lack of light beckoned the black edges of the evening to curl around me. A searing pain ripped across my brow, sharp as an icepick, crumpling me to the ground. Head in my hands, I closed my eyes.

Get it together.

Fight. For Ma...and Ashton.

I'd been in this situation before, and if there was one thing I'd learned, it's that you can't beat your enemy lying down. I couldn't give Phyllis the upper hand—and nothing led to defeat faster than crouching alone in the middle of a dark road without a plan.

When I finally had the strength to open my eyes, I calculated I was about twenty yards away from the only street lamp. Each dock had small safety lights along its walkways at consistent intervals, but they were dim and much farther away—not to mention dangerously close to the water. But if I could just make it to the lamppost at the edge of the road, I could regroup…perhaps, block everything out.

I struggled to my feet and ignored the sharp scent of macroalgae that tinged the air. Instead, I focused on the light squawking of gulls in the distance—a bitter reminder that there was life beyond this space—and slowly but surely muted my anxiety to steady myself.

I stepped toward the light with a renewed sense of purpose, that is, until I discovered a long, lean silhouette standing between me and the lamppost that lay ahead.

Chapter Twenty-Nine

"Oh, my gosh, Victoria. Are you out of your mind? What are you doing here?"

I recognized the voice as Mike's, which only intensified my nervous confusion.

"What are you doing here?"

"Trying to protect you," he shouted.

The brisk, briny air, once cool against my flushed skin, became heavy… ominous. We stood about thirty feet away from each other, but because the only light source was behind him at almost the same distance, I couldn't see his face.

"Put your hands in the air." I pulled out my phone and lit the flashlight in his direction. "How did you know I was here?"

"I didn't." Mike stood with one hand above his head while the other extended toward me at eye level. He held a cellphone that he waved back and forth in surrender. "I got a strange call and video message demanding I come down here."

Video message? Had he been contacted by Phyllis, too?

"Of my mother?"

"No," he inclined his head as if he couldn't understand the question, "of you."

My back bristled, and I stilled.

Had I been followed? I flashed my light three hundred and sixty degrees, searching the shadows for culprits, my heart pounding out the seconds.

"Victoria!" The urgency in Mike's voice brought me back to the present.

He gestured for me to follow him. "What are you doing? It's not safe here."

I lowered my light and ran toward him. I still didn't understand why he was here, but it meant I didn't have to go through this alone. His appearance was technically within the rules of Phyllis's twisted game—I hadn't called him, and he wasn't the police.

Mike pulled me into a hug when I reached his orbit. A practice we hadn't adopted with each other, but seemed appropriate in the moment with so much on the line.

"You need to see this." He led me over to the street lamp, which I noticed illuminated the sign for the marina, and opened a video on his phone. We both huddled over the screen.

The camera opened on a closed door. A gloved hand, the one I'd come to loathe, pushed the door open to reveal a bedroom...*my bedroom* with its tan shag carpet and angled white walls. My bed sat in the distance. The camera bobbed closer to reveal my sleeping face, and the hand reached out to brush a curl from my forehead. I stirred and disrupted the comforter that had covered me and my fuzzy red robe. The hand reached out to tuck the covers back into place. A beat passed while it disappeared, and the camera simply floated above me. A faint snap-click-swish sound occurred off camera, breaking up the ragged hum of my breathing. Seconds later, an open switchblade appeared, and the hand slid the point toward my unsuspecting eyes just as the video ended.

I gasped and looked up at Mike, whose face was twisted into a mask of confusion and horror.

"I thought he was going to take you away from me."

"He?" I looked over my shoulder. "Who are you talking about? Phyllis is the killer. The police have evidence."

"They're wrong. Ashton North is at the root of all of this."

"Mike, slow down." I put my hand over his phone, which had started to replay the video. "That's impossible. Ashton has been the main target all along. I just realized the other day the killer confused Yaris's truck with Ashton's. That's the only reason the President Judge was killed." I nodded to Mike's cell. "Phyllis is just messing with you to lure you down here. She has

Ashton's phone. He's been kidnapped."

"Why do you always bend over backward to defend him?"

"I'm not defending him. It just can't possibly be true. Ashton doesn't need to spy on me. He sees me almost every day."

Or rather, he *saw* me almost every day. I wasn't sure what tense to use at this point, but I knew Ashton was no murderer. I glanced at the video that replayed in Mike's hand. There were no overt context clues toward the date and time, as there had been in the threats sent to me. But I recognized the fuzzy red robe as the garment I'd worn the night I'd found the odd webcam recording on my laptop. Clearly, someone had broken in that day to go through the files on my computer and had apparently returned later that night, but the likelihood of that person being Ashton was impossible. He was in the hospital. I'd called him there myself.

"Victoria," Mike grabbed my arm, "stay focused. Ashton has a history of lying. He framed an innocent woman last year in order to avenge his partner and committed false arrest based on some trumped up drug charge. He's nothing but another corrupt cop. Why would you ever trust him? My mother fought her whole life against that kind of behavior."

"You're looking at it all wrong. I know you don't like Ashton, but why would he want to frame Phyllis for murder?"

"And as usual, you're missing the point." He clutched both of my shoulders with a slight shake. "This isn't about what Ashton did to Phyllis. This is about what he did to you and me."

"You and me?" I stared into Mike's dark eyes. "Ashton never did anything to us. You were always fiercely defensive of our friendship when he was around."

The words were barely out of my mouth before it dawned on me. Mike was right. Hadn't I come to the conclusion the other day that I was the common thread among the victims?

The killer called my office, attacked my boyfriend, broke into my computer, and abducted my mother. I was the root of all of this. The killer wanted me to suffer. And in terms of the potential suspects, that narrowed the field...

But I had overlooked the most obvious element in terms of the potential suspects.

Mike Slocum.

He'd texted me the day of the Yaris bombing, trying to lure me away from the courthouse and my lunch with Ashton. And when that failed, he knew that a threatening call to my office from the beachside pay phone would ensure that I unwittingly did exactly what he wanted—evacuate the building and renege on my lunch date.

He'd texted throughout the evening during my dinner with Ashton and fought with the man when I brought him to our clandestine meeting at the beach. By the next day, Ashton was in the hospital because someone tampered with his brakes.

And although Mike didn't deter me from picking up Ashton from the hospital, there was another accident that same day, in the minutes after Ashton professed his love.

Could Mike have been the figure who'd streaked through Ashton's yard with the Molotov cocktail? Was the cellphone video he'd just shown me a ruse? Had he actually been the person who'd held a knife over me while I slept?

Yes.

I exhaled sharply to steel myself against those thoughts and remain calm on the outside. As unnerving as it was to unearth the role he played in this never-ending nightmare, true clarity made space for action. If I kept my wits, maybe I could escape. It wasn't too late.

"Why are you so fixated on my relationship with Ashton?" I stepped back with a quick jerk of my torso, hoping the question and the momentum would catch him off guard. "If you had a problem with it, why didn't you tell me?"

"Didn't I?" His eyes grew wide.

I thrashed back and forth, struggling to break his grasp, but Mike held fast to both arms, twisting one until it was wrenched tightly behind me, and I was pulled back against him. He hooked his other arm around my neck in a choke hold, buried his face in my hair, and inhaled.

"Are you kidding me?" He pressed his mouth against my ear so the heat of his lips tickled my skin. "I've told you over and over again that Ashton is wrong for you. As a matter of fact, that's exactly why I called you down here—because you weren't listening. Since you seem so determined to take advice from everyone except me, I needed to do something to make you understand."

He pushed me toward one of the wooden thoroughfares where boats were docked on either side.

I dug in my heels and screamed bloody murder.

Mike released the arm that had been twisted behind my back, but held tight to my neck.

Snap-click-swish!

I didn't need to see the source of the sound to know that he'd drawn a switchblade.

My mouth closed immediately, and all sound ceased as he pushed the thin slice of metal against my cheek until it formed a cold, prickly line that made my entire body stiffen. His dominant arm tightened around my neck as he resumed pushing me down the length of the dock.

"See?" he hissed. "You're always defying me, forcing me to make things tougher on you."

"Stop it, Mike. This is crazy. If I defied you, I'm sorry. End this before someone else gets hurt. I didn't know our relationship meant that much to you."

"That's because you don't listen. You were too busy taking Johnny's side when I attempted to defend your honor at the beach during that moronic gun fiasco," he growled. "Another dishonorable person who should be behind bars for what he did. If anybody else in this community pulled a gun on innocent people in broad daylight in front of witnesses, they'd be shackled and humiliated—or if they were poor or brown…shot dead. But that frat boy elitist is given a slap on the wrist because his father owns half the waterfront." He steered me toward a small plankway that jutted out onto the water between two boats, one of which looked like a tiny floating house.

My chest constricted as the water sloshed against the slip's woodwork, causing the flooring beneath us to rock slightly. I kicked and thrashed my head from side to side, trying to bite Mike's hand, trying to knock us to the ground—anything to slow our progress—but he pressed the knife tip into my flesh until a ticklish trickle of warmth kissed my cheek.

"LOOK WHAT YOU MADE ME DO?!" His voice and body shook like a child about to have a tantrum. "You're always making me do things I don't want to do."

Before I could realize what was happening, he hauled me off my feet and tossed me over the small guardrail for the houseboat. I crashed onto the deck and rolled to the side to grasp at the knee that had taken the brunt of the trauma.

"Ashton had to be eliminated, and Johnny was going to be the fall guy. Just a shame Garrett Yaris had the same stupid-looking truck. I guess he chose the wrong day to come visit Trident County."

A loud thump alerted me to the fact that Mike was climbing aboard, but I didn't dare look at him for fear that this time he'd hit me...or worse, dig deeper with the knife.

"Of course, you wouldn't let the simple revenge plot unfold, you just kept digging and digging," his voice was a high whine, "and babbling about Phyllis, Phyllis, PHYLLIS! Nobody in this freaking town listens, no matter how many truths I expose!!"

I could hear him stomping around behind me, so I dared to open my eyes. The ache in my knee had grown into a stabbing sensation that made the thought of standing a distant fantasy, but I had to at least get some clear answers.

"Where's Ashton?" I flinched, covering my head, hoping the name wouldn't set him off again. "Is he still alive?"

"For now." Mike's face appeared over me. The once jovial façade curved into a hard mask of disdain.

"You messed with my webcam and made that video of me sleeping..." My stomach roiled at the next thought, "...and drugged my mother and stuffed her in a trunk, didn't you?" I could barely finish the sentence.

"Of course," Mike replied. "I've been following you. Keeping you safe from people who were trying to tear you away from me."

I jerked forward to retch up the bile that had formed in my empty stomach. The heaving brought with it a metallic bittersweetness that made me lightheaded.

Forgive me, Ma. This was all my fault.

"There, there, sweetheart." He grabbed my arm and produced a needle that he jabbed into it with a vicious thrust. "Let me give you a little medicine to make it all better."

I cried out and groped at the coarse floorboards, hoping to get purchase, willing myself back to the edge of the boat. I knew the guard rail had to be somewhere nearby, but the lines before me shifted so that down became up and forward led to nowhere. The air grew thinner, and the space around me tightened as the harsh angles of Mike's face dissolved into shades of nothingness.

Chapter Thirty

I awoke to the guttural drone of an engine, but it was Sam Cooke's voice that caused me to open my eyes.

A chilling string orchestration and haunting trumpet line drifted overhead while Cooke sang about finding the will to carry on. My head throbbed to the bass line metered out by the timpani as I gathered my wits and struggled to remove my blood-crusted cheek from the deck.

I had no idea how long I'd been unconscious, but Mike had apparently left me crumpled where I'd blacked out. He had the decency to cover me with a blanket, which I removed, relieved to find that I was fully clothed underneath—though a quick search of my back pockets revealed my phone and house keys had been removed. However, the tactical pen remained tucked in my breast pocket. I almost reached for it, but Mike's voice drifted overhead, mingling with the lyrics of "A Change is Gonna Come." Wherever he was, it was close but out of my line of sight.

"You know, my mother once told me that Cooke wrote this song because he couldn't stand to see the people around him struggle against injustice... and she devoted her brief life to that same concept. I was drawn to you because I thought you understood that basic idea, but you've done nothing but disappoint me at every turn."

I ignored him and stared at the starless sky above. Based on the salinity in the air, we were clearly on the water, but I was afraid to stand and discover how far out.

The best I could do was croak. "Where are we?"

Mike appeared above me and offered his hand. "My houseboat."

"No." I swatted at his palm. "How far from the slip?"

"Does it matter? This is the one place we can be together without interference or interruption, and I think the change in scenery will teach you some humility. Keep you sweet and docile like the girl I first met."

"Mike, this is insane." I struggled to push myself to a seated position, despite my pounding head. "You can't expect to keep me tucked away on a boat forever. You're going to get caught."

"By whom? You said yourself the police think Phyllis Dodd is to blame." He crouched in front of me and offered a handkerchief. "It's funny. This whole thing was meant to fall on Johnny or Ignacio Cardoza—another morally bankrupt individual who failed to pay for his crimes. Between my bogus phone call pretending to be his parole officer and the threats of revenge called into your office, I figure the cops would blame one of them for the bombing." His expression grew dark. "But if blaming Phyllis is good enough for you, it's good enough for me."

And before I could speak, he hopped up and walked to the area behind me. When I turned my head to see where he was going, my jaw dropped.

Hog-tied and silenced, with the same breathable ball gag I'd seen on my mother, was Phyllis Dodd. She lay on her side in a heap on the opposite side of the vessel. She'd clearly been tied for quite some time, as her hair was a wild tangle and her normally freckled face was stained with an odd mixture of sweat, lipstick, and smeared mascara. He'd apparently caught her coming home from work because she was wearing dress slacks and a sheer silk blouse, both of which were ripped and stained with blood.

"Framing her was easy enough, too." He bent down next to her, switchblade in hand, his mouth widening into a snarl. "And boy, do we know how she deserves it."

As he drew close to her, she jerked away. The movement clearly caused her pain because a strangled moan emitted from her throat, and anguish stretched across her features.

"What's that now?" Mike bent toward her as if attempting to interpret. "You want to atone for your criminal misconduct during the oversight of the Controlled Substance Lab?" He waggled the knife, then stabbed her in the side with the ferocity of a feral beast.

"Evidence tampering." *Stab.*

"Vehicular manslaughter." *Stab.*

Phyllis howled in response to each sin, but her cries were muffled as she struggled to breathe through her gag.

"NOT LIKE THIS, MIKE!" I crawled toward them, a hand outstretched in surrender. "Nobody asked for this. Can't you see that going this far isn't going to make anything right? You're becoming exactly what you claim to hate."

"I'm not a monster." He held up his bloody knife. "I only planted that evidence so you could get the conclusion you wanted. Everything I've done here is for you. I don't care about Phyllis."

"But if you did all this for me, why hurt my mother?"

Mike stood and paced the deck. "Yes, I'll admit that's a bit more complicated. She wanted to send you away." His voice grew high and sharp. "She was going to tear us apart. I couldn't have that. It was never my intention to cause permanent damage, but I had to do something to stop her and get you to stay."

"By drugging her and locking her in a trunk?" I screamed, "She's in a coma. That's not compassion, that's the work of a psychopath."

He lunged at me and hauled me to my feet. With the bay now in sight, surrounding the tiny houseboat, my head pounded and my legs flopped like rubber. The shore was still in view, but the way my mind had lost control over my body, land may as well have been a thousand miles away.

"Not everyone expresses themselves the same way." He snaked an arm around my waist and held the bloody switchblade to my neck as he pulled me into a half-embrace. "Sometimes it's easier to show it than to say it. You're just going to have to trust my methods."

The music from earlier had died away, but Mike still took to dragging me around the deck like a rag doll at a cotillion. I did my best to follow his lead, but my heart wasn't in it—neither was my soul. Being close to him had become more infuriating than the seasickness and panic attacks that rolled over me every few minutes. And of course, there was Phyllis lying bloodied and battered at our feet.

But worst of all, now that I had discovered the petty reason he'd attacked Ma, my blood boiled. Sure, there was some solace in knowing he had no intention of killing her, but she'd still been severely injured and now lay comatose in the hospital. If Mike was capable of attacking an innocent old woman and leaving her to die, what else was he capable of doing?

And what had he done with Ashton?

I had to act.

Chapter Thirty-One

While Mike continued to waltz us round and round the tiny deck, I clutched at my chest as if in pain, hoping it covered the fact that I was digging in my breast pocket for the tactical pen. Once I was sure I had its length concealed in the cuff of my jacket, I returned my arm to the side where it had previously hung.

My thumb and index finger worked feverishly to remove the nubby tip, just as Ashton had shown me during our dinner. I slipped the spare piece into my back pocket, careful not to run my palm over the curved blade that had been revealed. The sharp metal was only about an inch or so long—a far cry from the sturdier, lengthier weapon Mike held to my throat. But it was all I had…along with the element of surprise.

"Is Ashton dead?" I asked.

"Not yet." He ran the knife across my cheek, nicking the previous wound and causing me to wince. "I thought we'd have a burial at sea. A ritual cleansing of those things we no longer need. You ready?"

I nodded, not wanting to upset him.

"Don't move." He released me from the embrace and took a step back, pointing the knife at my face. "You don't want to miss this."

He laughed at his own brilliance, but I clearly had nowhere to go, so I crumpled back onto the deck while he disappeared into the cabin that occupied the center of the vessel. I waited with the pen knife tucked in my palm. The blade was at the ready with its hilt still hidden from sight.

Moments later, Mike wheeled in Ashton, who was still bound to a wheelchair and wearing the same blood-spattered clothes from the video.

His eyes were closed and his head was bowed, but I could still see that the blue and indigo bruises on his face were far more horrific in person.

"Ashton!" I scrambled to the side of the wheelchair and stroked his knee until he looked up at me. His eyes were vacant, and I couldn't help but think back to how horribly I'd treated him. "Oh, my God, this is all my fault. I should have seen it. I should have listened to you." He didn't respond, so I took his hand and squeezed, willing him to understand. "Mike sabotaged your truck and set your house on fire to punish us. Just remember, whatever happens tonight. I love—"

"Don't." Mike stepped from behind the wheelchair and leaned down to point a finger at my face.

In one sharp upward thrust, I plunged the pen blade into Mike's neck and twisted so the small edge would do as much damage as possible. Blood coursed from the wound, and Mike staggered backward, groping at the silver metal cylinder that hung limply from his throat.

"He doesn't love you," Mike rasped. Once his hand found the pen, he pulled it free and tossed it overboard. "He just likes the idea of you because you feed his ego."

"Isn't that what you're doing?" I eased to my feet and rounded the wheelchair so that Ashton, though mostly unresponsive, sat between us. "If you really cared for me, Mike, you'd let me go."

"Never." He brandished the switchblade with one hand and pressed a palm against his bloody neck with the other, his body crouched like a cat ready to pounce. "We're intellectual equals. I am giving you a chance to finally see me without any distractions." He waved his knife at Ashton. "I know that once you do, you'll make the right decision."

"Well, clearly, you don't know me at all."

And with that, I charged forward, pushing Ashton's wheelchair along with me, using it to ram into Mike with all the force I could muster. We collided with a violent crash that sent Mike flying into the rail, where he lost his balance and flipped backward into the water.

A loud splash and a wild scream followed, but I couldn't bring myself to look over the side. My focus was on Ashton, who had begun to moan.

"Are you hurt? Did I hurt you? Talk to me. Please."

My hands shook, and my fingertips were numb with shock, but I did my best to rip and pull at the rope and tape that bound Ashton to the chair. After I loosened the restraints as best I could, I shook him, but he didn't respond. He was, however, still breathing. I figured Mike must have drugged him as he had done with me, so I dropped to my knees to attend to Phyllis.

When I crawled to her side, her body was surrounded by a sea of red. The knots that bound her hands and legs were far more challenging, and I found myself wrestling with them for several minutes. As the rope around her wrists loosened, I realized I hadn't heard her make a sound, and the flesh along her arms was no longer flushed with sweat. The wounds at her side had seemed to cease their bleeding.

Oh, my God.

I took her pulse. Then I raced into the cabin where Mike had produced Ashton in hopes of finding a phone or a radio, but there was almost nothing in the room except a fire extinguisher, a couple of life vests, and a set of flares. I recognized it as the same white space from the videos, but seeing it in person led me to believe that it had once been a sitting area or sunroom that Mike had sealed off with drywall to create a studio that looked like a nondescript void.

"Looking for this?"

I whirled around to find Mike standing in the archway, dripping wet, bloody, and brooding. He held my cellphone in his hand, though I was sure it was useless since he'd just taken a dip in the bay.

"Stay back," I warned, feeling a little stronger now that I was inside and out of view of the water.

"Not a chance. You're going to pay for that little stunt."

He lunged at me, and I lunged for the fire extinguisher.

My hand wrapped around the metal valve just as he plunged the switchblade into my shoulder. The momentum of our combined efforts caused us to collide and stagger sideways into the wall with a collective crash.

The scorching hot pain of the knife radiated through my body, but I held fast to my new weapon and swung it in a wide arc toward Mike's head. The cylindrical tank connected with his skull, causing a loud and satisfying crack.

His eyes rolled back, then his legs buckled, causing him to topple over at my feet.

I clambered backward and tugged at the knife in my shoulder. Blood poured from the wound, and the searing pain caused the room to fade. I doubled over and slid to the floor.

"Victoria?"

I squinted in the direction where I remembered Mike had fallen, but the voice hadn't come from him. He remained still, sprawled prone on the ground.

"You need to put pressure on your wound." Ashton leaned down and knelt beside me. He clutched a wound on his side, and his face was still the mangled mess I remembered from earlier, but his lips held the faintest hint of a smile. "I'm going to get us out of here."

And with that, I lay down and closed my eyes. Finally, it was over.

Chapter Thirty-Two

After two more days of waiting in silence by her bedside, Ma showed signs of consciousness and emerged from her comatose state during a routine change in her IV. Although it would take another twenty-four hours for her to pass small milestones like responding to visual cues and speaking in full sentences, she eventually recovered enough for things to feel somewhat normal.

"Good morning, Angel."

My mother's voice had never sounded so beautiful. Hearing her utter those three words made me feel like my life was back on track. I wrapped my arms around her as best I could since she was still attached to a large variety of wires and tubes.

"I thought I'd lost you, Ma. I am so, so sorry."

"Shhhh." She squeezed me tighter and patted me on the back. "We were all fooled by that wolf in sheep's clothing."

"How did he get to you?"

"Leaving work on Friday evening." She released me from her embrace, and I pulled a chair to her bedside. "He caught me outside Town Hall after my interview with the editor of *The Bugle*. Well, I guess I shouldn't say 'he.' I didn't know who it was at the time. It was dark, and I was grabbed from behind."

"This is all my fault, Ma." I bowed my head. "He told me that he hurt you because—"

"Stop. The cause for what happened is not your burden." She put her palm on top of my hand. "He had us all fooled, but we made it through. That's all that counts." She reached out and lifted my chin. "And in truth, Angel, I'm the one who should apologize to you."

"Why?"

"Ashton loves you. He's laid his life on the line for you, time and time again. I'm sorry I meddled in your relationship." She leaned forward and kissed my cheek. "You need someone like him in your life. I am not going to be around forever, you know."

My eyes burned with tears. And when they began to fall, Ma changed the subject in classic fashion.

"You going to work this morning?"

"I think so. Things feel weird at the house without you, and my shoulder still feels pretty good. Besides, I know you don't want me hanging around here all day making a fuss."

"You got that right." She smiled and tucked a curl behind my ear.

Things at work, although still abuzz with gossip about my showdown with Mike, had returned to business as usual. My coworkers finally felt comfortable in our office because everyone finally knew the truth.

Once Ashton steered us back to shore and called the cops, troopers charged Mike with Phyllis's murder as well as an assortment of stalking and kidnapping charges in connection with all three of our lives. When they raided his home, they found the same materials used to create the bomb that took the life of Garrett Yaris, as well as several digital files, tracking devices, and videos proving that he'd surveilled all of our homes and plotted our movements around town using GPS.

After a few more pleasantries, I kissed Ma and promised to return on my lunch break. Then I took the elevator down to Ashton's room where he sat reviewing and signing his release instructions.

"Hey, handsome. You need a hand?"

Ashton looked up from his clipboard and gave me a megawatt smile.

Mike had ambushed Ashton after I'd gone on my wild goose chase looking for Ma. He'd beaten him pretty badly and dosed him with a mild cocktail of sedatives. All of this aggravated Ashton's recent head trauma and disrupted the internal sutures he'd received during his splenectomy, causing a wound dehiscence that doctors were afraid would lead to infection and internal bleeding. But most of the new damage boiled down to severe facial bruises and the type of dehydration that came from being held captive for forty-eight hours without food and water.

Once the nurse departed with his paperwork, he reached for my hand. "Are you going to be okay all alone in that house of yours for the next couple of days?"

"I'll manage." I settled on the edge of the bed beside him. "Ma will be strong enough to come home soon."

"I know I don't have a place yet, but the offer to move in with me still stands."

"I know, and maybe I'll take you up on it one day soon. Right now, I need to be there for my mom, but I am glad you decided to stay in Bickerton."

"Me too." He nudged me with his shoulder. "Driving forty-five minutes each way to work is going to be a bit of a beast, though. I hate to do it, but I might have to give up my baby in favor of something with some fuel economy."

I raised an eyebrow. Ashton's "baby," or rather, his monster truck, was still in the shop with front-end damage and a busted transmission from the incident with his brakes. Considering all the trouble that vehicle had caused, I didn't care if it was ever resurrected.

"A new car might be the best thing you get out of all this."

"No way. I think that distinction goes to you." He leaned over and placed a soft kiss on my lips, which sent waves of pleasure down my spine and into my toes.

When he pulled away, I stared into the cool pools of his blue eyes and marveled at how easy that had been after so long.

"Do you have any idea how much I love you?" I said. And this time, there wasn't a trace of hesitation or doubt in my mind.

"Yup, but it never hurts to hear it twice."

"I love you, Ashton North."

Acknowledgments

Special thanks to the late Dawn Dowdle of the Blue Ridge Literary Agency for believing in this project and helping the series find a second home even as she battled with her health.

Sincerest appreciation as well to Shawn Reilly, my editor at Level Best Books, for her hard work, support, patience, and sound advice throughout this lengthy endeavor.

In addition, much love to all of the faculty and staff associated with the Writing Popular Fiction program at Seton Hill University—especially my amazing mentors Sharon Short and the late Victoria Thompson, who would be so proud of how the heroine has grown.

And of course, none of this would have taken shape without the help of my critique partners Jennifer Mason, Katherine Dow, Lisa Sherman, and my accountability partner Suzanne Jessen.

About the Author

Andrea J. Johnson has worked as an entertainment writer for women's lifestyle websites such as *Popsugar* and *The List,* and she has developed content for genre magazines like *CrimeReads* and *The Romance Writers Report.* She currently teaches Creative Writing at the University of Maryland Eastern Shore. And when she isn't penning books about crime (or grading papers!), you can find her sipping peppermint tea and poring over old episodes of *Murder, She Wrote.*

AUTHOR WEBSITE:
  https://ajthenovelist.com/

SOCIAL MEDIA HANDLES:
  Instagram: https://www.instagram.com/ajthenovelist/
  Pinterest: https://www.pinterest.com/ajthenovelist/
  Twitter: https://x.com/ajthenovelist

Also by Andrea J. Johnson

Fiction:

Poetic Justice

Non-Fiction:

How to Craft a Killer Cozy Mystery
Mastering the Art of Suspense
How to Craft Killer Dialogue